Praise for

A *New York Time*

Winner of *SheRead*'s Best of 202

Named a most anticipated title by
*Harper's Bazaar* * NYLON * NBC News * LGBTQ Reads *
*PinkNews* * Lit Hub * The Lesbrary * Autostraddle

"Through *Old Enough,* Jakobson offers a guiding hand to her readers. If you're going through this mess, you're not alone, she seems to say, and if you've already survived, you'll understand."
—*The New York Times Book Review*

"Jakobson writes Sav with enough humor, heart, and nuance to make her feel simultaneously relatable and unique. . . .*Old Enough* is full of growth, heartbreak, and winsome bisexual chaos."  —Emma Specter, *Vogue*

"Equal parts funny and romantic."  —*Cosmopolitan*

"This is what bi readers say they're hungry for the most—a book that proudly and vehemently says it's a 'big bisexual book.'"  —*USA Today*

"An entertaining and quietly moving narrative about friendship, sexual assault, and remembering that what we owe ourselves comes before what we owe anyone else."  —Shondaland

"Jakobson's book is part coming-of-age story, part self-proclaimed 'big bisexual novel,' part treatise on the ways friendship and girlhood and brushes at love—or something like it—leave us bruised."  —*Teen Vogue*

"*Old Enough* feels like holding up a mirror to your younger self, no matter how far removed you are from that period in your life."
—*NYLON*

"Heartfelt and heart-wrenching . . . [An] unmissable debut."
—PopSugar

"*Old Enough* is the queer coming-of-age novel that most of us never had. . . . It's a heartfelt and humorous examination of the fractured and nonlinear nature of healing and becoming whole."  —*Them*

"Readers will down this breathless debut in one sitting, sending gentle prayers up to their twenty-year-old selves."   —*Booklist* (starred review)

"This poignant rendering of one young woman's journey out of denial and shame into a budding self-love is essential reading."

—*Kirkus Reviews*

"A campus novel as astute, funny, and loving as your best friend from college . . . A testament to the power, and the weight, of friendship, in all its messiness and its necessity."

—Isle McElroy, author of *The Atmospherians*

"Haley Jakobson brings to life a modern undergraduate experience in all its messy, cringey glory and gives Generation Z the queer coming-of-age novel it needs in the era of both social media and social anxiety."

—A. E. Osworth, author of *We Are Watching Eliza Bright*

"If you're looking for a group of cool queer friends, look no further than *Old Enough*. These characters jump off the page, transporting us into an immersive and heartwarming love story for a new era. Haley Jakobson shows us the power of chosen family, the nuances of bisexuality, and the strength it takes to overcome your past in service of your future."

—Jen Winston, author of *Greedy*

"I truly loved this book. Read it!"

—Rachel Brathen, bestselling author of *Yoga Girl*

"A deeply immersive, thought-provoking, and engaging exploration of identity and how and when we get the courage to be fully ourselves."

—Lynn Steger Strong, author of *Flight*

"This pitch-perfect story about queer coming-of-age is brilliantly observed, wildly funny, and full of insights into the way the past can snake through the present—no matter how hard we try to escape. I loved every word and can't wait for what Jakobson writes next."

—Julie Buntin, author of *Marlena*

"An absolute snack . . . A novel for anyone who's lost a friend, found themselves, and survived their twenties, *Old Enough* is a gem."

—Katy Hays, bestselling author of *The Cloisters*

# Old Enough

A Novel

Haley Jakobson

DUTTON

**DUTTON**

An imprint of Penguin Random House LLC
penguinrandomhouse.com

Previously published as a Dutton hardcover in June 2023
First Dutton trade paperback printing: June 2024
Copyright © 2023 by Haley Jakobson
Penguin Random House supports copyright. Copyright fuels creativity,
encourages diverse voices, promotes free speech, and creates a vibrant culture.
Thank you for buying an authorized edition of this book and for complying with
copyright laws by not reproducing, scanning, or distributing any part of it in any
form without permission. You are supporting writers and allowing
Penguin Random House to continue to publish books for every reader.

DUTTON and the D colophon are registered trademarks of
Penguin Random House LLC.

THE LIBRARY OF CONGRESS HAS CATALOGED THE HARDCOVER EDITION OF
THIS BOOK AS FOLLOWS:
Names: Jakobson, Haley, author.
Title: Old enough: a novel / Haley Jakobson.
Description: New York: Dutton, Penguin Random House LLC, 2023.
Identifiers: LCCN 2022038129 (print) | LCCN 2022038130 (ebook) |
ISBN 9780593473009 (hardcover) | ISBN 9780593473016 (ebook)
Subjects: LCGFT: Novels.
Classification: LCC PS3610.O437 O45 2023 (print) |
LCC PS3610.O437 (ebook) | DDC 813/.6—dc23/eng/20220824
LC record available at https://lccn.loc.gov/2022038129
LC ebook record available at https://lccn.loc.gov/2022038130

Dutton trade paperback ISBN: 9780593473023

Printed in the United States of America
1st Printing

BOOK DESIGN BY ALISON CNOCKAERT

This is a work of fiction. Names, characters, places, and incidents
either are the product of the author's imagination or are used fictitiously,
and any resemblance to actual persons, living or dead, businesses,
companies, events, or locales is entirely coincidental.

For my mom, who listened.

# Author's Note

A note before reading—

This is a work of fiction that navigates the messy, painful complexities of long-standing trauma. To my fellow survivors—as well as anyone who carries a tender heart—I ask that you go forth gently and with great care. As you hold this book, may it hold you too.

# 1

IT WAS THE first day of Gender and Sexuality Studies 101.
There were only six of us and the pressure of forced intimacy was
palpable. The first person I noticed was a long-necked girl sitting
with perfect posture, tapping her manicured nails on her notebook. Coffin-shaped, pink polish, with thin gold bracelets on both
wrists. She was very pale, with a light smattering of freckles across
her nose. A single small, pear-shaped diamond dotted the center
of a gold band on her left ring finger. It was a promise ring, I could
practically smell it, but I wanted to give her the benefit of the
doubt. Maybe it was a feminist move to reclaim her ring finger,
a kind of "I'm-married-to-myself" fuck-you to the patriarchy. I
hated that word now, "patriarchy." All I could think of were over-
priced graphic tees and white liberal mothers on Facebook updat-
ing their status to "WE'RE STILL WITH HER" and "PANTSUIT
NATION!" Not that I'd prefer timelines littered with American
flag beer koozies and Bible quotes. Although, I did love the liberal
Christians—the ones who believe Jesus is a woman and include
their pronouns and a verse from the Corinthians in their email
signature.

Promise Ring Girl was sitting next to a person in a navy button-up, ironed meticulously so that the collar was stiff and crisp. They were Black and wore a maroon beanie, a tight fade peeking out from underneath. I didn't want to assume their gender, not that I should have assumed Promise Ring's. They side-eyed her tapping nails and didn't seem amused. They lounged in their seat, legs spread, resting one elbow on the back of their chair. They took up space. There wasn't an ounce of self-doubt about them. I checked for rainbow paraphernalia. I didn't see any, but they didn't really seem the type. They shifted in their seat, and I heard the jingle of keys from underneath the table. I strained my neck until I clocked a silver carabiner hooked around their belt loop. Bingo. Ugh. Problematic that I was doing this, but I'm sure everyone was assuming that I was straight and in a sorority, so.

I looked around. The classroom was old and outdated. Desks the color of manila folders and uncomfortable plastic chairs. The kind with the two metal circle screws near the top, which always snagged my hair. The floor was shiny linoleum, but not shiny enough to cover years of scuff marks. There was a new wing at school that had been renovated over the summer, all plush carpets and ergonomic everything. I heard the STEM kids all had standing desks.

"Hello hello hello!"

Professor Tolino flew into the room carrying a tote, a purse, a leather backpack, and what looked like a burlap sack hanging all over her person. I knew who she was because I had looked her up on one of those teacher rating sites. Four and five stars, reviews that said things like "fair grader" and "final wasn't crazy" and one that said "loose cannon, but in a good way." That sold me.

I only knew one person in the class, Candace Kelpin, also a sophomore who lived on my floor. She was very short, had a dimpled chin, and could be spotted a mile away because of her mess

of frizzy curly red hair. Her Instagram bio read, "yeah, carpet/
drapes." We'd been friends since last semester. The first time
we talked we were both in the bathroom, and I was brushing my
teeth. I saw her glance down at my Birkenstocks.

"You gay?" she asked.

I nearly choked on my toothbrush.

"Yeah," I blurted.

It had just come out. I had just come out. I had only told a few
people I was bi. Izzie knew, and my mom, and Nova, obviously.
After Nova ghosted me over the summer, I decided I should make
an effort to look gayer, so I had gotten my septum pierced in July
and bought a pair of Birkenstocks. Besides that, I was pretty
femme and my nails weren't even that short, and I was too tall to
cuff my jeans without them looking like capris. I thought Doc
Martens were absurdly expensive for a wildly uncomfortable
shoe. Candace was the first person at college I had come out to.

"Sweet," she said. "Come over later. Like sixish. Bring wine or
cookies and weed if you have any. I'll introduce you to the queers.
I'm in 217."

I showed up at 6:07 with wine and cookies and no weed. I entered the room to find, as Candace had promised, the queers. A lot
of them. They were laughing and smoking, and a few people with
technicolor hair turned to see who had walked in. Candace hopped
up from her twin bed and threw her arms around me.

"I totally forgot your name, dude."

I laughed. "It's Sav," I said, presenting her with the wine and
cookies.

She gestured toward her desk, and I added my snacks to an already heaping pile of cheap wine and a lot of weed. Candace put
her fingers in her mouth and whistled, jumping up on a chair.
Everyone turned toward her.

"Queers, this is Sav! Sav, these are the queers! Pronouns, Sav?"

"She/her!" My voice squeaked a little.

"*Hey, Sav!*" bellowed the queers.

A drink was shoved in my hand and I was pulled onto a floor cushion and into a conversation about why tops-and-bottoms rhetoric was bullshit.

"Wait, everyone is secretly a switch, right?" argued someone with oversized wire glasses and a silver mullet, definitely self-dyed and self-cut.

"Absolutely not! Touch-me-nots are real and valid and so are pillow princesses!" This from someone who looked like a cross between a young Sigourney Weaver and a midthirties Freddie Mercury.

I had literally no idea what they were talking about, let alone which category I fit into. My eyes wandered around the room. There was a large print on the wall with many squiggly lines that looked like a wave. I had taken a meditation class once where the instructor told us to imagine our breath like the tide rolling in and out. Meditation made me feel like I was going to die, but the wave image had stuck. I took a deep breath. There were little stalks drawn on the bottom of the print. They looked like what I imagined a broccoli tree to look like. Wait, did broccoli grow on a tree?

"It's a tarot card." Candace interrupted my thoughts. "It's all about joy and, like, celebrating success. Good vibes. My ex got it for me. No good vibes there, but I like the print."

"What happened with your ex?"

Oh, well, that was forward of me.

"I cheated. Not my best move. Don't worry, though, she cheated too. *Right, Mitchie?*" Candace cupped her hands around her mouth and screamed across the room. Someone with a long black braid swung her head around and flipped her off.

"Fuck you, Candy!" she yelled before turning back to the joint she had been passing around.

"You . . . still hang out?"

"Ah, young, sweet queer." Candace swung her arm around my shoulders.

"You have much to learn about the inner workings of the gay group dynamic."

•

"COOL IF I sit here?"

I looked up to see very white teeth attached to a curly-headed person with a soul-crushing jawline and the kind of lashes no amount of castor oil could promise me.

"Yes, of course!"

I snatched my denim jacket from the desk next to me.

"Sweet, I'm Wesley. I use they/them pronouns." They sat down next to me. "I like your water bottle."

"I—thank you—I'm—Savannah. She/her, it's from Amazon, I feel guilty about it."

What had happened to my ability to string together a normal sentence?

"Ah, the clutches of capitalism and the quest for hydration and a dope aesthetic. I feel you."

They spoke like a quippy Twitter feed but somehow it was endearing. I resisted the urge to shout, "I'm good at banter too, you just have very green eyes!!" Before I could respond, a pile of syllabi was dropped onto my desk.

"Pass these around, my dear." Professor Tolino was already on the other side of the room, fiddling with the blinds.

"Vitamin D is an essential element of the Socratic debate, don't you think?"

She directed the question to someone wearing an oversized tee that read NOT YOUR BABYGIRL. They were Asian, with those very blunt bangs that only ten percent of the population pull off, and I saw platform combat boots sticking out from under their desk. A neon orange backpack rested near their feet. I had no idea how some people could wear their personality so effortlessly. I had regular panic attacks deciding if I could pull off gold hoops.

Not Your Babygirl nodded, but Professor Tolino had already bounded toward the other side of the room. She started scribbling on the whiteboard with a blue marker.

"Names, pronouns, why you're here." She swung around and pointed at Promise Ring.

"I'm Lara Wentworth." Her voice had a singsong quality. "She, um, her."

I tried not to judge the pregnant pause between her words.

I also tried not to think about the trademark curve of her designer nose, her Gucci belt, or how I could see her collarbones peeking out beneath her knitted black top. She had an Alpha Phi sticker on her computer. Of course.

Shit. I was being so judgy. Not everyone in a sorority was a horrible person. I mean, Izzie wasn't. People just want friends, I reminded myself. A community. I wanted that too.

"I'm an anthropology major. I study people. And, like, people have genders, so. Ha ha. I'm here!"

Dangly Keys was up next, but they currently had their head tilted toward Lara, not even attempting to unfurrow their brows. They sucked in their breath before turning to look at the rest of us.

"Yeah, it's Reg. She/her. Psych major with a focus on restorative justice. Needed this class to fill a requirement, but, uh . . ." Reg looked over at Lara again, no expression on her face. "Happy to be here." She then forced a smile at Lara, who beamed back.

This was going to be interesting.

"Whatsuuuuuup. I'm Candace, she/they. You can call me Candy if you think I'm sweet." Candace laughed at her own joke.

"Undeclared and still shopping around. But this class is a prerequisite for being gay, so I had to take it!"

Everybody chuckled. It was impossible not to like her.

Candace winked at Not Your Babygirl, who was seated next to her.

"I'm Vera, she/her. Fine arts major, exploring the impact of satanic worship on feminine liberation. Through textile."

My phone buzzed. I peeked under my desk. It was from Candace.

I'd sell my soul to Satan for her to step
on me.

I snorted.

"Bless you, Sav." Candace bowed her head in prayer.

Professor Tolino's eyes landed on me, one eyebrow raised.

"Hi! She/her. Creative writing." The words tumbled out.

There was a beat. Professor Tolino looked at me expectantly.

"Oh! Um. Savannah. Sav. Either. Yes."

There was a laugh from Green Eyes, and I blushed. They jumped in.

"Hey, y'all! I'm Wesley, they/them, I'm a sociology major. More specifically, the sociology of gender. Basically, gender is a thing in my life that is interesting!"

I laughed too loudly.

"Thank you, everyone. I'm thrilled to meet you all. I hope in this room we can cultivate a sense of collaboration, critical thinking, and respect for the individual experience. Let's take a look through the syllabus, shall we?"

There was nothing more mind-numbing than going over a syllabus. I peeked over at Candace, who was now pretending she didn't get her own copy and was sharing with Vera instead, the two of them crowding over one desk, knees precariously close.

"I guess I'm seeing that a lot of these books are older, and very focused on the gender binary."

I turned to see Wesley speaking. I scrambled to flip through the pages in my syllabus to find the reading list.

"There are some dope essays and books that have been published in the past decade, give or take, that are really good. A lot of perspectives from folks of different cultures that have a more nuanced relationship to gender than the US does."

"I'd love to hear more, Wesley! Let's find a time to chat in the coming week and see if we can change up the list a bit?" Professor Tolino seemed genuinely excited.

Wesley beamed. I realized I was also smiling and immediately became very invested in the zipper on my jacket.

"You'll see that at the end of the semester you have a final project, and I'd like to plant the seed now to start thinking about it. I want you to be my teachers and present on something you feel truly passionate about. Gender and Sexuality Studies covers a wide range of topics, so there are plenty of subjects to explore. It's my hope that as we trek on, you'll be inspired by the conversations we have together. So, be vigilant in our discussions and really start to ask yourself where your passions lie, yes?" She looked around at all of us.

I nodded eagerly, despite having no fucking clue what I was passionate about.

Lara asked if she could be excused to the bathroom. Her voice was chipper, peppered with invisible question marks at the end of her sentences. I resisted the urge to scour her Instagram right then and there, already making a bet with myself about how many posts featured pumpkin spice lattes and how many captions read "Saturdays Are for the Boys" unironically.

"Actually, Lara"—Professor Tolino interrupted my thoughts—"I think this is a good stopping point for all of us. I'll let you out a bit early today. It was lovely meeting you, new friends. Get to work on the assignment for next week; it should already be up on Blackboard, Lord willing. See you next class!"

"Thank you!" Lara and I spoke at the same time. Goddamn it.

Candy's hands thudded onto my desk and she rocked back and forth, tipping my desk with her.

"What are you doing tonight? I just ended things with Maya."

"Who's Maya?"

"Maya. You know, that other orientation leader I was paired with over the summer?"

"Is she the one who bit your shoulder too hard?"

"Dude!" Candace shushed me and looked around the room. Vera had left.

"I still have a fucking bruise."

"Did you end it over that?"

"Over what?"

"The bite!"

"Oh, nah. The sex was amazing. But she wanted to switch dorms to be on my floor. Plus, I'm pretty sure I'm polyam now."

Candy was dating someone new every other week. I knew not to get too attached to anyone unless they made it to the month benchmark; otherwise I ended up with a bunch of random information about how to make kombucha in your closet or why Jenny from *The L Word* is a queer reclamation of the manic pixie dream girl trope and that is why it's okay that everyone secretly wants to fuck her. I had only watched season one of *The L Word*, but that was more than enough to know that nothing justified wanting to fuck Jenny.

Candace and I walked toward the door. I glanced behind me at Wesley. They were slinging a green backpack over their shoulder and I wondered if they had color coordinated it with their eyes. Their backpack straps were so tight, it was so nerdy.

"Being. Too. Obvious," Candace growled under their breath and yanked me through the doorway.

"Shut up!" I blushed hard.

Candace was looking at her phone. Someone had texted her something very long and with a lot of cat emojis.

"Maya talked to her therapist and wants to have a check-in." I rolled my eyes.

"I know, but I'm such a sucker for a theater major. So intense. The brooding kills me."

I laughed and headed for the quad. "Bye, Candy if you're sweet."

"Nothing compared to you, sugar!" Candace waved.

When I reached the quad, I stopped and closed my eyes, turning my face up toward the sky. It was an unseasonably warm day, one that I decided to blame on chance when I knew very well it was because the earth was burning. I picked the bench with the least shade and sat. I shook out my bag, looking for the apple I had taken from the dining hall this morning. My phone tumbled onto the grass and the screen lit up. I felt a little twinge in my stomach as I picked it up. I had two missed calls from Izzie. We hadn't talked in a week or so. I was just busy, I told myself. I'd call her later. I absentmindedly opened Instagram to a post of a manicured hand sporting a gigantic diamond ring. I squinted from the sun to see who had posted it.

SparklingLikeIzzie. 12 minutes ago.

Fuck. What? No fucking way. I scrolled to see the caption.

"Ring by spring, anyone? Sooooo lucky to get to spend the rest of my life with my best friend."

My phone screen burned against my fingertips. It had become too hot on the bench. Beads of sweat were gathering around my hairline. I dropped my phone in my lap and scooted to the far end of the bench, where a lone branch did its best to block the sun. My heart was drumming espresso-infused palpitations against my chest despite the lack of caffeine I'd had that day. I closed my eyes, but it did the opposite of what I'd hoped for. The movie I had been avoiding started to play.

Izzie is in an ivory gown. He stares at me while he stands in line with the groomsmen, holding the rings. During the pictures Izzie insists on, his blue eyes scan the slit in my skirt. He leans against a beam by the dance floor as Izzie loops her hands around my neck, he's seated at the edge of the bar while we take tequila shots, he's opening the restroom door for us as I grasp the train of Izzie's dress in my arms. He watches me, never blinking, while I do everything I can to avoid his gaze.

# 2

### Sixteen
### July 12 — Morning

THERE WAS NEVER enough tanning oil. The sickly-sweet smell of it, burning against teenage skin. We spent the bits of summer you were home baking by the pool. All day long I'd run from the pool to the house, "bathroom!" trailing behind me as I snaked my way across the lawn, avoiding the patches of grass gone prickly. In the mirror I'd peer at my nose, waiting for my eyes to adjust from the sun, blinking hard. And there in the quiet of your bathroom, wallpapered in beige and lit by iron sconces, I'd search for my freckles. The mark of summer, proof that winter was behind us and we were no longer cold and pale and bored. No longer stuck in math class with our chins on our palms, willing the clock to tick faster. Our skin was like a sundial, each shade we burned darker meant time well spent. We found a worthiness in being tan, like being made anew, even with the warnings that it would ruin us one day. But we wanted to be ruined; all teenage girls do. A tan meant summer, and summer an endless promise.

"I feel crispy!" you yelled as I traipsed my way back up to the pool.

"Me too, I just checked! I want to be the tannest I've ever been," I said, unlatching the fence to the pool.

"Same! I'm so pale, I look like a vampire. I want to go back to school looking like I spent the summer in Aruba. No, Jamaica. No, the South of France!"

"Oh my god, the South of France!" I shouted back. I dipped my fingers in the pool and scrunched them through my hair like I'd seen in a magazine, willing beach curls to come. In those days, I believed that changing my hair could change my whole life.

"Ooh, good idea," you said as you bounced off your chair to join me by the edge of the pool. Our knees dug into the chipped concrete.

"We're beach goddesses now!" You blew a kiss toward me. I giggled and shook my hair in response.

What I wanted, you wanted. And the same in reverse. But when we weren't together, when you were off at summer camp riding horses and spreading chocolate and marshmallow fluff on white bread, I spent most of my time reading. Safely behind the glass doors of my childhood home, the siren call of wealthy suburban summers seemed to quiet. My dad used to joke that he'd leave in the morning for work and say goodbye to me while I read on the couch, and he'd arrive home that evening and find me in the same spot, a new book in hand. At home I was a totally different person, so much so that I had to remind myself that I wanted the lifestyle you said you wanted. Most girls in our town did. Money and husbands and Burberry trench coats. Hints of anything else were tiny flashes I tried to forget. Even when I won the poetry competition in third grade. Even when I spent a summer at art camp and sobbed the whole car ride home, dreading going back to school. Even when we took a class trip into the city and saw a woman perform spoken word and I leaned very far forward in my seat because I didn't want to miss a single word, even when she looked right at me when she spoke and her face was pretty but her voice was so deep that she was at once both beautiful and scary, even when I whispered her poetry to myself in the mirror every night after for a whole week. Even then they were all just tiny flashes. Little moments. Nothing I couldn't dismiss by shaking my head and calling them weird.

I lay on my side and poked the flesh of your arm, testing your skin for sunburn. We were safe, for now. There was no little splotch of white rising from where my finger had been. When I looked up, I saw him approach the pool, bounding up the hill with his arms stretched out wide. He wore his red bathing trunks, the same as the summer before, frayed at the edges from too many washes. I was suddenly aware that my mouth felt extra wet, like I had sucked on an ice cube. I swallowed hard. At fifteen yards away I could tell his skin had already turned caramel from a winter at a California university, which my parents insisted was not a real place to go to college. They said sunshine and school did not go together. Before unlatching the gate, he looked over his shoulder and I could make out another person in the distance. My belly soured; I could taste the sweet potato fries I had for lunch at the back of my throat. I swallowed hard. It was an Older Girl, I could tell, hips swinging as she catwalked toward us. When she was close, his arm flopped over the stretch of her shoulders. He claimed her, and she was happy to be claimed. She was everything I wasn't yet, her thin frame bikinied and belly ringed. She yanked at his hair as he struggled to unlock the gate, now both arms around her and reaching from behind. A townie, you called them, girls he knew from growing up who never made it out of the suburbs.

"Dizzy Izzie!" he shouted, cupping his mouth with his hands.

"Finally!" you called out to him, jumping up from your lounge chair and lunging for his neck. The Older Girl laughed, but it wasn't a real laugh.

"You're so greasy! What is that?" he complained, feigning disgust as he pushed you away. You streaked his chest with your fingers, leaving a slug trail of oil behind, your laugh an antidote to Older Girl's, full-toothed and maniacal.

"Oh my god, I used to use that stuff," said Older Girl, who picked up the bottle with her long red nails. She spoke like sandpaper was stuck in her throat. She turned to you. "It's really important to use sunscreen, Izzie. Like, my mom had skin cancer once." You shot a look at me.

I stared at her, realizing her tan had an orange tint. Older Girl's name was Kelsey. I remembered her from my freshman year; she had been a senior. She was on the dance team and held the coveted spot at the front of the group. She could drop it low and undulate her back on the way up, showing off her butt. She had one of those stomachs that turned into a four-pack when she laughed, and a long torso and long legs. A totally unfair genetic jackpot. Her thighs didn't touch. I peered down at my own legs. My inner thighs had sprouted little squiggle marks earlier that spring. I had noticed them sitting on the toilet, how they spiraled out from underneath my paisley shorts. I was shocked. I didn't think you could get stretch marks at fifteen.

"You fucker," he cried, trying to wipe away the glop of tanning oil you had smeared on his chest. Then he was picking you up, which made you screech, and dangling you over the pool. The threat of being thrown in was always worse than the throw itself, and your screams grew louder, your laughter uncontrollable. Your big brother. Your idol.

He put you down and dove into the pool, and when he came up for air, he whipped his head from side to side, leaving his hair in a semi-Mohawk. He looked at me for a prolonged moment and then flicked water at my feet. I glared at him and rolled my eyes. Those two seconds of silent communication would feed me for a week.

I had turned sixteen the month before. I had always been obsessed with the age sixteen; it was my lucky number. It signified maturity. It didn't mean I was old but at least it was old enough. Old enough for him to notice me. He was twenty.

I grabbed the slick bottle from the table next to me and reached for the slope of my calf, careful to suck in my belly as I did. I prayed he could not see the folds of my stomach.

"That stuff smells like fake coconut," he groaned, wrinkling his nose. He hopped out of the pool, ignoring the ladder, just using his arms to lift his body out. Within moments he was standing and the weight of the water on his shorts tugged them down across his hips. I saw the creases peeking out of his bathing suit, the shape of a V cutting into his skin. I quickly looked away. *Cosmo* magazine had rated hip Vs the hottest part of a man's body.

"It's the best smell," I offered, squinting my eyes at him, hoping it looked like a twinkle but knowing it probably looked like my contact was bothering me. This was the first thing I'd said to him in the ten minutes since he'd arrived. "It smells like summer."

"We're trying to look like we spent the summer in the South of France," you explained, using a haughty accent with no specific place of origin.

"Weird. Gimme some," he growled and lunged for the sticky bottle. "Yeesh, gross," he said, sticking his tongue out. "How much should I put on?" The question startled me, because he was looking at me. The way he had asked, with innocence in his voice, warped time. I was the Older Girl and he was a little boy. Suddenly, it was possible, fathomable even, that he could want me.

"Just a couple sprays." I tried to sound nonchalant. "I'll tell you when you start to burn."

He threw his body onto a lounge chair and made a mess, oil spraying everywhere. He spit, it had gotten into his mouth, and the Older Girl laughed. She was such impossible competition. *No,* I told myself. *You're sixteen now. Things are different. You are different.* I stood up, careful to suck in my abdomen, and walked over to where he was sitting. I stuck my hand out and stole his eyes back; he acquiesced and handed me the bottle. Propping myself close to his chair, I made a big show of spraying my calves again, the layers of oil now so thick I could barely feel my skin underneath. But I would do anything to keep his attention on me, and on what I had been told were the best parts of me.

"You don't need any more of that." Your voice cut through my fantasy. My face reddened. "Think you're starting to burn. Remember what happened last time? I don't want you to have a fever during the party." I put the tanning oil back on the table.

"When do we start drinking?" you demanded, poking your brother's belly button.

He grabbed your hand away, pinned it down against your own head.

"Never," he teased. "You'll get too dizzy, Izzie."

I shrank back against my towel. We were still little to him. His little sister. His little sister's best friend.

"Oh, please." You rolled your eyes. "Dad lets me have wine at dinner, and it doesn't matter because by six p.m. they'll be so blasted they won't be able to tell if it's me at the bar or Mrs. Westerly."

"You're not wrong," he conceded. "Mom's already on her third gin and tonic, and it isn't even five yet."

"Classic," you said.

And it was. You could never rely on your parents for parenting, but you could always rely on the parties. Wildness was expected, demanded, and I relished that recklessness. What was routine for you was rebellious for me. My own parents were strict and boring and frustratingly reliable. My mom always called before the party to make sure the parents were home; my dad always picked me up after. Parenting, at your house, was a constant flip between lofty declarations of outdated ideals: sometimes it was all about how a young woman should be, should be seen, how to dress and flirt and talk about God, what dreams were prescribed and how to achieve them; the rest of the time it was a fervent blind eye. Well, not so much blind as drunk. And that sort of worked when we were just kids, when the nannies were around, when alcohol wasn't interesting. But we weren't kids anymore, and alcohol made everything interesting.

"So what are we drinking?" I asked.

"Fine, whatever," he said, rolling his eyes. "What do you want?" His eyes were so blue I forgot how to speak.

"Something super sweet! Girly! A Manhattan!" you squealed, and I exhaled. I had no idea what I wanted.

"A Manhattan is not, like, very sweet," said Kelsey, who had taken out her pink headphone bud just long enough to grace us with her attention.

"Have you ever had one?" he asked you, laughing.

"No!" we said in unison, suddenly hysterical, suddenly eleven and caught staying up past bedtime.

"You guys are so weird," he said, holding back a smirk. I could tell he was trying to impress Kelsey. "I'll be right back."

I watched him sprint down to the main house, noting he didn't have any hair on his back. He really wasn't that old, I thought, checking my phone. My home screen read 2:22. I closed my eyes tight and begged the universe for luck.

"Did you know a Manhattan wasn't sweet?" you whispered to me, lying on your side away from Kelsey.

"No, I definitely thought it was."

"Right?"

"So weird. We'll just add sugar."

You nodded, relieved that I didn't know something you didn't know.

"Yo, I got the goods." I turned to find your brother balancing cups and Diet Coke and a giant bottle of vodka. You clapped and ran to help him.

"You better not be lightweights," he said to you, filling the red plastic cups with clear liquid. My eyes widened.

"We're not. We drink all the time." You glanced at me for reassurance.

"Yeah. We're not babies anymore," I added, lifting my chin high.

"Whatever you say." He shrugged. "Cheers." He tapped my cup with his.

I took a sip and tried not to grimace. I looked up and found him watching me.

# 3

IZZIE WAS GETTING married.

My head was spinning. I needed to get to my room. I scooped up all my shit and ran toward my dorm. Why was she getting married? What was the rush? We were nineteen, for fuck's sake, and we grew up in *New York*. I mean, yeah, Izzie's mom was from Georgia and was in a Bible study group and was desperate for Izzie to have a boyfriend, but I had never known her to push marriage. She never pushed anything but martinis. But Izzie had trouble with boys throughout high school, and when she met Ben last year, she fell stupid in love. But still. Marriage? I thought of Lara and her promise ring. Suddenly that seemed like a much more laissez-faire approach to long-term commitment.

I knew I needed to call her. An hour had passed since she first called me, and there was a way these things should go. The best friend is supposed to know first. I mean, I should have known way before this. I should have been consulted by her boyfriend—fuck, her fiancé?—to help pick out the ring (diamond cut, with tiny emeralds), and I should have taken her to get her nails done, and I should have been hiding in the bushes while the proposal was happening. Nothing was going according to plan, our plan, the plan that we had carefully crafted since we were twelve years old. What had happened to the plan?

I was pacing around my room. My throat felt increasingly dry even though I was taking tiny sips from my water bottle every few seconds. Every minute that passed meant that our plan was getting screwed up even more. I needed to fix this fast. I could do the few-hours-post-proposal celebratory FaceTime. It was a call reserved for a second-tier friend, but it would work. I could reroute the plan. I had to. I could call now, say I got caught up after class, that I wasn't looking at my phone or it was dead. I stared at my phone, which I'd thrown on my bed as soon as I got to my room. It was taunting me. I didn't want to touch it.

It started ringing. I basically jumped out of my skin.

It was Izzie. Not a FaceTime, just a regular phone call.

It rang.

It rang.

It rang.

I knew it was about to go to voicemail, and I tried to think of reasons why I could let it. My throat was very dry. Maybe I was getting sick. Izzie would understand if I couldn't call her because I was sick. I felt a wave of guilt wash over me.

I lunged for my bed and swiped at the screen.

"Hey!" My voice came through clear.

"AHHHHHHHHH!"

I winced. On the other end I could hear nothing but screaming and heavy breathing. I shifted the phone away from my ear.

"Hi! Hi! What? What's happening?"

I couldn't admit that I had seen the post first.

"Savvy, I'm getting married. Ben proposed!"

Even though I already knew it was coming, my heart sank.

"Oh my god, Iz, congratulations! I can't believe—"

"I know, I know. It's fast," Izzie cut me off. "But I know he's the one, and he's graduating, and once ROTC ends he has to report to his base, like, right after, and then deployment is after that and it's just, like, crazy. And we already know we want to be together, so we might as well get the benefits now, you know? I just love him so much, and I know it's fast but—"

"Iz. I'm so happy for you." I tried to keep my voice cheery. "I totally understand."

"Ugh, Sav, I knew you would. And I know you've only met him once, but he totally loved you, and he knows you're my other half, and I'm just so fucking excited to spend my life with him."

I took a deep breath.

"That's so wonderful. He's a great guy, and I know he loves you, and whatever makes you happy makes me so happy too."

He was a great guy. And he really did love her. And for Izzie, that was huge. She wanted love so badly, and Ben loved all of her. He liked that she couldn't whisper, that she told the same stories over and over again, and when she suggested they dress as sexy Mr. and Mrs. Claus for Halloween, two weeks after they first hooked up, he drove two hours to a year-round Christmas store to buy the costumes. The guy was it. Most importantly, Izzie's biggest dream was to marry a man who was nothing like her father, and Ben wasn't.

"Fuck, Sav, my aunt's on the other line. You know how she gets. I have to go but I'll call you later or tomorrow and we'll talk about everything. I'm going to need your help. This thing is gonna be a fast turnaround, but it'll be so worth it."

"So worth it."

"I love you so much."

"I love you too. Congratulations. I'm hugging you from here."

"Hugging you back!" she squealed.

The line went dead.

I sat back on my bed, still gripping my phone.

Well, this was not how I thought my day would end. I had a writing assignment due tomorrow, but I couldn't shake the feeling of dread that had been growing since I saw Izzie's post this afternoon. I needed to distract myself. I needed Candace. I leapt from my bed and grabbed a bag, stuffing my phone and wallet inside. I headed down the hall and banged on Candace's door.

"It's Sav!" I spoke into the crevice between the door and the wall.

"Hi, Sav!" Candy's voice called out.

"Can I . . . come in?"

"You may!"

I swung open the door and saw Candace sitting on the floor with a person dressed in all lavender, wearing a dress so full it seemed to billow out from every angle, covering the floor like a carpet. Sort of a cross between a petticoat and a ball gown. This must be Maya.

"Sorry to interrupt—I totally forgot . . ."

I had not forgotten, but I was hoping their check-in was over.

"I was just preparing to leave." Maya's voice was deep, and she enunciated each word she spoke. Her eyes were dark, and her mouth seemed to be stuck in a perpetual pout.

"This was good, Maya. Thanks for, yeah, you know. Thanks." Candace smiled widely at Maya, who did not smile back. Instead, she unfurled from her carpet dress and glided out the door, not a single glance in my direction as she walked past me. She did not close the door behind her.

Candace took off her shoe and threw it at the door, barely missing my shoulder. It slammed shut.

"Goaaaaaaal!"

"Candace!" I yelped. "You almost hit me!"

"Don't worry, babe. Softball days." She flexed her arm.

"So how did that go?" I pulled out the chair tucked under Candy's desk and sat down.

"Yeah, we basically just broke up again. But she wanted to do it through a monologue she wrote in her acting class."

"You're kidding."

"I'm so far from kidding, I can't even tell you."

"Are you okay?"

"All good. She's a sweet girl. But her bark is actually very much *not* worse than her bite." Candace pulled up her shirtsleeve to reveal her left shoulder, which bore the bite mark Maya had left months earlier. It was a yellow-brown color and the tooth marks were still distinct. I closed my eyes. The bite made me queasy.

"I'm never gonna be able to wear a tank top again." Candace sighed.

"I'm very sorry, and I love you, and I need you to pull your shirt back down." My eyes were still closed.

"I understand."

I peeked one eye open. Candace was sprawled out on the floor again, hands tucked behind their head.

"So what's up?" she asked.

I thought about telling Candace about Izzie but decided against it. Too complicated. Besides, I didn't want to think about it anymore. I started doodling on a notepad sitting on their desk.

"Just bored. Is there anything happening tonight? Any parties?"

Candace narrowed her eyes at me.

"You want to go to a party on a Wednesday?"

I didn't usually go *out out* before the weekend.

"I do." I batted my eyes innocently.

"All riiight! I'm not even gonna question that. Let's do it to it. Let me text the network." They pulled out their phone and started typing vigorously. It dinged in an instant.

"Bingo." She flashed me the phone. Thirty minutes later we

showed up at an apartment just off campus. We trekked up four flights of stairs and, to my relief, I heard the chatter from down the hall, which meant there were enough people in there to talk to, or talk about, or fall in love with, so I could actually get my mind off the Izzie stuff. The apartment was a studio, with big crunchy-granola vibes. At least seventeen plants were crowded into the room, and a hammock was hung up in one corner. I recognized quite a few people there, people who frequented the monthly queer night at a bar in town, two of Candace's exes, and one person I had taken a writing class with last year. I think her name was Ludi. I hadn't realized she was queer, but we never interacted much in that class anyway.

A group of people surrounded Candace, so I was introduced by default, and before I knew it, I was chatting with an Italian major named Andie who was currently writing her thesis on the inherently gendered rhetoric of Romance languages. She was a senior.

"Do you speak any other languages?" Andie asked.

"Oh, um, a little French. From high school." I actually spoke a lot of French, but on the off chance that someone at this party was actually French, I did not want to be dragged over to them to do the whole "Hey! You're French! Sav speaks French! Talk!" thing. I always clammed up when that happened, which was a bummer, because I enjoyed practicing.

"Cool. Did you like it?" Andie inquired, genuinely interested.

"I did! Yeah. I did. For sure."

Candace elbowed me in the ribs and coughed into my ear. "Flirting."

"What?" I turned to her, confused.

She opened her eyes wide and glanced over at Andie.

"Oh."

Oh. Okay! Andie was cute. I could flirt with Andie. I could definitely flirt with Andie.

"So, what are your big three?" I turned back to her.

Andie blinked at me for a few moments, and then a look of recognition washed over her face.

"Astrology!"

I laughed. "Yes, astrology!"

"Got it. Okay, let me think. My sun is in . . . Aries? Yes, Aries."

"Amazing."

"Is it?"

"Keep going and I'll tell you."

She looked impressed.

"Moon in Cancer. And rising in . . . fuck, I always forget this one. Something about balance?"

"Libra!" I shouted.

"Yes! Libra." We both laughed.

"So? Did I pass the test?" She leaned in slightly.

"Let's see. So you can get really heated in a fight but also love to cozy up and make dinner for your friends, and you secretly love a beautiful Pinterest board and when people make decisions for you?"

Andie's mouth dropped open.

"You're good."

"Thank you."

Andie took a sip of her drink.

"I also like to make pretty girls dinner."

Instant blush.

"Well, I, um. I like dinner."

"Cool."

"Yo, lovebirds, I need to interrupt for a second." Candace poked her head between us. They squeezed Andie's shoulder. "Hernández, we're thinking about karaoke. You in?"

I looked at Andie, who threw up her hands. "Who says no to karaoke?"

"Only the worst people."

I loved nights like this, where one fun thing led into another and it felt like the universe was conspiring to show you a good time, to show you that you were worth having a good time.

"Let's do it."

Somebody called an Uber and five of us piled in, Candace insisting I sit on Andie's lap, which made both of us incredibly uncomfortable. I tried to make myself as light as possible while craning my neck to listen as Andie gave me a detailed review of the newest album by a band I should be gay enough to know about but didn't. Every time we went over a bump in the road I grimaced and said, "Sorry!" and the third time I did it she leaned in and said, "Hey, I'm really not complaining," and the hair on the back of my neck stood up.

We got to the karaoke spot and Candace practically leapt over the bar to get the songbook, apologizing to a bartender with a neon orange pixie cut who seemed terrified. Candace turned back to look at me and mouthed, "You and me, bitch." I rolled my eyes and reluctantly mouthed back, "Fine." The last time we were here she'd roped me into a rousing performance of the *Twilight* theme song, which has no lyrics, and demanded that we use only our bodies to portray the song's power.

"Can I get you a drink?" Andie handed me a frayed paper menu.

"Thank you, but I'm good. I'd love a water, though!"

"You know what? Water sounds great. I have an eight a.m. tomorrow."

"Exactly, me too."

That wasn't quite true, but it got us off the topic.

"Okay, so, what are you going to sing?!" I reached down the bar to grab the songbook. The pages were sticky.

"Look, I don't want to intimidate you, but I was in choir for all of middle school and high school." Andie spoke in a low voice, as if she was telling me a dark secret.

"Am I in the presence of a superstar?"

"Truth be told, you are. A lesbian superstar who got the solo on not one but two different songs in the annual Christmas performance. I was the talk of, like, my whole Long Island public school district."

"A Long Island girl, huh?" I mashed "Long" and "Island" together, making it sound like "Longaiiiiland."

"You're not from there, are you?"

"No, no, unfortunately I'm from the other direction. The ever-humble county of Westchester."

"Nooooo! Our classier nemesis! Bet it was fun to be gay there!"

"If only I'd known I was gay there!"

I played it off like a joke, but it was true. I came from the land of I Want to Be Her and had no idea that was a telltale cover-up for I Want to Date Her.

Andie laughed and I saw that her bottom teeth were a little crooked. I liked that.

"Same, dude, same."

"I'm your dude, huh?" I raised my eyebrows at her.

"Oh yeah, bro." She leaned in closer to me.

"Okay, Hernández," I whispered, staring at her mouth.

She laughed and shook her head.

"No way. Cute girls get to be on a first-name basis."

"Hey, newlyweds! The show is about to begin!"

Candace was standing center stage holding a mic.

"We better go over there." I grabbed both of our waters and headed toward the back of the room. I felt Andie's hand on the small of my back, guiding me there.

Candace's first solo pick was a sultry rendition of "Wrecking

Ball," during which she attempted to climb onto the bar and swing at the cheap-looking chandelier in the center of the room. The bartender was not having it and pulled the plug to the speakers until Candy got down.

"I can't take another second of this. I'm gonna go pee," I whispered to Andie.

I snuck toward the bathroom at the front of the bar and accidentally bumped into a giant group of guys coming through the door.

"Sorry," I mumbled, and then kicked myself for apologizing for nothing.

"Yoooo, Savannah!" I looked up. Oh boy. It was Matt.

"Hey, Matt." I prepared myself for a bear hug.

"What's up? I haven't seen you in a minute!" Within seconds he engulfed me, crushing my body in the process.

"Dude, we have like five minutes before the dollar beers are done." A tall Black guy in a sports jersey elbowed Matt in the ribs.

"I'm coming, but wait, Kev, this is Savannah. Remember, the girl I worked with over the summer?"

It was true. Matt, of all people, had worked the same shift at The Spine, the bookstore in town. Matt, who was very proud of being Irish, perpetually had a sunburn on his nose, and was ridiculously upbeat all the time. He seemed to have no real interest in reading but every interest in talking to each customer who came in about what they wanted to read. He said "sure, sure, sure" a lot while nodding very fast, whipping his lacrosse boy hair off his forehead. What I gathered from our shifts together were three things: Matt loved beer pong, golden retrievers, and his fraternity brothers.

"Oh shit, hey, dude, you write and shit, right?" his friend asked.

I blushed. Why had Matt told Giant Jersey Man that I was a

writer? I had read him one half of a poem on our lunch break, once, after he badgered me about it for twenty minutes.

"Nah, dude, Sav's a *poet*." Matt beamed at me, as if being a nineteen-year-old poet meant anything at all.

"Cool, cool. That's actually very cool." Jersey Man was nodding but had his eyes on the bar.

"It was great to see you, Matt." He jumped in for another hug. He smelled like Old Spice.

"We should def hang out, though. Add me on Snap?" He pointed at me, his eyes awaiting my approval.

"Totally." I absolutely was not going to add his Snap.

I waved and made my escape to the bathroom. Matt perplexed me. He was exactly the kind of guy I went to high school with. But for whatever reason, Matt lit up every time he saw me. I think he probably just wanted to fuck me. He had chalked me up to be a sort-of-nerdy-sort-of-hot liberal arts student and wanted to check me off his list. I hated that I felt a little smug about that. As if it was worth anything that exactly the kind of person I tried to avoid wanted me at all.

I peed and fiddled with my hair and put on more ChapStick and then headed back to my group. Matt and his friends were each holding two beers and were talking at an unpleasant volume.

Right as I got to our table, "Mr. Brightside" started blaring on the speakers and Andie jumped up.

"That's my song!" she shouted.

"Then you better go sing!" I shouted back. She ran up to the stage and grabbed the mic.

"God, she's hot. Nice job, Sav." Candace thudded into Andie's seat, beer in one hand, and chugged the rest of my water with the other.

"Yeah, she's very cool." I stared up at Andie, who slid to her knees and was giving it her absolute all. I cheered loudly.

"Sav, why did you just get a DM that says *'did I just see you at Chords?'*"

I looked over at Candace, who was holding my phone. Sure enough, it was lit up by a DM. novagonnahappen had messaged me three minutes ago.

No fucking way.

I grabbed my phone from them, dumbfounded, staring at the unread message. She was reaching out *now*? No, no, no, no. I couldn't deal with her. But maybe? No. This was not good news. It was another one of their games. Which were sometimes very fun. And sexy. But mostly very painful. But also . . . very fun and sexy. Fuck.

"Wait—I know that handle." Candace leaned over and tried to take my phone.

"Do not open that message!" I slapped my hand over the screen.

"I'm not! I'm just looking—Holy fuck, Sav, you're talking to Nova Chatto? You cannot get caught up with them."

My head jolted up in surprise.

"Wait, you know each other?"

"We know of each other."

"How?"

"Let's just say we have dated in the same circles."

"Isn't that how being gay works?"

"We have dated the exact same circle. One circle in particular."

I gasped. "Natalie?"

Candace closed her eyes and sighed.

"Natalie."

"But you both have red hair?"

"That's what you're getting from this?"

"Sorry, no, I just had no idea. You've never mentioned it."

"It's not my favorite topic of conversation. Why are you talking to Nova? Didn't they graduate or, like, go on some cross-country tour?"

"European tour, actually."

"Why do you know that, Sav?" Candace looked suspicious.

"Remember when I said my last girlfriend was an asshole?"

Candace's eyes widened.

"From over the summer? You told me she didn't go to school here! I thought you met at the bookstore!"

"I may have told a small lie." I bit my lip.

Candace crossed her arms in disbelief.

"They are bad fucking news."

"Believe me, I know."

"You're still talking to her?"

"No! Seriously, I'm not. We haven't talked since before she left for the tour. Well, she hasn't talked to me. She completely ghosted me."

"God, I knew they sucked. What a fuckboy. And that's a lot, coming from a recovering fuckboy."

"Who said you've recovered?"

"Fuck you."

"Wait, so besides dating the same girl, what happened? Why do you hate Nova so much?"

"Ugh, I don't even like talking about it. I hate giving them my energy."

"Please? It's communal hatred. Let me commiserate with you," I begged.

"Fine." Candace relented. "But only because she left you to drown in your babygay tears and that really bummed me out."

She wasn't wrong.

"I met Natalie early on first semester freshman year, at a party, and I was just a total puppy dog for her. She was so cool, and a senior, and so hot, and we had this really intense connection.

We're also both from Vermont, and we kind of nerded out about that, and she was just so great to be around. We started talking a lot and I completely fell for her, and I felt like she really liked me, and we started hooking up and stuff. We were going to parties together, basically as a couple, and we even went back to Vermont for a weekend, and I told her I was in love with her, which is completely mortifying now considering her response."

"Which was?"

"And I quote: '*Your energy is really amazing.*'"

"No."

"Yup."

"Okay, so then what happened?" I asked.

"Fucking Nova happened. I had met her at a couple parties, and we'd gone to one of her concerts, and they were always hanging around Natalie and obviously flirting with her. Natalie kept reassuring me that they were just friends and had been since their sophomore year, but I didn't really believe it, and then right before winter break, I saw that Nova was texting her a bunch at like two a.m. I looked at her phone while she was in the bathroom and Nova was saying shit like, 'She's so young for you. Are you sure you're getting all your needs met by her?' And, like, 'We have so much history together. Our connection is magnetic. I can't get you out of my head.'"

My jaw clenched. Thinking about Nova talking about someone else that way stung.

"I'm so sorry."

Candace chewed on a fingernail.

"Yeah. Thanks. It's whatever."

I could tell it was very much not whatever.

"And you know what's so fucked up?" Candace whipped their head toward me. "When I confronted Nat she said nothing had happened, physically, but she was really confused and sad and graduating and she didn't want anything serious, with Nova or me. She said she didn't want to hurt me."

I knew what was coming.

"They started dating right after, over winter break."

"Fuck."

"No, fuck Nova."

I was starting to understand why Candy didn't stick around in relationships for too long.

"You did not deserve that, at all."

"Thanks, buddy." Candace wasn't looking at me now. She was trying to play it cool, but I could tell she was sad. "You're not gonna respond, are you?" She looked down.

"What?" I asked, confused.

"To their DM." Candace cocked her head toward my phone.

"No." I shook my head. "Of course not."

"Good. 'Cause they're a waste of our time."

Candace drained the last of her beer and wiped her mouth. Her face broke into a devilish smile.

"What?" I asked.

"It's time."

"Time for—?"

Candace pushed me out from the booth and leapt back up onstage, beckoning for me to join her, just as the intro of "It's Raining Men" began to play.

# 4

WHEN I FIRST got to school my freshman year, I had many plans to burst out of my shell and find myself, whatever that meant, but where I actually found myself was glued to a couple of girls I met in my orientation group. Julia and Victoria.

On the first day of orientation, we were sectioned off into smaller groups. As I smoothed my name tag onto my chest, Julia gasped and pointed to her own.

"Oh my god. All of our names end in an 'uh' sound. That's fucking crazy."

"So crazy." Victoria nodded, eyes wide.

"Oh yeah. It's like fate, I guess!" I joked.

Julia grabbed my wrist and squeezed.

"That's literally exactly what I was going to say."

They were nice enough, and included me in their plans, and reminded me of Izzie. But most white girls with blond hair reminded me of Izzie. We went out together on the weekends, frat parties and whatever upperclassmen house party they could get the details on, but during the weeks I mostly kept to myself. I wasn't used to not having a built-in best friend, and for the first time I realized there could be benefits of having a bigger friend group. But I had no idea how to find one. Izzie was having the time of her life in North Carolina and was in the middle of rush. I tried to keep my voice cheery on the phone with her and did my best to keep up with all the updates she sent me, like how she saw a guy in Phi Kappa Phi eat a live goldfish and then throw it up, still alive, one minute later. And how she wasn't allowed to post any photos of herself holding a red plastic cup, even though she could barely keep up with how much the rest of her sorority drank. "I thought we were bad, Sav, but if I'm gonna make it through four years of this I'm going to need to buy a second liver." I cringed when she said that. I purposely arrived late to pregames with Julia and Victoria, pretending I had already had a few shots before I arrived.

In March of our second semester, Julia invited me to a movie night with this guy she had met at a toga-themed party we'd been to the previous weekend. That's where I met Josh. Josh was friends with Julia's toga lover, and he was a journalism major, and a sophomore. Julia and I got there a few minutes after the movie started. She made a show of pointing to the empty seat next to Josh. He gave me a quick wave and then turned back to the movie.

It was a Marvel movie. During an action scene with lots of explosive noises, Josh turned to me and offered me some popcorn. A bomb went off on the screen, and it lit up our faces. He was wearing eyeliner and had a little scar jutting from his bottom lip toward his chin. He looked like a slightly emo Matthew Gray Gubler.

"Thank you," I whispered, digging out a handful of popcorn.

"Sav, right?"

"Yes."

"I'm Josh. He/him."

A cis boy wearing eyeliner who introduces himself with his pronouns is fucking bisexual catnip.

"She/her," I added.

"Dope. I like shes and hers." He grinned.

Josh was from Oregon, played bass guitar, and told me he missed hiking every weekend. I did not tell him I would give up sugar for a year if it meant I didn't have to go on a single hike ever again. I also did not tell him that I thought bass guitar was boring. He wore rectangular black glasses that slouched a little on his nose, and he wrinkled his eyebrows a lot when he was listening. When he asked for my number at the end of that night, I couldn't tell if I actually liked him or if I just liked the idea of having someone else to spend time with on the weekends. Julia and Victoria were becoming insufferable.

Josh was the reason I came out. Not directly, and not because I wasn't into him, but because he took me to the open mic night where I saw Nova play for the first time. Gorgeous, magnetic, treacherous Nova. Nova, who had the power to make the summer after freshman year one of the most electrifying times of my life, and managed to totally ruin it too.

The open mic was at an apartment off campus, but instead of the poorly-decorated-except-for-a-beer-pong-table-and-neon-sign two-bedroom I had become accustomed to, I found myself in a cozy living room with scuffed leather couches and soft twinkly lights strung across the ceiling. There were black-and-white photographs on the olive-green walls, and a massive cream tapestry, and a whiteboard was hung in one corner. On it was a monthly schedule of chores written out neatly in pink and purple. According to the board, four people lived there. Names like Seven, Ash, Rain, and someone called Super Nova. It was a potluck-style party, and two people had even made their own bread, complete with an ingredient list next to the cutting boards, in case anyone had any allergies. An assortment of rugs and blankets had been rolled out onto the hardwood floor, making it look like a giant patchwork quilt. I chose a light blue fluffy blanket just in front of the wall, so I could rest my back against it.

"Some of this stuff can get kind of weird. My band is playing somewhere in the middle and then we can leave right after."

"Isn't that kind of rude? Not to stay?"

"Nah, it's cool. People do it all the time. Trust me, you'll want to leave."

Josh had told me it was a folk night, which didn't mean banjos, just that anyone could perform. I don't know why, but I was expecting Ed Sheeran covers interspersed with dramatic readings of Rupi Kaur poems. Instead, I found myself mesmerized by every performance, everything from a jazz quartet to a Dolly Parton cover band to a slam poet who talked about the underground BDSM scene in Berlin, which sounded terrifying yet thrilling.

Josh's band was better than I thought it would be. I was nervous he would make a weird music-playing face, which would be a guaranteed ick for me, but he didn't. His upper lip quivered a little, making him look like he was snarling. It was kind of cute. After his set, he snuck back over to me and kissed me. He squeezed my shoulder and looked at me eagerly.

"You all were amazing," I whispered, trying not to distract the performer who had just started playing.

"The vibes were on tonight. We were really feeling it," Josh said at full volume.

"Totally. I could tell. You're so talented." He was lapping up the compliments. I wanted to roll my eyes but instead I leaned in and kissed him again, and then scooted over to make room for him to sit back down.

"Yo, we can go now." He glanced toward the door, where his bandmates were waiting.

"I want to stay. Everyone's been so great so far."

Josh's face grew sullen.

"You were obviously the best, though." I grabbed his chin. "Thank you so much for bringing me," I said, coating my voice with sweetness.

"Of course, babe. I knew you would dig this."

Satisfied that he was the catalyst for my joy, he sat back down. He waved his bandmates out the door. I settled into his shoulder and he linked his fingers into mine.

The host of the open mic came on to introduce the next act. They were wearing bright fuchsia overalls, striped socks, and a bucket hat. They couldn't have been more than five foot two, and they kept having to adjust the microphone back down after each act.

"Our next performer is allergic to guava, hails from Fort Apache Reservation, and is double-jointed. It is my honor to introduce my lover, my brother, my favorite Aries, the beautiful nightmare that is: Super Nova!"

The crowd erupted in applause and at least five people whipped out their phones to record. I had a feeling that a lot of the people here had come specifically to see this person play.

When Nova walked onstage, which was just a corner of the living room designated by a line of decorative pillows in a large square, I was surprised. I don't know who I was expecting, but the person in front of me didn't look like a nightmare. She wasn't wearing any makeup, I didn't think, maybe tinted ChapStick, or her lips were naturally very red. It wasn't profound or anything, not to wear makeup, it was just. I don't know. Different on her. She had a sheath of black hair hanging down her back, and her face was sharp. Harsh features, not exactly feminine, but I didn't know how to describe her. Were there masculine girls? Could you be both masculine and beautiful? Before my mind could spiral too far about gender versus presentation, Nova was walking into the crowd and headed in my direction. "Can I grab that?" She was looking right at me, but all I was holding was a cider and a plate of assorted cheeses. I looked around wildly, trying to figure out whom she was talking to.

"I gotchu." I had almost forgotten Josh was sitting next to me.

He handed her the capo attached to his guitar and she bowed in front of us.

"Thank you, sir," she said and made her way back to the stage. She grabbed a stool against the wall and positioned it just in front of the pillows, in line with the front row of the audience.

"Let's be close," she whispered. Everyone laughed. She sat there for a while, attaching the capo to her guitar. I felt nervous watching her. It felt intimate. I couldn't stop staring at her hands. I took a sip from my drink and peered around the room. My eyes landed on a white, redheaded femme person whose eyes were also focused intently on Nova. One side of their head was shaved, and there was a tattoo on their arm that read DYKE. They were wearing a black oversized tank top, and definitely no bra, and black leather pants. Everything they wore was black, actually, except their boots, which were cherry red with frayed yellow laces. My eyes glanced back to Nova, and then back at the redhead, and I heard myself mumble "oh" under my breath.

"Is that person going to perform?" I leaned toward Josh.

"Who?"

"Um, I don't want to point. But, uh, red hair? Arm tattoo?" I tried to subtly nudge my head in their direction.

"Uh, don't know. I've seen her here before, but she's never played. Why?"

"The whole rock-star vibe, I guess."

"What? I don't have a rock-star vibe?" Josh pouted at me and pushed his glasses up his nose. He was wearing a multicolored Patagonia and well-worn jeans.

"Not quite rock star, but definitely still cute."

"I'll take it." Josh took a swig of his beer and my eyes traveled back to Nova, who was taking her sweet time tuning up her guitar. Her mouth moved slightly as she fussed with the tuning pegs. She looked up for a moment and saw me looking at her. I felt my face go slack. Without thinking, I turned to Josh and kissed him. He looked surprised, but pleased, and before I had a chance to mentally slap myself for being so fucking weird, I heard strumming.

Nova's eyes were closed as she was finger picking her guitar. I was on edge, waiting for her to open her mouth, holding my breath as I did. And then I heard her sing. Her voice was low, like gravel, and her fingers gained speed as she sang, the heel of her shoe tapping against the leg of the wooden stool she was sitting on. The style of music she played was kind of like folk pop, but also sort of bluesy. Her voice could jump from baritone to falsetto within seconds, and at one point she sang a riff so long it reminded me of an orgasm, and I had to pull out my phone and pretend to check my email.

The longer she sang, the bolder I felt watching her. I propped myself up on my heels and tapped my hand against my thigh, following the beat. My mouth had dropped open slightly, and my throat felt kind of dry, and at some point I realized I had learned the chorus of the song and was mouthing the words along with her. When we reached the bridge, she put her guitar down in her lap. She snapped her fingers against the backside of her black guitar and kept her head low, voice deepening once again. The room was silent, and I swear everyone leaned forward in unison. It was in that moment that Nova lifted her head and locked eyes with me.

> "*When your eyes are closed, that's when you
>     miss me*
> "*And when he turns away, that's when you think
>     of kissing me.*"

Fuck. I couldn't move.

"All right, who knows it?"

She broke away from my gaze and gestured to the crowd. Everyone started to sing along as she jumped back into the chorus. She was just having fun now, barely singing, listening to the audience shout her words back at her, and I found myself hoping way too much that she would look at me one more time, but she didn't.

## 5

TWO WEEKS BEFORE summer break, we went to another open mic night. It was May, and the weather had started to warm up. For the first time in years, I decided to let my hair dry naturally instead of straightening it. It was wavier than I had remembered, albeit a little frizzy, and for some reason it gave me a little boost of confidence I wasn't used to having. Ever since I had seen Nova play, I had felt this mounting adrenaline, like I had had a little too much coffee, but not enough to make me regret it. I was having trouble imagining going home for the summer, especially because Izzie was staying in North Carolina. I wondered if I should rent somewhere cheap off campus and get a boring summer job. There was a bookstore in town that had a WE'RE HIRING sign out front, and I had almost gone in the last time I passed it.

As soon as we got to the party I staked out my spot. I chose a green-and-white-striped beach towel in the center of the room.

"That girl is so talented." Josh nudged his head toward the door. Nova had just walked in. My stomach did a little flip.

"Yeah, they are."

"What do you mean, they?"

"Oh, um, she uses she/they pronouns. So, like, you can say 'she' or 'they.'"

Since the last folk night, I had scoured every form of social media available to me and discovered Nova's Instagram, a Twitter account that hadn't been updated for five years, and a very brief Wikipedia page that told me that Nova had won a local singing tournament when she was twelve.

"That's kinda weird."

"I don't think it's weird."

"I've just never heard of anyone doing that. Like, using both."

"It's really normal."

"Hey, are you pissed at me?" Josh furrowed his brows.

"No, we're just having a conversation!"

"You seem stressed."

"Well, you were just being a little transphobic." My voice rose slightly.

Josh whipped his head around to see if anyone was listening.

"Yo, that's not cool."

"Yo, that's my point." I stood up and grabbed my bag. "I'm going to the bathroom."

I walked straight past the bathroom and tucked into the small kitchen instead. There was some liquid concoction in a yellow pitcher. I grabbed a plastic cup next to it.

"Ooh, watch out for that stuff. You want some of my wine instead?"

I turned to see Nova talking to me, holding a bottle of red wine. The front parts of their hair were blue now.

"I like the blue," I blurted.

She looked confused for a second, and then her face lit up.

"Willy Wonka special." They winked, already pouring some of her wine into a real glass. She handed it to me, and I took a small sip.

"So good. Thank you."

"No worries. I like your hair too. It was different the last time I saw you."

I almost choked on my wine.

"You're the most amazing singer." I didn't know what else to say.

"Oh, dude, thank you. I'm not, 'cause, like, Bowie and stuff, but that means more than you know." She tapped at her heart.

"Is your girlfriend here?"

*Holy fucking shit what the actual fuck Savannah.*

Nova was quizzical, twirling a ring around their thumb.

"Now, what makes you think I have a girlfriend?" She was still smiling. I honestly had no proof that the person with the DYKE tattoo was their partner. I had found zero evidence online, even in tagged photos.

"Redhead. Amazing boobs?"

"Ah yes, that would be my girlfriend! Natalie. Nat."

"Nat." *Fuck. Natalie and Nova? Barf.* I tried to hide my disappointment.

Nova looked at me for a few seconds, as if they were trying to size me up.

"So, I'm gonna go play some more," they finally said.

"Cool. I, uh, yeah. I'll probably listen . . . some more."

"I hope you do." Nova clinked her glass with mine.

She scooted past me in the small room, which wasn't quite small enough that she needed to press her body against me the way they did. I held my breath.

Once she was gone, I sank back against the kitchen island and pinched the bridge of my nose, embarrassment mounting.

I heard a knock on the wall and opened one eye. Nova was back, just her head visible at the entrance to the room.

"I guess I want to tell you that, uh, we're open."

"Open?" I repeated, confused.

"Yes, open." She laughed and her head disappeared.

Open? Open to what? Did she own a business?

I took out my phone and hurriedly typed into my browser.

*What does it mean when someone says they're open?*

I scrolled down to the bottom of the search page, until an *Atlantic* headline caught my eye:

THE PLEA FOR OPEN RELATIONSHIPS:

WHY SOME COUPLES SAY IT'S THE BEST THING

THAT'S EVER HAPPENED TO THEM

*Open.*
*Relationship.*
*OPEN.*
*RELATIONSHIP.*
*OPENRELATIONSHIP.*

Open relationship. Nova was in an open relationship. With Nat. That meant. Oh my god. And if they came back to *tell* me that she was open, did that mean? Oh my god. Was Nova interested in me?

"Sav?"

I whipped around and smacked my body into Josh's, spilling red wine all over him.

"What the fuck, Savannah?"

Without thinking, I burst out laughing.

"I'm so sorry, here, let me—"

I grabbed a dish towel off the countertop and started to mop up Josh's shirt. He looked pouty and kept sighing.

"I'll make it up to you, okay?" I mustered up an innocent face.

He narrowed his eyes at me.

"How?"

"I'll think of something," I said, leaning in to kiss him, letting his tongue find mine just long enough for him to forget he was mad. I pulled away and kissed his nose, then tossed the towel back onto the countertop. I took Josh's hand in mine and dragged him back to the living room.

Over the next few weeks, I couldn't get Nova out of my head. Five days after the party I had half of a pot brownie that Josh had left in my room and followed her on Instagram. Three days later she followed me back. On the last night before summer break, Josh and I went to the movies. Halfway through he tried to finger me, but I pushed his hand away. He leaned closer to me and whispered in my ear.

"I know you like it."

"No, I really don't." I spoke at full volume.

He pulled away from me, embarrassed, and crossed his arms for the rest of the movie.

When we walked back to campus, he apologized and said he didn't mean to be pushy.

"It's cool." I slipped my hand into his to comfort him, even though it actually wasn't cool.

"I never want to do anything you don't, um, consent to." He looked earnest, but something about the way he said it felt scripted. As if he were repeating what he'd learned from a video about sexual harassment in health class.

"I know."

That night we slept in my dorm room, a rare occurrence, and my body bristled when he tried to spoon me. I tried to shake it off and turned to face him. I pressed my chest into him and kissed him, trying to ease into foreplay. He snaked his hands down my pants and I startled, hitting my head against the wall behind me.

"Whoa, whoa, you okay?"

I winced as I felt for the back of my head.

"Sorry, yeah, I'm fine. I, um. I feel anxious, I guess."

He looked annoyed.

"We don't need to do anything," he mumbled.

"I know."

"Well, I'm just saying, you kind of, um."

"What?"

"Nothing."

We both were quiet.

"Just, like, you initiated." He filled the empty space.

I froze.

"Um, yeah. Sorry."

*Notsorrynotsorrynotfuckingsorry.*

My head felt hot where I had bumped it. I wasn't sorry. I knew it was okay to initiate sex and then not want to have it. I lay down on my pillow and turned away from him. I wiggled my backside toward him as a sort of peace offering, a way to placate him. The air in the room was still.

"You good?"

I felt like I was watching us from above, not in my own body.

"Yeah." I could barely choke out the response.

My head was buzzing with so many things I could say, but nothing would come out.

A minute later, his body twitched. I knew he had fallen asleep. I stared at the wall for a while, unable to close my eyes. An hour must have passed, maybe more, and I replayed our interaction over and over. I wasn't going to be able to sleep. I reached for my phone and mindlessly looked at Twitter, then Instagram. Someone had messaged me. Nova had messaged me. My mouth dropped open.

**novagonnahappen:** staying here for the summer?

Well. Now I was.

## 6

PROFESSOR TOLINO HAD us switch seats every class. She said it was like feng shui, but with bodies. Today I sat next to Reg, who was drawing in her notebook. From what I could make out, her illustration looked suspiciously like a naked woman licking another naked woman's ass, but if it wasn't, then I really needed to hook up with someone soon. I had seen Reg on Hinge last weekend. It wasn't that weird for her to pop up on there, there were a lot of queer people at school, but not enough to not have your classmates show up during your late-night swiping. I was desperate to know what kind of gay she was, as if her profile would tell me anything more than what music she was vibing to (Willow) and her go-to queer pose in pictures (she went for the arm slung around her friend and the looking-hot-while-I-pet-my-dog kneel). Her profile linked to her Instagram, where I learned that Reg hosted monthly movie screenings featuring Black femme directors. She seemed to love her friends; there was a marked ease between them. I had really only had that kind of ease with one person at a time. I wondered if it was hard to balance a whole group of friends, if you had to parse out bits of yourself to each person. It seemed exhausting. But looking at that photo of Reg, I saw no signs of fatigue. If anything, she seemed to explode with joy.

It was good that we had to switch seats, because it meant that I didn't have a panic attack every time Wesley walked into the room, wondering if they would sit near me. I had tried to calculate how many times we might sit next to each other over the course of the semester, but my ability to do math disappeared the second I graduated from high school. My dad and I used to fight about that, whether I would ever end up using math out of school, and he always said it wasn't about that—it was the principle. "If you're taught it, you should learn it. It's good to have principles, Savannah." My mom would scoff at him and we'd both roll our eyes. She never went anywhere without a travel calculator in her purse.

"Let's talk about the reading." Professor Tolino thumbed through our assigned book; the cover of hers seemed to have a wine stain on it. Today she was wearing bright red slacks and matching heels, and her glasses were a silver-rimmed cat's-eye. Note to self: be incredibly hot and smart when you're older.

"I think it was really important." Lara's hand was still raised while she spoke. Professor Tolino nodded. "Because?"

Lara tentatively brought her hand down and cleared her throat.

"Well, because the kits need to be more accessible." She glanced down at her own book. "For, um, different. Communities." The way she said "different" was like the spoken version of *italics*. Reg let out a small sigh, barely audible to anyone but me. Lara was looking intently at her notebook, using a purple highlighter to underline what I presumed were her own notes from the reading. I always started the semester with a fresh pack of pens and multicolor Sharpies, but by the first round of midterms I would be nudging Candace to borrow one of hers. Candace was an out-and-proud nerd. She made the dean's list every semester and somehow still found time to show face at every party she was invited to and keep three to four girls on rotation every week.

"Honestly, I thought it was messed up. The whole thing was written by an ex-cop, who was, like, dead set on making assault recovery 'efficient,' as if there's some formula to catching abusers. Access to kits doesn't matter when survivors don't even want to get them in the first place." Vera was tapping her boot under her desk.

She was right. Nothing sounded worse than showing up at a hospital and having strangers make you relive the unthinkable. I didn't know anyone who had. I looked over at Candace, who was chewing on her lip. I knew by now that meant she had something to say but was holding back.

"Candace?" Professor Tolino looked over to where she was sitting, her professorial sixth sense leading the way. "What was your perspective on the reading?"

"Yeah, so." Candy twirled her pencil in their hand. "I've brought people, from the shelter I volunteer at, to get one. It sucks. The wait can be hours, and the whole thing is just a reminder of why you're there. And if it's right after, people want to shower, change, sleep. I understand that this guy"—she gestured to her book—"is trying to avoid that to some extent, but it doesn't change the fluorescent lights or the intense questions. It's . . . I don't know . . ."

"Inhumane?" Reg asked.

I looked over. Her elbows were on the desk and she was gripping her knuckles with one hand. She looked irritated.

"They can make you pay for it," she went on.

*Wait, what?*

"What?" Lara asked. Her eyebrows shot up. She looked like Reg had just spoken in another language.

"Sometimes they bill you. Later. For the kit." She wasn't

looking at Lara when she spoke. She wasn't looking at anyone. The air in the room suddenly felt stiff.

Wesley was nodding at Reg.

"Reg is right," they said, swooping in to take the attention off her. "I just read an NPR article about it. It's federally prohibited, but there's a disconnect between what happens in the emergency room and the billing department. It happens all the time."

I realized that my face must have looked as shocked as Lara's, so I started nodding too. On the inside, I was fucking horrified. How could I not have known this? I looked over at Reg, who had resumed her drawing, as if she hadn't said a thing. *Of course you didn't know this, Savannah.* Why would you have to? I'd never seen a single hospital bill in my life. A swell of guilt washed over me.

"It's like a second trauma," I said quietly.

Professor Tolino looked over at me.

"Go on, Savannah."

"It just seems like, from start to finish, if there is even a finish . . . it's traumatizing. The initial violence, the hospital, the questioning? To have someone touch you, um, when you've just . . . and after all that . . . you're asked to pay for it?"

"Well, that doesn't happen when you know the person," Lara said, self-assured.

My heart lurched. I swallowed hard.

"Right?" Lara went on. "It's different in that situation, isn't it?" She looked around the room.

"No." Vera didn't miss a beat.

"Well, that doesn't . . . like, why would you need a kit when you already know who it was? That doesn't make sense."

Vera laughed out loud. "Make sense? None of it makes sense." She shot daggers at Lara with her eyes. "It's not always some guy in a ski mask at a shitty gas station. It's mostly people you know."

Vera didn't break her gaze from Lara. "You still need proof. Just in case."

"In case of what?" Lara looked confused.

"In case the police think you're making it up," Vera said plainly.

My cheeks felt hot.

The room fell silent again.

"Let's take a break, yeah?" Professor Tolino's voice broke through the quiet. She sounded very calm. Intentionally so.

I glanced at my phone. My mom had texted me.

> Hi sweetie! Just got the save the date
> for Izzie's wedding. It is SO CUTE!!!
> Took a pic 4 u! Luv, Mom.

As promised, my phone buzzed with a second text. I didn't bother to tap it, but I could tell right away that the card was now displayed directly next to Izzie's and my joint sweet sixteen invitation, which had been resting atop a shelf in our living room for the past few years. I started to text my mom back when I noticed Vera stand up from her desk and shove her AirPods into her ears. She busied herself picking a song and walked out the door. Before I knew it, I was trailing behind her into the hallway. She was at the far end of the hall, leaning against a radiator, her body turned away from mine. I could faintly hear the music coming from her AirPods, which meant she was blasting it. Why did I follow her out here? It would be weird for me to say something, wouldn't it? And how would I even get her attention? I'd have to walk up behind her and tap her on the shoulder, or worse—loop around her and wave. Besides, I didn't want her to think I was playing therapist. Maybe she was totally fine and I was just reading into it. Before I could turn back around, she saw me.

"What's up?"

She popped the bud out of one ear and cringed.

"Shit, that's loud. So emo of me." She took the other one out and stuffed both in her pockets.

"Sorry, I, uh. Yeah, well, hold on." I was basically yelling. I awkwardly started to make my way toward her, not knowing at what point of distance it would be appropriate to start speaking again.

"I just, um, wanted to check on you," I said, stopping a few feet in front of her.

Her face softened.

"Oh. Yeah. Thank you. I'm okay. That girl, though, sometimes she just doesn't get it, you know?"

I nodded.

I mean, I did know. Kind of. I knew that what Lara was saying, and how she was saying it, was wrong. She made my skin bristle when she talked, and I was always on edge when she raised her hand in class. But I didn't know the stuff Vera was talking about. I didn't know you needed proof. I, like Lara, thought if you pointed a finger the jail cell would automatically open.

"I just want a milkshake." She rolled her eyes at herself, shrugging her leather jacket back up over her shoulders. She looked like she was going to head back to class.

"What's your favorite kind?" I asked.

"Of milkshake?" she asked, a small smirk playing across her mouth.

"Yeah!" I was being overly enthusiastic. This girl was going to think I was nuts.

Now Vera grinned.

"Strawberry."

My jaw fell open. "It's my favorite too."

"No way! I secretly love pink." She looked down at her ankle and pulled up one leg of her oversized black jeans. She was wearing a bubblegum-pink sock, with little red hearts embroidered around the ankle. "Don't tell anyone."

"I promise. I love them."

"They're great, aren't they? I get them from this novelty shop in Koreatown, back where I'm from in LA. I bought a pair for all of my partners."

*All of her partners.* I forced my face to remain neutral.

"They killed it." I played it cool.

Vera let her pant leg fall again and checked the time on her phone.

"Better go back. You coming?"

"Yes! Actually. No. I have to pee."

*Overshare.*

Vera smirked again.

"'K. See you in there."

"For sure."

She turned around and walked back to class. I gunned it for the bathroom; I only had a minute. I peed quickly and then rushed to the sink. My hair was doing exactly the opposite of what I wanted it to be doing. "Fuck," I muttered under my breath, trying to finger curl a thick unruly wave that had disrupted my middle part and created a zigzag across my scalp. Someone like Vera could pull off a zigzag part. An ironic throwback. She could crimp her hair too. I just looked like a middle schooler who woke up too late to shower before class.

"You have such pretty hair." I whipped my head around to see Lara coming out of the last stall. *How fucking long has she been standing there?*

"Oh, um, thanks. It doesn't really do what I tell it to."

"I like it a lot. My hair doesn't do anything interesting. And if I don't wear it in a middle part, you can tell that the left side of my

face is really wonky." She pointed to her cheek. Lara's face could
be a scientific model of human symmetry. I doubted there was
anything even slightly wonky on her entire body. She was beautiful. Classically, reliably, cover-of-*Elle* kind of beautiful. The
thing about Lara that was frustrating was that she wasn't intentionally shitty. She was ignorant, and I had a feeling she had never
had a reason not to be. I probably wouldn't have either, if things
hadn't turned out the way they did in high school.

"I'm sure it looks amazing," I said.

She shrugged and finished washing her hands. This whole interaction was bizarre. We had just gone from talking about sexual
violence to forcing compliments. It made me feel like a robot.

She tapped her watch, indicating that we should go.

"Be right there," I said, waving her away.

I didn't want anyone from class to see us together. I waited
until I couldn't hear the tap of her heeled boots on the linoleum
floor, and then I made my way back to class.

## 7

# Nine

YOUR BROTHER HAD a patch of white hair, in the shape of a triangle, by the nape of his neck. Everyone asked him about it. Did he dye it? Was he born like that? Premature grays? It was Lyme disease. A weird tidbit to share with the girls he fucked in college the morning after, when the sun came out and he turned over on his pillow. Boys like him don't usually have quirks. Golden boys who are good at sports and make friends easily and get their braces off quickly, who are mostly nice in the way that boys are expected to be nice and therefore rewarded for that niceness, who aren't really funny but whose straight-toothed smiles trick you into thinking they are, because boys like that are always smiling. Boys like that always have a reason to smile.

I was nine and he was thirteen when I fell in love with him.

"Yo, you have a mad gap between your teeth." Donny Maldino had sprung up behind me on the bus, looking over the top of his seat down at the two of us.

We had been playing the try-not-to-laugh game and failing miserably.

"That's really mean, Donny," you said, crossing your arms at him and sticking out your tongue.

"I mean, her teeth are better than yours. Your braces have gunk between them, don't you ever brush your teeth, dude?"

Izzie slammed her hand over her mouth, hiding her teeth and slouching in her seat. I gripped a bag of Doritos and crinkled the wrapper. That got Donny's attention.

"Lemme get those chips," he said, hand outstretched. His fingernails were bitten to the quick.

I shook my head no.

"What? You didn't hear me the first time?" He started to come around to our seat, standing in the aisle of the bus and leaning over us. "I said, give me the fucking chips."

"No!" I shoved them in my lap and used my backpack as a shield.

"Fucking gap-tooth," he muttered, reaching over to yank my bag from me.

And then, magically, your brother was there. I saw a flash of the back of his head as he came between Donny and our bus seat, blocking him from us.

"Donny, dude, quit it. That's my sister and my friend."

*His friend.*

"Stop being an idiot."

Your brother had come all the way from the back of the bus to defend us. He was watching us. He was watching me.

Donny looked over your brother's shoulder and narrowed his eyes at us. "Whatever," he said. The two of them started walking to the back of the bus. I propped up my knees on the leather seat and peered over the edge. Your brother turned around one more time and saw me looking. He pointed to his teeth and then mine.

"I like the gap," he mouthed. "It's cute."

And just like that, I was unmoored, devoured, and decimated by the throes of my first crush.

# 8

AT SIX P.M. I was in my room trying to get homework done when I heard a knock at my door. I figured it was Candace since she was the only one who ever came by unless the RA was doing random checks. But when I opened the door, Vera was standing there.

She had her hands in her pockets; she was wearing a beat-up oversized denim jacket with red paint splattered all over it. The letters *ACAB* were written across her chest.

"Let's go," she said, looking devious.

"Where? Also, how did you—"

"It's a surprise. And I have work-study in the admin office, so I know where everybody is at all times. It feeds my inner stalker. Come on, put a sweater on, your tits look amazing but it's kind of cold out." She was staring at my chest, but there was no glimmer of objectification in her tone.

"Got it. Give me a second."

I ran into my room and started tearing through my closet. I didn't have any anti-police gear. I did have one sweatshirt that read TRANS RIGHTS ARE HUMAN RIGHTS, which was—as far as politically pointed sweatshirts go—the absolute bare minimum.

But it was better than nothing. I grabbed my wallet and rushed back to the hallway. Vera was drawing on the community white-board. She had scribbled, "I'm a slut for Satan."

"Hi," I said.

She glanced back at me.

"Sick sweatshirt. You should let me bleach it."

"Sure!"

"Cool. Come on."

Vera avoided the elevator and went for the stairwell, which was ambitious considering I lived on the eighth floor. She was surpris-ingly quick. I had to run down the steps to keep up with her. She took me through the exit that led to the parking lot and walked straight to a bright red van. Like a big, three-row, soccer-mom minivan.

She shrugged.

"Not on brand, but it does the trick."

She gestured for me to get in, and as soon as I buckled my seat belt, she proceeded to drive extremely fast until we left campus, only to drive even faster on the way into town. I didn't even know minivans could go this fast. My parents always drove at precisely the speed limit. Vera looked over at me and must have sensed that I was petrified because she slowed down, slightly, and stopped changing lanes every two minutes.

"Sorry, I'm from LA, and nothing thrills me more than not dying of boredom in traffic. I feel like I'm making up for lost time every time there's an open road."

"It's totally fine. I like driving fast!" I did *not* sound con-vincing.

"Cool."

We ordered strawberry milkshakes at the ice cream shop and drank them in her car with the heat blasting.

"So, sea or space?"

"What?"

"Which one scares you more?" she asked, like it was the most obvious thing in the world.

"Oh, um." I thought for a second. "Space."

"Mm, interesting. I'm sea for sure. Why space?"

"Honestly, everything about space kind of freaks me out. The time thing is mostly what gets me, though. Like the fact that things take years on certain planets and for others those years are seconds. That's terrifying to me."

Vera nodded. "But time's kinda made up, you know?"

"Oh, yeah. Definitely. A construct." I tried to say it like it was something I really believed.

"But I get that. It is freaky." Vera tipped her cup into her mouth. Her lips were dotted with pink froth. She wiped her mouth with the back of her hand.

"Okay, why sea?"

"Oh, you know. Endless darkness. Sea creatures bigger than buildings. Even scientists are scared of the ocean. That's when you know it's legit terrifying." She shuddered.

"Well, fuck, now I think I'm scared of both."

Vera laughed.

"So do you like class?" she asked, shoving her empty shake cup in the cup holster, smushing it to fit.

"I do." I nodded. "It's intense sometimes."

"Yeah. I feel like everyone in that class has some shit they're working out. Like sometimes what we talk about feels *too* relatable."

My stomach churned a little. I wanted her to say more.

"Totally."

"That's why talking academically about this stuff is hard. Sometimes I just want to cut the crap and be like, yeah, this actually happened to me."

I didn't respond.

"Sorry if that's too much to share."

"No, it's not, it's, um. It's refreshing. I, uh, relate, as well."

Vera's face softened.

"I figured. I grew up in a family that didn't talk about mental health stuff. A lot of Korean families are like that. I guess I'm trying to counteract that in my life now. With partners and friends, you know?"

I nodded. "That makes sense."

"Plus, I can tell that Lara fucks with your head."

I bit my lip. Was it that obvious?

"Me too, clearly." Vera sighed. "She means well, though."

*Does she?*

"Well," Vera went on, "you can always talk about anything with me. If you want. I'm an open book."

"Thank you. Do you have any idea what your presentation will be about at the end of the semester?"

She chewed on her straw.

"I don't know. This shit makes me think about a lot of stuff. I feel like I have so many things rumbling around up here"—she pointed to her head—"but I never know what I really wanna say until the last minute. But I'll definitely do it through art. And I'll definitely make it freaky." She stuck her tongue out, still shiny with strawberry milkshake.

"Definitely. Yeah, same. Thinking about a lot of stuff."

Absolutely no stuff had been thought of.

"So." She shifted in her seat to face her body toward me. "Tell me everything about the first time you had gay sex."

WHEN NOVA FUCKED me for the first time, I saw stars. She had those little glow-in-the-dark stars taped to her ceiling, which felt particularly uncool for someone who was, well, incredibly cool. When she got on top of me and slipped one, two, and then three fingers inside of me, I grabbed the back of her head and pressed her face down into my neck. I stared at those little green stars until her fingers felt so good I had to squeeze my eyes shut. When I came, the first time, she got close to my pussy and said, "Good girl," her voice low and hoarse from singing all night.

"Again?" she asked, although she knew the question was rhetorical. I came again within seconds, this time with her tongue pressing against my clit and my hips bucking into her mouth.

I still hadn't opened her DM. I got heart palpitations every time I checked my messages. Lately, Izzie had been flooding my inbox with inspo for floral arrangements, and every time I swiped to my messages Nova's handle stared me in the face. If I tapped it, she would know I had seen it. Which would sort of be a power move, to read it and not respond, but I had a feeling if I opened it,

I would respond. And after talking to Candace, I really couldn't do that. I didn't want to respond, or at least my brain didn't. My body was saying otherwise.

I was also ignoring texts from Andie, who had invited me over for dinner and sent me a photo of her cat, Maude, who she said would be making the appetizers. It was a cute move, but I had a nasty cat allergy and preferred dogs. A dicey take in the queer community, but I didn't have time to bother with creatures who were hard to get. That's what I had enjoyed so much about Nova, at least at the start. How easy it was for them to express their desire for me. I had never experienced unbridled, unapologetic wanting quite like that. Having sex with Nova had been sort of exhausting, though. In part because there was no definitive end point, so it usually lasted all night, but mostly because every time we fucked I was reminded of how every moment of my life, since puberty, had been spent making myself desirable for a man. With Nova, my body was no longer a mannequin and I didn't know what to do with it. How to even be a sexual person if a man wasn't on the receiving end of my orgasm? Could I flirt the way I did with guys? Could I make the same sounds in bed, say the same dirty things? Were those even my fucking sounds, or were they sounds I learned through porn? And if I did make those sounds and say those things, would Nova think I was antifeminist?

It turned out that Nova liked all those things, and she didn't seem invested in unpacking if the moans I made when I came were actually my own or a Pornhub imitation.

I asked her once, nervously, if she ever objectified me. She laughed hysterically.

"Of course I do," she said. "I zoom in on every photo you send me just to look at your tits."

I was relieved, and then I felt guilty for being relieved. If I was actively *not* fucking the patriarchy, then why couldn't I undo my desire to be totally fetishized? Shouldn't I invoke some sort of gay body neutrality?

"Sav, I don't know what to tell you." Nova shrugged when I asked her this question. "We like what we like. It's hard enough being gay as it is; try not to judge yourself for liking it when I call you a dirty slut."

*Maybe she's born with it, maybe it's brainwash!*

Aside from the exhaustion, being with Nova was incredible. I never had to worry about her thinking I was clingy, she texted me nonstop, her apartment was clean and with no two-in-one shampoo in sight, and there were so many things that we just didn't have to talk about because we had a shared experience. Our relationship was filled with long summer mornings in bed; surprise picnics at an overlook near campus; talking for hours on the phone at night when she had a gig out of town; and really, really, *really* good sex. I was so happy.

A month after we started sleeping together, she announced she was going on a tour across Europe and didn't know when she'd be back. I asked her if I could come with her until school started again and she said no, Nat was coming, and she wouldn't be comfortable with that. I asked her if she wanted to do long-distance and she looked at me for a long time, squeezed my hand, and told me I had a beautiful heart. It took me another three days to realize that was her way of breaking up with me.

I spent the rest of the summer in a soul-crushed daze. At first, I convinced myself that I actually wasn't gay and just had completed the prerequisite experimenting that women were supposed to do in college. But then I thought a lot about Shane from *The L Word* and changed my mind. If I wanted to have sex with Shane, I probably wasn't straight. And then I contemplated being a lesbian for a while, but *I Love You, Man* popped up on Netflix and I thought a lot about Paul Rudd too, so I decided that wasn't right.

After consulting a Healthline article, I decided that queer felt okay. And bisexual was okay too. When Nova ended things, I called my mom scream-crying. Something like:

"ThegirlIamDATING" / SOB / "justBROKEUPwithme" / SOB-SNOT / "andIfeellikeI'mDYING" / HEAVE SOB / "alsoI'mBISEXUAL / SOB-SNOT HEAVE SOB.

"Oh, sweetie," she said, "I'm so sorry."

After that, my mom started recommending movies I should watch, but I passed on her suggestions after watching *Kissing Jessica Stein*, where a straight woman basically leads on a lesbian for the entirety of the film, only to renounce her queerness and leave her for a man. Whatever that genre of gay was, I wasn't it.

And then I met Candace. After that first party she invited me to in her dorm room, I was completely overwhelmed. I went back to my room and googled all the phrases I hadn't understood. I was directed to a plethora of queer digital mags, and subreddits, and one site dedicated to The Golden Age of Lesbian Tumblr, which apparently had gone downhill after Tumblr had changed its nudity policies. I followed as many radical queer Instagrams as I could find, and I added a bunch of books that were considered "queer canon" to my Christmas list. I knew my mother would love nothing more than to buy them for me, and subsequently read them with me, as she had told me over the summer that she wanted to be a part of "my community" and added a tiny gay flag to the pencil cup on her desk. My dad was quieter about his support; coming out to him was entirely anticlimactic and ended in one of his classic speeches where he said something like, "I don't care who you date, as long as the person respects you, has a job, and is forward thinking."

I didn't admit to my mom that I had no idea how to be a part of my community, because there seemed to be a whole second step after coming out, and that was finding your people. I mean, I had cis gay male friends, I did community theater growing up, but they didn't really feel like my community. And Nova certainly hadn't invited me into her community, and even if she had, I was pretty sure I didn't want to be a part of it. But that night at Candace's felt like I had inched closer to the thing that I wanted. They were just. So. Gay. Effortlessly so. Each with their own iconic style and vibe and fluent in a language that made my head spin. But unlike Nova's elitist group of self-proclaimed Celesbians, I felt welcome here. Wanted. It was thrilling, and terrifying. It had been four months since that queer hang, and I finally looked forward to having weekend plans. Candace invited me everywhere, like Gay Bowling Tuesdays at the alley in town, and queer book club, and she binged all of *Atypical* with me in two nights. But even though we were close, there was still something that made me feel distant from everyone else. Like if I got too close, something terrible would happen.

## 10

## Thirteen

"I CAN'T WAIT to get married," you said dreamily, tracing your finger against a worn page in our one, holy copy of *Cosmopolitan*. It was our favorite page. A bride getting ready with all her bridesmaids.

I turned over on my back, lifting my copy of *Seventeen* into the air. We were both allowed to read *Seventeen*. I wrinkled my nose at a photo of a couple getting married at city hall. How stupid not to have a gigantic party. How dumb not to wear a long dress.

"Are you sure you still want to get married in the city?" I asked, trying to make it sound innocent, like I really was just making sure. Even though I knew for sure.

"Yes!" You kicked my magazine out of my hands with your pink-socked foot.

"Hey! The pages could rip!" I scrambled to grab the magazine and carefully smoothed the pages.

"At the Plaza. Like Eloise," you said, for the millionth time.

"But the city is dirty," I said, flopping down next to you on the carpet.

"Not the nice parts. Not the Plaza! You've never been, that's why you don't know." You jumped up and made your way to your vanity, the one you got for Christmas, and piled your hair on top of your head. Your eyes caught mine in the mirror.

"We're still doing updos, right?" Your voice became very serious.

"Of course! I think it's so tacky not to."

"So our necks look really long." You stuck your chin up and out, straining a muscle in your neck.

I joined you, mimicking the updo.

"Here! Wait. I'll hold your hair for you, so you can really see." You leapt behind me and replaced my hands with yours, and then crouched so you were invisible. You peeked your eyes up over my shoulder and gasped.

"You look like a model!"

I didn't. We both knew I didn't. I didn't like the updo. But we had decided on how our hair would look early on, back when we first started planning our weddings together. But my neck wasn't as long as yours, and my ears stuck out, and my hair was starting to look nice now that my mom finally let me grow it out past my chin. I stared at my reflection, mainly the huge zit that had erupted smack-dab in the middle of my forehead. I made a face like I was going to puke.

"I look gross. No one is gonna want to marry me." I turned to avoid the mirror.

You dropped your hands from my hair and popped back up to full height.

"Savannah Henry, you're the most beautiful girl in the world." You spun me back around. "Repeat after me, Savvy!" You planted your hands on my shoulders.

I rolled my eyes.

"I saw that, you butt."

"Saw what?" I batted my eyes.

"Promise you'll say what I say."

"Fine." I sighed.

"Okay. Repeat after me: I am beautiful from the inside out."

"I am beautiful from the inside out." I said it as dramatically as I could, sweeping my arms into the wind.

"No, Savvy, you have to mean it!" You pleaded with me with your eyes.

I groaned. I dropped my arms and looked in the mirror.

"I am beautiful from the inside out." My voice was small.

"A little louder, noodle head," you urged.

I tried not to look at the pimple. Instead, I looked at my eyes. Brown, like my mom's. You had blue eyes; everyone in your family did. Down to my nose. Not crooked, which was good, you assured me. You had the tiniest curve to yours, and you pressed on it each night before bed, hoping it would flatten. I looked at my mouth. Pink, sort of, more orangish. And then my teeth. Which were also not crooked. No braces for me. You, on the other hand, had gotten yours on six months ago. Your mouth was a mess of pink and green and rubber bands that sometimes snapped if you forgot to take them out before eating an apple. You hated them, never letting anyone but me see your real smile anymore, instead stretching your lips around the metal to conceal them. I felt guilty, but I liked that I didn't need braces. I liked my teeth. They were nice. My dad said I had a smile that looked just like my heart.

For a brief moment, I saw what you saw. A flash of me, pretty, or at least someone who could be. It was easier to see me through you.

"Sav," you whined. "Say it!"

"I am beautiful from the inside out." My voice was firm.

Without thinking, I stomped my foot this time, which made me laugh. But a tiny bit more of me meant it.

"Okay, now you!" I ran behind you and clamped my palms on your shoulders.

"Okay! Me!" You turned to face the mirror. I knew instantly you would catch your smile in the mirror, and sure enough, your face fell. Your eyes filled with tears.

"I'm the ugly one," you said, looking down at your hands.

"No, you're Eloise." I poked your shoulder. "But even better."

"No one's better than Eloise," you said quietly, and poked me back.

"Ow!"

"That didn't hurt!" You looked up, accusing.

"I know," I said.

"You b-word!"

"You're a b-word, b-word!" I poked you again and you squealed, gearing up to get me back. I screamed and ran around the perimeter of your tiny room, giggling and out of breath, clambering on top of your bed and trying to make a pillow barricade.

"No way, you can't escape me!" You knocked the pillows away and lunged for my ankles.

"Mercy! Mercy!" I cried, unable to stop laughing, and collapsing onto the bed. You climbed up with me, panting, and poked me one more time, for good measure.

"You'd never survive with brothers," you said. "You always give up so fast!"

"I don't want brothers. I have you!"

"You're right. I'd choose having a sister any day."

"Same."

You hoisted yourself off the bed so you could reach for the *Cosmo*.

"Okay, let's do the quiz again."

"Which? Which wedding dress are you?" I said the next bit in a whisper. "Or which kind of seductress are you?"

"Both. But wedding first!"

We pretended like we didn't have the questions, and their answers, memorized. We were the same. We both got the elegant dress, the classic.

The first day we got the magazine, I did the quiz again by myself while you were in the bathroom. I picked my real answers. I got the bohemian dress. The model in the picture had her hair down. When my mom took me to the bookstore later that week, I found the magazine and tore out the picture of the bohemian dress. I slid it in the back of my favorite Judy Blume book, *Starring Sally J. Friedman as Herself.* I knew you wouldn't look in it. I had given up on trying to get you to read it; by then you were team *Twilight* or bust. Sometimes, after we got off the phone at night, I slipped the picture from my book. I did my best to make my hair like the model's. It looked nice.

## 11

"I JUST THINK it's more complicated."

We were more than halfway through class, and this was the first time Lara had piped up. She tapped her fingernails on the desk, a singular chip in the pink polish. I noticed she was no longer wearing the promise ring. She had the reading we were discussing out in front of her, most of it thoroughly highlighted in blue and pink. The reading was about reported rates of sexual violence in cities verses suburban and rural areas.

"Like, um, people do things when they're drunk, and they . . . regret it, but like. They keep living and are happy and, like, do the next thing."

"That's not how trauma works," I heard myself blurt.

"What?" She turned toward me.

"All those things, keeping on living and happiness and doing the next thing—that's, that stuff can live alongside trauma. I mean, it usually does. That's why it's called being a survivor."

Lara stared at me. My heart was beating fast. I knew I should back down, but I couldn't.

"Okay. Um, I guess, I don't know. I feel like you have, everyone has, a choice to, like—of what you call it. It's just really easy to make it sound way more serious than it . . . was. Not every person decides that they need to label it."

She started to pick at the chipped nail. I had never seen her on edge. Rage and pity bubbled up inside me. I saw myself in her and so I could not hate her; it would be too easy to hate her, too lazy, too convenient, too cheap.

"Sure," I said, more ice in my voice than I had hoped for.

Lara brought her fingernail up to her lip and bit down.

•

I WAS TALKING to Izzie once, on the phone, sometime during the end of our freshman year. She was in North Carolina, getting ready for a frat party. The theme was Anything But Clothes, she told me. I was avoiding writing a paper. She was already a little tipsy, and she mentioned something that happened during Thanksgiving earlier that fall. She ended up in the kitchen with one of her brother's friends, Charlie Mackavoy, at three a.m. They were teasing each other, drunk and high, eating fistfuls of Cool Ranch Doritos. She stole the last chip and he kissed her, a kiss she had been wanting for years, and then he turned her over on the kitchen island and entered her. The way she told me this was so casual, punctured with that kind of Valley girl upspeak we still dipped into with each other, like we were gossiping on the back of the school bus. The line got quiet for a moment, and I felt an apology prick my lips. I swallowed. I knew if I said something it would make it real, and I knew she wouldn't engage. It had been the first Thanksgiving I hadn't been home for since we were ten. I had gone to Florida with my parents instead.

"How did you feel about it?" I asked.

"I mean, I wasn't trying to have sex. But, like, it happened."

"Yeah."

"Whatever. He's hot."

"Mhm," I said, shutting my eyes tight.

"I gotta go, Sav, I can't duct tape my boobs with one hand. Love you."

"Love you," I said, but she had already hung up.

•

"I THINK IT'S a choice, yeah."

I turned to see Vera was speaking. Today she had tiny *x*'s painted on her cheekbones and had changed her phone case for a neon green plastic one with DADDY emblazoned in white block letters. I would just never, in this lifetime, be so fucking cool.

"Most people don't talk, you know. If they go through that shit. People don't believe you most of the time. Or they want to kill the dude or make sure he gets life and that whole process is bullshit and backfires. Like it's enough to get, yeah, it's just enough. You can tell yourself whatever the fuck you want." Vera looked out the window, then up at the ceiling. No one said anything.

Wesley broke the silence. "Little pivot, y'all, respectfully. I think if we're going to talk about sexual violence, we have to acknowledge—or I would like to acknowledge—that not only men are assaulters. And believe me, I am not trying to argue the reality that the vast majority of rapists are cis men. That's true. But there are all kinds of predators."

Wesley glanced at me quickly, imperceptibly, and I grinned and nodded so fast my head could have rolled off my neck and onto the desk. Embarrassment rushed to my cheeks. What kind of person grins in the middle of talking about assault? They didn't see me, or if they did, they politely looked elsewhere to allow me to suffer humiliation alone. At least I didn't do a thumbs-up.

Professor Tolino leaned her hip onto her table and crossed her ankles. "Wesley brings up a good point. While there are published statistics of all genders committing sexual violence, those stats are believed to be widely inaccurate because fewer survivors come forward to report the abuse—"

Reg jumped in. "Wait, why are we changing the subject? How common is it that women are abusive in that way? Men are inherently violent in a way women are not. And even if they are, they learned it from men. Men are bred to be attackers and possessive and think they own us and our bodies."

"Cis men," Wesley slipped in, sort of under their breath.

Reg blinked at them.

"Right. Cis men."

Candace interjected. "It's still valid to talk about, though, Reg. Right? People of all genders do fucked up things and they need to be held accountable no matter what." Reg leaned back in her chair and interlaced her fingers behind her head, contemplating Candace's offer. She shrugged her shoulders.

"Candace uses the word 'accountability.' I'm curious what that means to all of you. How do you define accountability when it comes to sexual violence?" Professor Tolino looked over at Lara, who had regained her statuesque posture and sense of calm.

"Like, justice," she said, tipping her head to the side as if to add "Like, obviously."

"Justice," repeated Professor Tolino. She paused and looked around. "And what is justice?" Lara's hand shot up. Professor Tolino ignored her and glanced at the clock instead.

"I'm going to break you out into groups now. I have a reading that I'd like to get to. But we should continue this conversation around justice, so let's have your responses be your assignment, shall we? Find a partner and have this conversation together. I'd like you to record yourselves talking about the concept of justice for ten minutes. Then you'll transcribe what you've said as best you can, and we'll discuss it next class. Got it?" We all nodded.

"On second thought, I will assign partners. I'll email you all by the end of the day." There was a nervous flutter around the room. I glanced over at Wesley and felt my heart start to race again. In a good way, this time.

We spent the rest of class reading a mind-numbing excerpt from a text called *Devices and Desires: A History of Contraceptives in America*. It was, unfortunately, as depressing as it sounded. I found myself peeking over at Wesley more than I should have been. They were so animated, talking Lara's ear off about something I couldn't quite hear, occasionally jabbing at the article between them. She seemed completely uninterested. I could see she had her phone under her desk, swiping through what looked like selfies on her camera roll. Wes didn't seem to notice. My heart went thump-thump-thump.

"All right!" Professor Tolino clapped. Class was over. "Thanks for a fruitful conversation, everyone. Enjoy your weekends, and I'll send over those emails shortly. Please be on the lookout for your assigned partner."

I slipped my laptop into my backpack. What if Wesley was my partner and we had nothing to talk about during our recording? What if they wanted to talk about the intersection of queerness and assault and I hadn't read any of the theories they wanted to bring up? Should I wear my shirt that read BICON that I had panic-ordered during Pride or would that make it seem like I only like *two* genders, "bi" meaning "two." I needed a shirt that read BI AS IN HORNY FOR GENDER EXPANSIVENESS. Maybe I could get that custom-made on Etsy.

"Whatcha up to this weekend?" My head shot up. Wesley was

standing above me, one hand running through their mess of brown curls. My heart gave out completely.

Was this a "what are you up to this weekend" that was going to lead to a "cool, I wanted to invite you to *insert gay activity here*" or a "I'm just making polite conversation because I'm a Good Person™ and saw that you got really heated during class when we were talking about unspeakable violence"? What was I doing this weekend? Oh fuck, wedding dress shopping with Izzie. At the literal *Say Yes to the Dress* store. So, basically, the most heteronormative activity I could possibly be doing, besides Santa Con. Just lie. Just lie, Savannah.

"Nothing crazy. Seeing a friend from home; we're going to get tattoos."

WE

ARE

GOING

TO

GET

TATTOOS?

*You don't have any tattoos, Savannah. Are you implying that you are going to get your first tattoo?* Do you realize that the follow-up to a question like this is, "Oh dope, of what?" Followed closely by, "No way, I love that! Where?" WHAT TATTOO, SAVANNAH? WHERE TATTOO, SAVANNAH?

"Oh dope! Of what?"

Fuck.

"A tribute to my grandmother. Um, her favorite chair. That she always. Sat in."

Oh, okay, I had a brain once, but I guess it's gone forever now.

Wesley leaned forward on my desk, grinning.

"That's so special. Where are you going to get it?" Not a single human on earth had eyes as green as theirs.

"My hip!" I basically screamed. A perplexed look replaced Wesley's grin.

Oh. Oh no. I had paired something very sentimental with a very sexy tattoo place. So now, now Wesley was intertwining the image of my grandmother's *chair* with my bare *hip*, which was my own special form of boner-killing witchcraft.

"Cool! Cool, cool. Well, I hope you have fun with your friend. Appreciated what you said today, by the way."

Ah. There it was.

"Thank you." I stood up, slinging my backpack over my shoulder. I was about three inches taller than them, which was so fucking cute to me. I hoped they thought I was like, model tall and not puberty-really-went-for-that-optional-last-growth-spurt tall. We both walked toward the door.

"I'll see you next week, Wesley."

Wesley pointed finger guns at me and clicked their teeth. Their eyes widened in panic. Wait. Had Wesley just . . . been very . . . not cool? They blushed and chuckled, walking backward slowly down the hall. They shook their head. Bashful was *hot* on them.

"Bye, Sav."

They turned the other way and I watched them walk down the hall. Maybe it hadn't been a sympathy ask. Maybe they really did want to know what I was doing this weekend. Which was, of course, getting a tattoo. Of a chair. A tribute to my grandmother. On my hip. I groaned loudly. My phone buzzed in my pocket. I slipped my hand into my jeans and clawed it out. I had a text from Izzie and an email from Professor Tolino.

> So excited for this weekend. I know
> you hate day drinking but we're doing
> mimosas before and I'm the bride so
> you have to have oneeeeee. ILYYYYY.

I sighed. Saturday was going to be a very long day. I swiped to open the email from Professor Tolino and groaned again.

> Hi Savannah and Lara! Please find a time to get together this week to record your conversation on the topic of Justice. I look forward to reading your responses.—Prof T

## 12

I LOVED MY metaphysics class. Well, I didn't love the actual class as much as I loved that Vera was in it. Vera, who sat with her legs crisscrossed on her chair, who was perpetually eating gummy worms at ten a.m., who was always five minutes early and saved my seat with something new every time. Today it was a giant plush stuffed octopus, like the kind you might win at a carnival, wearing a bucket hat that read FRESH OCTOPUSSY, which Vera had undoubtedly embroidered herself. I let out a small, mortified shriek and rushed to snatch it from the seat before Professor Frankel could clock what the hat read. I attempted to stuff it under my chair.

"V!" I hissed. "This thing is huge!" Vera looked at me deadpan. Last class she had placed martini glasses filled to the brim with water, garnished with two olives, in the center of both our desks. Professor Frankel was a bald, short king with ruddy cheeks, who was—like most men, it seemed—tremendously intimidated by Vera. When she offered him a sip of the cocktail, he had spluttered in confusion and, potentially, flattery, and then mumbled something about his class not being an open bar. I had apologized profusely and assured him it was just water. Without knowing how else to absolve the situation I proceeded to down the entire glass while Vera screamed, "CHUG, CHUG, CHUG!" as I tried my best to cover her mouth with my free hand.

Desk pranks aside, Vera was crushing this class. V was smart, like mega-fucking smart. She had let it slip one night in my dorm that she had been valedictorian at her high school. But AP art was the only class she had genuinely cared about. She swore that she would devote herself to her craft in college and leave her academia days behind. In our gender studies class she could blend in during group discussions, but in metaphysics her hand was always raised first. After our second week in Professor Frankel's class she made me swear not to tell Candace.

"They would never let me live it down," she explained, as she forged ahead of me down the hall. "No one answers his questions! It's agonizing." She was talking with her hands now, gesticulating wildly. "I mean, it's not a hard class, is it? It's like no one pays any attention. We're going over basic philosophical concepts!" I swerved to avoid a flying hand. She glanced back at me. "Sorry, no offense."

I laughed and shrugged. "None taken. Seriously, even when I try to pay attention, all that stuff is still gibberish to me. I won't tell Candy, but just so you know, it's pretty badass how smart you are."

V's mouth twitched slightly; she looked pleased. I had meant it: it was badass. I loved her confidence, how she would schedule office hours and debate with teachers about antiquated theories. I also relished hearing about her high school years, loved the stories she told me about her crew of friends, who were equally competitive and focused, but whom she would go to house parties with just to steal the alcohol and go hang out in a city park until three in the morning. I wished I had known her then. I wished I hadn't

been the one who stayed at the house party, waiting for some future frat boy to notice me and finger me by the washing machine.

No one I grew up with was anything like Vera. She was so
many things at once. A witch, an artist, an activist, a sadist, a
savant, deep thinking, hugely loving. She had a tattoo that read
HEDONIST in big block letters across her calf. Life, to Vera, was
about pleasure. And she derived a lot of that pleasure from her
partners. She was the first polyamorous person I had ever met. At
the moment, she had two serious partners, Ellis and Raz. Ellis was
a cis Black bisexual man from Nigeria who stood at a casual six
foot three. He had a slight gap between his teeth and studied the
ecosystems of mushrooms. He also had just signed with Ford
Models. Whenever he talked to me my voice got a little pitchy and
I laughed too much. Vera always teased me and reminded me I
could go out with him if I wanted, but that just made me more
nervous and I usually ended up pretending I hadn't heard her. Raz
was Korean American, a nonbinary lesbian with they/she pronouns, and preferred Vera call them her boyfriend or partner. Raz
was a budding chef who won Vera over with a series of home-
cooked Korean meals in their apartment off campus. They were
five three on a good day, the good days usually co-occurring with
their passion for wearing sky-high combat boots, and wore a tiny
vial strung around their neck that I knew was filled with Vera's
period blood. This was revealed to me earlier in the semester, after
she and I shared a very strong weed gummy. When I woke up the
next day, I was (1) very thirsty and (2) thoroughly freaked out.
Seeing Vera with Ellis and Raz, the way the three of them bal-
anced a life together while still allowing exploration with other
people, was beautiful. After my breakup with Nova and her elu-
sive open relationship, I had become pretty jaded about ethical
nonmonogamy, but getting to know V and her partners showed

me that some people could really make it work. That loving more than one person at once could be a sacred, expansive thing.

Vera squeezed my arm. "Thanks, Sav. The academic institution is soul sucking, classist, and a capitalistic machine. But hey, just because we participate in the system doesn't mean we approve of it."

"True," I agreed, though I had only begun to integrate her take on higher education. It was yet another thing I hadn't given thought to growing up.

"Okay!" Vera grabbed my hand. "Let's log in to Candace's Instagram and follow a bunch of conservative mommy bloggers. I figured out they use the same password for everything. It's Kate-Winslet143!"

I snorted.

"Of course it is."

## 13

IT WAS ONLY an hour train ride home. I could have looked at fall foliage and written in my notebook. Instead, I spent it dreading the next day with Izzie. I had received a full-blown itinerary that morning, complete with what to wear and what not to eat before arriving. I wanted to cancel, fake food poisoning or meningitis, but guilt had made me pack my bag and rummage through the back of my closet for the only pair of ballet flats I still owned. They were covered in a dusty film. I thought about what Candace would say if she saw me in them. Probably pretend to faint and then pronounce cause of death heterophobia. Vera would probably light them on fire and sacrifice them to the demons of capitalism. Wesley wouldn't say anything at all, and that, somehow, caused embarrassment to sear through me. I shoved the flats to the bottom of my bag and settled for my least ripped jeans and a fuzzy black sweater. I sat on the floor for a while, lost in all the reasons why going home would suck—having to explain my nose ring to Izzie's mother, feigning interest at retellings of rush from Izzie's sorority friends, and worst of all, the look of pride Izzie would have when she saw me, her best friend in the entire world. She had drowned her guilt about what had happened our junior year of high school and replaced it with feverish loyalty. She felt bad, so bad, and sometimes I wished she didn't. It would be easier that way, if she could be the villain. But her remorse haunted every elaborate gift she gave me, made her eyes well up just before we left for a party, and made her tell anyone who would listen that I was going to be the next Nora Ephron. I had to google who that was after the fifth time she said it. I didn't really understand the comparison, but Izzie hadn't read anything I'd written since high school. Her most recent gift, a blanket embroidered with the phrase GOOD AT NAPS, was still in the plastic sleeve it came in, shoved in the corner of my dorm room. At first, I thought the gift was ironic. I never had been able to nap, even as a kid. But Izzie had monologued about having found "the most Sav gift ever" and had texted me every day to see if it had arrived at school. I pretended to love it when I opened it over FaceTime. "I got one for me too!" she squealed, showing me her own. Izzie napped every day.

Izzie called me to invite me to her dress-shopping day. It was early; she was at the gym.

"Savvy, I've been putting this off, but I really want to talk to you about the bridal party." I could hear the whir of the treadmill through the phone. I had known this was coming.

"I know it's still, like, weird with you and my brother." She panted.

*That's one way to put it.*

"Mm-hmm."

"And you would have to be involved in so many of the wedding events. I don't want you to feel uncomfortable. And honestly, I think I would be thinking about you being uncomfortable and then I would be uncomfortable."

"Sure."

"I don't want to put us through that, you know?"

Izzie liked to use the word "awkward" to describe my relationship with her brother. And I let her. It was too complicated otherwise. I was fine with this plan. It meant that I didn't have to be near him. After my junior year, he seldom came home. He stayed in California after graduating, worked a finance gig with crazy hours. He hardly made it home for holidays. Recently, though, he had moved to the city. I knew it was only a matter of time before we crossed paths, but I was determined to avoid it until the wedding.

"I get that. I think that's smart." My tone was even.

"I know it isn't what we planned." Her voice was quiet.

"Yeah." I didn't know how to respond to that. It was just true.

"But we'll still be together for the shower!" Izzie's voice lit up again, filling the dead air. "And you'll come to the bachelorette party! The rest of the stuff is boring, anyway."

*The rehearsal dinner. The dress reveal. The maid of honor speech. Boring.*

I pushed myself to agree with her. "Totally. It's all fine! This is your special day. Whatever makes you happy makes me happy."

"You're the best. Really. I love you." I heard the relief in her voice.

"Okay!" she continued. "I'm gonna sprint now, okay? I had the drunchies last night and need to burn it off—I want to look perfect for dress shopping." I heard the treadmill beep as she upped the speed. I sighed.

"Don't overdo it, Iz. Love you too."

For the rest of the day, I had this nagging feeling. I kept thinking about the wedding, going over the day in my mind. I had imagined it so many times, as many times as my own, but now my mind had gone blank. I couldn't imagine myself doing my makeup, or drinking champagne, or fixing a wisp of Izzie's hair caught in her lip gloss. Maybe it was just because it was finally real, finally happening. Or maybe because it was happening in a way I could never have imagined.

It wasn't just that I couldn't imagine the series of events; it was that I couldn't imagine myself at the wedding at all.

·

"YOU CAN'T HAVE your legs up like that." A conductor with a thick Brooklyn accent was talking to me. Her mouth hung slightly open to reveal a wad of blue gum.

"Sorry, sorry." I yanked my feet down from the seat across from me. I would put my legs back up as soon as she left. Izzie always chided me for that. She said it wasn't ladylike. This from the girl who once ate an entire T-bone steak with her fingers. She was vegetarian now.

"Tickets?" The conductor looked at me expectantly, smacking the gum.

"Yes, sorry, my phone is, um—" I dug around my seat before realizing I was sitting on it. Cool.

I activated my ticket and shoved my phone toward the scanner. The machine made a little dinging noise, and the conductor shuffled off to the next train car. My phone rang. It was my dad.

"Hey," I said.

"Making good time?" he asked. Mom must have told him I was heading into the city.

"Yes. Got the express train. How are you, Pops?"

"Oh, you know. Helping your mother with her various dilemmas. I bought the wrong trash bags, apparently."

I gasped dramatically into the phone. "Shame on you!"

He laughed. "Are you ready for Izzie and her debutantes?"

Dad loved Izzie. But Dad did not love Izzie's choices. And he really didn't love the choices Izzie and I made together. He didn't like the way her family flaunted their wealth, didn't like that she had no bedtime, didn't like how I'd come home from a sleepover with a new lilt in my voice. "Did a Valley girl just climb into my back seat?" he'd ask as I clambered into the car, running on no sleep and a sour-gummy high. "Oh my god, Dad, just stopppppp." The voice thing wasn't Izzie's fault anyway; we had just watched too much YouTube. My dad loved how smart Izzie was, how silly she could be, how much she loved me. But when Izzie got a designer bag, I wanted one. When Izzie's parents let her have wine at dinner, I asked for some too. But when Izzie told me she wanted to rush a sorority, I had no interest at all. My dad was thrilled.

"Kappa Kappa Bullshit," he said. "You don't need to pay dues to make friends."

I thought about all that now, talking to him on the phone.

"They're not so bad when they're off their home turf. Panhellenic can't see them, you know?"

"Good point." He paused. "Well, just wanted to call and see how the ride was going. Wish you were heading our way."

"I'll be home for break very soon, Dad. I miss you too." I played it cool, but it made my heart ache. I'd have killed for him to pick me up from the train. I'd swap mimosas and scones for Diet Coke and pizza any day.

"Okay. Sounds good. Love you."

"Love you," I replied.

I peered out the window and suburbia stared back at me. Squinting, I could see a skyscraper in the distance. I put my feet back up on the seat across from me and closed my eyes.

•

"THERE SHE IIIIIS!"

Before I even had the time to look up from Google Maps, Izzie's arms were wrapped around me and I got a mouthful of blond hair. It was freshly washed, very floral. Very Izzie.

"You look skinny. Please tell me I look skinny, I know you won't, but can we not be body-posi for, like, one day? Like, this day, specifically?" She squeezed my cheeks between her hands.

"You look beautiful." I smiled, cupping my hands over hers.

"Can you *believe* it? I'm getting *married*!" Izzie threw her arms into the air and jumped.

"I can't! I can't." I forced some excitement into my voice, but I wasn't lying.

"I know. I'm so happy you're here, Sav. Come, come, everyone's waiting for you!" Izzie yanked my hand, rushing me over to a bright green awning with lots of kitten heels crowded underneath it.

I braced myself for an onslaught of "hiiiiiiiiiii's" and weak embraces. I wondered if Izzie's friends all thought I wanted to fuck them now that I was gay. I mean out as gay. I was always gay. Right? Nope, no, I could save my bisexual crisis for the train ride back.

"Izzie!" It was Kenzie, which was a relief. I could relax, slightly, with Kenzie. She and Izzie had met at a summer internship in DC, between freshman and sophomore year of college, back when Iz was on a women-in-politics kick. Kenzie was smart, and she led with that, and she hung back when calories became the topic of conversation, which they inevitably did, and I had never heard her say a shitty thing about another woman's appearance. She was Izzie's maid of honor.

"Kenz, hey!"

I reached out to hug her, a real hug, and she hugged me back.

When she pulled away, I could tell she was a little nervous. Not because she thought I was a Big Lesbian for her, but because I knew she felt guilty for being Izzie's maid of honor. I squeezed her hand.

"It's so good to see you," I said, and I meant it.

Relief flushed her face.

"So good to see you too. I love your nose ring."

I laughed. "Me too. Thank you."

The rest of the girls crowded around me all at once, and I bounced around from hug to hug, enveloped in Chanel No. Something and fake cheek kisses from Noelle, who had spent the previous semester in Paris.

"Okay okay okay! My day! Just kidding. Kind of." Izzie wiggled her tongue at us. "We're doing high tea, but, like, with alcohol!"

The rest of the girls squealed. Fuck. I hated drinking during the day. I wondered if I could sneak over to the server when no one was looking and ask for plain OJ.

"My mom and Ben's mom, I know, I'm obsessed, are in the back. Cooooome!" Izzie skipped toward the back of the restaurant. There was no one in the entire place. I had a feeling that Izzie's mom had rented more than just the back room.

"Oh, this is so fancy!" This was from Melissa, who was a newer friend of Izzie's. She was also engaged, to one of Ben's friends in ROTC, and she had a slight lilt to her voice. Izzie said she was from Alabama, but not, like, scary Alabama, whatever that meant. The restaurant was hardly fancy, not by Izzie's standards, anyway.

*Get it together, Sav. A back room at a restaurant on the Upper East Side is fucking fancy.*

"It's so beautiful, right?" I whispered to Melissa.

She nodded vigorously. "Like, gorgeous."

I was the last one in the room, purposely, hoping that Izzie's mom, Mrs. Kirtz, would run out of her chirpy comments and painstaking once-overs by the time she got to me. I hadn't seen her in person for what felt like forever, just quick hellos over FaceTime when Izzie was visiting home.

"Savannah, my love bug! Oh, it's so good to see you, sweetie! I've missed you so much. How's your mom? She never answers my calls! Oh, would you look at that gold thing in your nose? Like a sweet little cow!"

Wishful thinking.

I hugged Mrs. Kirtz and quickly sidelined for Ben's mom, who looked slightly overwhelmed, and thrust my hand out to her.

"Hi, I'm Sav!"

Mrs. Kirtz didn't miss a beat. "Lorraine, Savannah is Izzie's best childhood friend. You should have seen those girlies growing up! Inseparable. I could never take them anywhere; they were always laughing themselves into fits." Mrs. Kirtz was stroking my hair. I forgot how suffocating secondhand guilt could be.

"Lovely to meet you, Sav." Lorraine shook my hand. Izzie bounded over.

"Look at my two mommies, Savvy! Can you believe? Both so beautiful."

I nodded. "So beautiful."

I slid into my seat and saw my phone light up in my bag, but I knew Izzie would kill me if I checked it. She was really into being "present" now, after taking a yoga elective first semester. I thought about something Reg had said in class a few weeks ago, about white women appropriating yoga, and I cringed at the thought of her sitting at this table. Actually, the thought of anyone from school being here made me queasy.

"So are you dating anyone?" I looked up to see that Kenzie had taken the seat across from me. She looked so earnest, but I couldn't help but feel that she was trying to earn ally points.

"Oh, um, no. Not right now!"

"Weren't you dating someone over the summer? A singer or something?"

Oh good, Izzie had told everyone about her Gay friend dating another Gay person.

"Oh yeah, that was casual. She ended up being kind of a dick." I didn't feel the need to go into detail about having been plunged into the vortex of a toxic polyamorous love triangle and my first soul-crushing queer heartbreak. But who knows, maybe I would open up more after tea.

"Oh, that sucks. I'm sorry! I'm sure you'll meet a new girl soon."

*Or boy*, I thought. *Or human.* Wesley's face flashed into my head, and I gripped the edge of my seat. Absolutely not, Sav, no pining. Not the time, certainly not the place.

My conversation with Kenzie was cut short as a group of servers swarmed the table with bottles of expensive champagne. A round of clapping erupted around me.

"Oh my god, speech! Speech, s'il vous plaît!" Noelle screamed across the table at Izzie, who was at the head. Everyone joined in, clapping louder and echoing Noelle.

"Okay, okay!" Izzie stood. Her hair was blown out and barrel curled, and her nails were painted her signature Ballet Slippers nude. Her dress was cream and scalloped around the skirt. She did, in fact, look skinny. I wish I didn't notice.

"I can't believe this day is here. I feel like I've dreamed about this forever. Like, wedding dress shopping? Me? Now? It's surreal! And I couldn't be happier to be here with my favorite people ever. And I'm so excited to have my new mama here too." Izzie beamed at Ben's mom, who blew her a kiss.

"It feels like yesterday that Savvy and I were dreaming of this moment when we were, like, thirteen years old, clipping pictures from *Cosmo*. I'm so happy you're here, Sav." She turned to me, her upper lip quivering. Cue the tears.

"I just, like, feel, like, so lucky." Izzie was full-blown crying now.

Kenzie jumped up and dabbed Izzie's cheeks with a linen napkin. Izzie laughed between sobs and gestured to Kenzie. "And I couldn't do any of this, obviously, without my maid of dishonor, the fabulous McKenzie Bloom. You're my literal savior in all of this." The two embraced. My hands felt clammy.

"To the strong women in my life!" Izzie held up her champagne glass, and everyone followed suit. When I reached my glass toward Kenzie's, she clinked mine, but I could tell she was avoiding my gaze.

Izzie looped her arm around my neck and whispered into my ear.

"Remember that time you peed a little at that party and I had to give you my literal underwear?" Before I could answer, Izzie started cackling like she did when we were kids, without control, and I started laughing too. We had the same blueprint. Our faces were close together and I could see saliva frothing around her lips and I almost gagged from how fast my chest was heaving. For a split moment everything was totally normal, and I thought maybe none of this was weird. Maybe this was just the kind of shit that went on in relationships. Maybe time really did heal all. Maybe I was just too in tune with my feelings. Maybe my school was too liberal. Maybe I needed a better therapist, or maybe I never needed one in the first place.

"So, wait, Iz, is your brother going to bring that girl to the wedding?" Noelle turned to Izzie.

I stopped laughing.

"I think so! I'm so happy for him. They are so cute together. I just feel like she's the only girl who has ever really *gotten* him, you know? Like actually been good enough for him."

I bit down on my lip and tried to hold back the tears forming in my eyes.

# 14

I ENTERED THE house and felt dizzy, blinking the sun from my eyes and steadying my red cup, now half empty. You were close behind me. Your hand reached out and pushed me forward, toward the kitchen.

"Come on! Let's get sugar before they come back. You're not gonna take a million hours to get ready, are you?"

"I have to do my hair."

"It looks fine if you let it dry natural," you said, shooting me a look.

"I don't feel hot like that. I like it straight." Annoyance spiked my reply.

"Who are you trying to look hot for?"

"No one. That's not the point. Jeremy might come over, if he can get his sister to drive him."

"Tell him to bring a friend. Or five."

"Once I get service I will. I wish your parents would get better wi-fi."

"They're cheap. They just sold a six-million-dollar house, but they're cheap."

You stood on your tiptoes to retrieve the ziplocked bag of sugar from the cabinet, green bikini strings hanging from your bathing suit. One butt cheek was rosy.

"I think your butt got burnt," I observed.

"Fuck, really?"

You groaned, slapping the sugar down on the kitchen table. You dropped your bikini bottoms to inspect your burn just in time for the door to swing open. I grabbed the sugar and a spoon, and we dashed up the back staircase, your ass crack visible, bare feet padding on wood stairs, creaks following our footsteps. Your house was 250 years old.

Once in your bedroom I sank down onto your plush blue carpet. It felt good against my skin, my calves now a reddish tan, soft from the oil, prickly from a couple of days without shaving. I winced. Had he noticed that? The hair hadn't been as visible by the pool, had it?

You were busy playing bartender by the dresser, spooning white crystals into our red cups and stirring fast, licking the spoon between jumps from cup to cup. "Let's shower. Bring your drink with you!" you called from the bathroom.

I pressed my way back up to stand and giggled when my vision blurred.

"I'm a little drunk," I whispered, peeling my bikini off in the bathroom. You were already standing in the shower, testing the water with outstretched hands.

I pushed my way into the shower and tipped my head under the spout, as you danced in and out of the stream. As soon as the water hit my skin, I knew I'd gotten a sunburn.

"Switch, bitch," you said, handing me the shampoo. "Should I shave my legs? Do you think Jeremy will bring friends?"

"He said he'd try. Do it just in case." I shrugged.

I cringed as you reached for your disposable pink plastic razor, knowing you wouldn't use shaving cream. I took a long time to shave my legs, always in the bath, using thick conditioner. I imagined foreign hands sliding up my thigh. His hands.

"Do you think you'll have sex?"

I startled; your voice was too loud, echoing inside the glass doors of the shower.

"What?"

"With Jeremy. He hasn't been home for a month—aren't you dying to fuck?" Jeremy had gone to guitar camp.

"I don't know, we only did it that one time. He has such a skinny penis."

"But he went down on you for a long time, right?"

"Yeah. But I don't like that as much as fingering." I distracted myself with the loofah, rubbing at my stomach.

"But you came, didn't you?" Your voice was insistent.

"Um, yeah. But I had to focus really hard."

I reached for my towel. I left the bathroom before you had time to grill me with another question. Thinking about having sex with Jeremy made me nervous, and I wasn't sure if it was in a good way.

He and I spent the bulk of tenth grade IMing back and forth, staying up late on school nights talking about music, college, and his love of guitar. He and I had been close since middle school. Even back then I had an inkling that he was enamored with me, but I wasn't interested. He was too nervous, his eyes often darting back and forth in the middle of a conversation. He seemed calmest in our guitar class, and it was only there that I'd imagine kissing him. But soon enough he got a girlfriend and our conversation turned to her. He employed me as relationship coach, and I relished his need for my advice. He'd call me after each date, and we'd pore over every detail of what happened.

"Dude, I think she wanted me to finger her during the movie."

"She definitely did. Scary movies are fingering movies."

"I fucked up, then. 'Cause I didn't do that. We held hands, though."

I considered this for a moment, weighing hand-holding versus fingering.

"I actually think that's even better," I told him.

"Really? Fuck yeah." I could hear him beaming on his end of the phone.

"You're mad good at this, Sav."

I don't remember if it turned me on, but I knew I liked the power. I wasn't his girlfriend. I was his confidant, and somehow that was better. When I broke up with my first real boyfriend at the end of that year, Jeremy waited five months before he asked me out. By then he had shot up three inches and grown out his hair enough to semi-mask his darting eyes, so I said yes.

I sat down on the carpet in front of the full-length mirror, my towel dropping to my lap. I inspected my tan line, tracing the triangles left by my bikini.

"Do you think I have pepperoni nipples?" I shouted, leaning my head back toward the bathroom.

"What?" Your voice was muffled. You wrapped your hair up in a towel as you came through the door.

"Pepperoni. Nipples."

"You have big nipples. Should I wear my yellow dress or the one that you left here, with the off-the-shoulder sleeves?" You dropped your towel on the floor and swung open your closet.

"Yellow." I turned back to the mirror and fastened the hooks of my bra, hoping the fabric would make my nipples hard, so they looked smaller.

"What did you bring? Can I see?"

You were already riffling through my bag. You tugged my makeup case from the left pocket, scooping out the contents until you found my lip gloss, the one that stung a little and made your lips puffy. You painted your mouth with it and then handed it to me, smacking your lips loud, as if to say, "Your turn, slut."

"Just that black dress I always wear, the one with the frays at the bottom." I retrieved it from the bag and held it up to my chest.

"I love that one. So cute. I really want to borrow it, but my mom hates when I wear black."

I held up my drink. "Can we chug? I can't sip this, even with the sugar." I stuck my tongue out.

"Okay, on three, we do six big sips. Ready?"

"No, but okay. You count."

"One, two, two and a half . . ."

"Fuck you."

"Three! Chug!!"

I gulped my drink, now tepid and too sweet, the alcohol cutting across my tongue. Between sips I made gagging sounds, and you held up your middle finger, closing your eyes.

"Finished!" you screamed, fisting your cup into the air in victory.

"Ugh. My fucking nightmare." I slammed the cup down on your dresser.

"It'll be easier once we're drunk. Besides, the champagne will be out soon, and you love champagne."

"I do love champagne. When it's the good kind."

"You know my parents only buy the good kind."

I pulled on my dress, goose bumps forming on my arms as the cotton ran over my skin. The alcohol bloomed in my belly.

"I'm so crispy." I giggled, throwing myself on your bed.

"I'm crispy and tipsy!" You flopped next to me; your wet hair smelled like a fresh smoothie.

"Are you gonna put makeup on?" I asked, batting my lashes. You had recently conquered the smoky eye.

"Which is really you asking if I'll do it for you?"

"Exactly."

You rolled your eyes and gestured for me to come sit.

"Gold and bronzy, right, beach goddess?"

"Yes, please." I scooted to the edge of the bed, my legs dangling over the mattress as I leaned my face closer to you. You pulled open your vanity drawer, grabbing a pack of gum, handing me a stick.

"Vodka breath."

Dabbing concealer onto my skin, your fingers were warm and a little clammy. My phone vibrated. I pawed the bed, searching for it.

"Stay still, bitch," you growled.

"It's probably Jeremy," I whined, squinting at the screen with my one open eye as you smeared gold powder over the other lid.

"He's coming. He's bringing Sam H. and Luke."

"I hate Sam H."

"We don't know for sure if he's the one who drew that horse and put your name next to it in the boy's bathroom."

"I do know. I can just tell. And I hate him."

"But Luke is coming."

Your face reddened. In May, you and Luke had made out on a coach bus on the way home from Gwen's sweet sixteen. The gifts were monogrammed blankets and Luke pulled his over the both of you before launching himself at your face. You hadn't spoken since.

"I don't think Luke is interested."

"Of course he's interested. He won't be able to resist you."

You finished applying lip gloss to my lips and peered at yourself in the mirror. You pouted.

"I do look cute."

"You are cute! You're perfect!"

You tipped your forehead toward mine, landing softly against my skin. "Thanks."

I hopped off the bed and looked out the window. Your brother was playing catch with Kelsey, palming a beer with his free hand.

"She's not that pretty," I said, watching her miss the ball and stumble back on the grass, laughing.

"Yeah, right. She's gorgeous." You had joined me at the window. "Even before the nose job, she was literally perfect-looking."

"I guess," I muttered.

"Why do you care?" You narrowed your eyebrows.

"I don't." I shrugged.

"You can't get with my brother, Savannah."

I tried not to freeze.

"I'm not going to!"

"I'm not an idiot. You act stupid around him." You were staring at me now.

"Whatever, Izzie. It's a dumb crush from when we were little. Obviously, that would never happen."

You weren't sold. You put your hand out to block the window.

"I'm serious. You can't hook up with him. That would be fucked up."

"I'm serious too. I won't."

"Okay, good."

"Okay, good," I mocked back. Your mouth twitched. I felt relieved.

"Let's go, slut. I'm hungry," you said. "Let's get drunker before the boys get here!" You grabbed your sandals and left the room. I followed you, resisting the urge to look out the window once more.

We trailed downstairs and out to the appetizer table. I shoved celery sticks with ranch dressing into my mouth. I felt a tap on my shoulder and turned to find Jeremy standing behind me, a lop-sided smile stretching across his face.

"You're so fucking pretty," he whispered, hugging me tightly.

I knew I should kiss him, but I didn't want to risk your brother seeing, so I told Jeremy I wanted to show him something on the tennis court. I quickly poured us two vodka Cokes and shoved the drink in his hand, much more confident with a boy my own age. I laced my fingers with his as we walked up the big hill.

I took him behind the court. I leaned in fast to kiss him, unable to withstand the in-between. Within seconds his hands were on my lower back and his tongue slipped into my mouth. It was too much, and I pulled back, offering smaller closed-mouth kisses as a nudge that he was doing it wrong. He pulled me down to the grass with him, muttering something about how much he missed me. I wished we had a towel; grass always made my skin itchy and red. I rolled on top of him instead, masking my discomfort with what I hoped seemed like a power move.

"Did you bring a condom?" I asked, breathy.

"Heck yes," he replied, smirking. He tried to reach into his pocket with me still on top of him, squirming, knocking me off him in the process. I landed with a thud next to him.

"Shit! My bad, are you good?"

His voice was dangerously close to cracking, revealing his nervousness. He coughed, low and deep, to cover it. I felt a quick wash of nausea and pushed past it by diving in to kiss him again. He pulled me back onto him. I took the condom from him, feigning know-how, ripping it open with my teeth. I had watched enough porn to act the part, but I secretly recoiled at the slippery leak of lube. I scooched farther down onto his thighs so he could undo his jeans, which were basically glued to his legs, black and ripped for the aesthetic. I tried to look sexy as I rolled the condom over him, but the sight of a penis still shocked me a little, and I focused on his face instead. I felt clumsy as I wiggled him into me. I lowered myself down too fast and felt my vagina resist. I took a sharp breath. What was he hitting? I wasn't a virgin. Was that my cervix?

"You okay?" he asked. His voice was gentle and somehow that made it worse.

I nodded, adjusting a little. I felt too exposed sitting on top of him like that, so I leaned down and let my hair create a sheath around us. He slid his hand around my neck, making little grunting sounds. He was, objectively, so handsome. *I should be really into this*, I thought. *He likes me. He says he loves me. Isn't that the point of this? To have sex with someone who loves me?* That's what my mom had told me. Jeremy shut his eyes tight, nearing closer to coming, and instinctively I reached down to touch myself. I refused to let myself have sex without finishing too, and tried to catch up. Jeremy asked me if he was going to make me come. I wished he would shut up. He wasn't doing anything to help, but I lied and told him, "Yeah, you are, baby, you're gonna make me." And I did. He came immediately after, his grunting now a higher-pitched moan, revealing that he was, in fact, just a teenage boy. I swallowed hard, rolling off him. I wanted a hamburger, and another drink.

# 15

I WOKE UP to my phone alarm. It was set for my typical eight thirty wakeup, but it was Sunday and the sound was ungodly. I thrashed around my bed for my phone, finally locating it under my pillow. I wondered if the toxic chemicals penetrating my brain all night were making my hangover worse. My mom would kill me if she knew I sometimes slept with my phone under my pillow. She still made me duck if I was heating something up in the microwave.

I had a text from Candace, and another from a number I didn't recognize. I blinked hard and tried to read the words on my screen, still bleary-eyed, my vision spinning.

Candace had texted at three a.m.

> I love party Sav. See you in the
> morning, babygirl.

I tried to remember the order of events leading up to today's hangover. I had decided to come back to school early, not wanting to stay over in the hotel suite Izzie had booked for the group. I just couldn't handle having to recap the day, the hours spent trying on what felt like millions of different dresses, schlepping from bridal boutique to bridal boutique, holding up tiny signs that read YES 2 THE DRESS or THAT DRESS IS A MESS. My jaw ached from pretending to smile. I took the earliest train back I could, and I ended up in Candace's room at nine thirty that night. A small human with a buzz cut greeted me at the door, offering me a shot of clear liquid.

"She doesn't drink!" Candace called out, but before she finished the sentence, I downed the shot. It was vodka, but especially horrible vodka, and I dove for the liter bottle of OJ I saw on the nearest desk. I drank right from the bottle. Warm orange juice had never tasted so good. I looked up to find Candace staring at me, her hand clasped over her mouth. I rolled my eyes at her and walked over.

"I can drink sometimes, you know."

"Of *course* you can." I could tell she was thrilled. She'd never seen me drink more than a glass of wine, once, when her parents took us out to dinner last semester.

I had a lot more than a glass of wine last night. I groaned. My phone buzzed again. The number I didn't recognize had sent another text.

The first: Library at 2? XoL

The second: ??? XoL

XoL? What was this, *Gossip Girl*? Who the fuck was XoL? Had I signed up for one of those volunteering things again? The last time I had done that I had been coerced by a very attractive boy who looked like Walmart Harry Styles at best. When I showed up, he wasn't even there, and, more suspiciously, all the other volunteers were also quite feminine and wearing too much bronzer for eight in the morning.

> Oh, I guess if we're recording we
> shouldn't be in the library. Where do
> you want to meet? XoL

Oh. XoL as in "hug and kiss, Lara." A wave of nausea hit me. I hastily responded.

> Let's do Owen's on the patio. It's
> supposed to be sunny today.

I opened my weather app after sending the text. Partly cloudy. It would do. I needed to be outside; I couldn't be stuck in a stuffy classroom with a headache this bad. And at Owen's I could inject an IV of coffee into my bloodstream. My stomach growled. As if on cue, Candace barged through my door.

"*Bagels, bitch.*"

She practically body-slammed onto my bed.

"Thank you, you're an angel." My voice was hoarse. "Gimme."

She tossed a bagel into my lap, the wax paper already laden with grease stains from what I prayed was bacon. I unwrapped it and wolfed down the first bite of bagel.

"*Yummmm.*" My eyes rolled back into my head.

Candace doused her bagel with hot sauce, throwing me a handful of packets. I ripped through one with my teeth. We ate without speaking and chewed with our mouths wide open.

"Last night, huh?" Candace finally managed through mouthfuls of her bagel.

"What?" I looked up mid-bite, panicked at the thought of what she might say.

"What did I do?"

"You don't remember last night?"

"Um, sort of, yeah." I really didn't.

"Oh my god, Sav goes wild. My little lightweight!" She poked me with the straw of her iced coffee. I bit my lip, waiting for the worst.

"Dude, you were great. You're a menace when you drink tequila. In the best way."

Relief washed over me. I grabbed the coffee and chugged it.

"I couldn't get you away from the speaker all night. You dance hot." Candace wiggled her eyebrows.

"I dance hot?"

"Yeah. There's, like, good dancing and hot dancing. You do hot dancing."

"So you're saying I'm not good?"

"Who wants good when you can be hot?"

"Fair."

I loved to dance. I especially loved to dance when I was drunk, but I never let getting drunk happen anymore. Last night was, apparently, an exception.

Dancing was the only thing worth a hangover. Sitting around to drink for the sake of drinking was a waste of time and brain cells.

"How was your night?"

"Good, good. Nothing too crazy." Candace looked down at her shoe, hiding a smirk.

"Liar. Big huge liar!" I threatened to throw my bagel at her.

"Maya may have made an appearance."

Oh my god. I remembered now. I had gone to the bathroom and found Maya and Candy by the door, peering closely at each other's hands.

"She read my palms. It was so hot."

"You've got to be kidding me." I laughed and lay back on my pillow.

"I saw Wesley there too."

I shot up again.

"What? Did I?"

"No, no. They only came for a few minutes. They said they had a thing in the morning. Wesley's friends with Jari."

I stared blankly.

"We were at Jari's house, Sav!"

Oh, yes, Jari. Jari had the blue buzz cut.

"Blue buzz cut!"

"Yes, blue buzz cut."

"So how long is a few minutes?"

"Ten? Fifteen, tops."

I tried not to look disappointed. It was probably better that they hadn't said hi, who knows what I would have said.

"They were for sure watching you, though. Like, a lot."

My eyes widened.

"A lot a lot?"

"A *lot* a lot."

My cheeks turned bright pink. Well, they probably turned a regular shade of pink, considering all the blood inside my body had congealed inside my very angry liver.

"You really don't remember?"

"I'm just tired. I'm sure it will all come back to me." I knew it wouldn't. It never did.

"Tequila will fuck you up like that. That's why I stick to vodka." I suddenly remembered the shots of Svedka. No wonder my body freaked out.

"What's wrong?" Candace was looking at me funny.

"Nothing, nothing." I shook my head. This was a story I didn't have time to explain right now.

I looked at my phone. It was 1:42. I jumped out of my bed.

"Fuck, I have to go. I'm meeting Lara at Owen's. Unfortunately. Wish me luck."

Candace had already crawled under my covers and opened my computer to Netflix.

"She's hot."

"Candace."

"Annoying and problematic, but hot."

I grabbed my towel and stripped down to my bra and underwear.

"Can I nap here?" Candace's eyes were already closed.

I headed to the communal bathrooms. I had left my shit on the counter again, in an apparent drunk attempt at my skincare routine, and scrambled to put it in my shower caddy. Someone had left a very passive-aggressive note on the mirror last semester and I did not want to make that a repeat occurrence.

I took the quickest shower in existence, scouring my body with the nozzle turned all the way to H, and brushed my teeth three times. Right before I got out, I twisted the nozzle to C, hoping to shock the hangover out of me.

"FUCK!" It was fucking frigid.

I slammed the shower off, shivering. I dried my hair with a ratty T-shirt and slapped a handful of moisturizer on my face. Back in my room, Candace was snoring as I got dressed. I pulled on my loosest jeans and a black hoodie and ran for the door. It was 1:54.

I made it to Owen's with a minute to spare, totally out of breath. On the way I briefly scrolled through my texts to see if I had messaged anyone on my tequila bender. Just a few texts to Andie, the girl from karaoke night. I groaned. At eleven thirty I had written heyyyyyy there cutie, and at two a.m. I had sent you're so hot we shoukd get Thai djcod. Slick of me. She hadn't responded, but I couldn't blame her. I shoved my phone in my pocket and ran down toward the backyard of Owen's. Lara was already there, fingering a piece of blond hair, curled to perfection. I felt cold water from my bun drip down my neck. I wiped it away quickly as I sat down.

"Hey, how are ya?"

"Hello." She smiled weakly.

Ah. I was going to be the one to lead this conversation. Great.

"How was your Friday night?"

"It was nice. I went to Roberta's with my boyfriend."

I noticed the promise ring was back.

"It's this little Italian spot in town?" she added.

I knew about Roberta's. It was the only restaurant in town with real linen tablecloths and a menu that changed every week. It was expensive—not Friday-night-date expensive, like graduation-dinner-with-your-parents kind of expensive.

"That's so nice."

"You?"

"Oh, I stopped by a party. Nothing wild."

I swallowed a burp and tried not to make a face. It tasted like tequila.

"Which frat?" She cocked her head to the side.

"What?"

"Which frat did you go to? SAE was having a party and so was Kappa Alpha. Which did you go to?"

"Oh, I, um, I didn't go to a frat party. I went to a house party, at an apartment off campus."

Lara looked confused.

"My friend Candace brought me."

"I know Candace."

"Right! Yes. Candace. From class."

There was a pause. She looked embarrassed.

"So nice!" The syrup in her voice was back.

"Really nice."

God, this was awkward.

"Should we start?" Lara asked.

"Yeah, definitely. Let me just get my—"

"We can use mine."

"Oh, sure."

Lara pulled her iPhone out of her purse. Chanel. Who brings a Chanel purse to our campus café on a Sunday? She opened the voice memo app and hit record. She slid her phone between us on the table, slowly, as if she was scared I was going to grab it and run.

"So, like, what does justice mean to you?" She looked at me, her lips tight and eyes expectant.

"Honestly, I—don't know . . . I . . ."

"Well, it's when the law—"

"Right, no, Lara, I know what justice means from the point of our legal system. I just don't exactly know what it means to me."

"Well, rapists need to be put in jail."

I cringed slightly. How crazy it must be to be able to say that word so loudly and without much thought attached to it. Lara glanced down at her notebook, folding the corner of the page she had it opened to.

"I mean, so they, you know. Don't do it again?" she continued.

"Sure. Yeah. That's important."

My cheeks were getting hot. I didn't want to come off like I didn't want abusers to go to jail. I just, I don't know; something was missing from that logic. But I wasn't sure how to say that, how to explain myself.

"How long should a rap—I mean assaulter go to jail for?" Lara asked.

"I, um, I don't really know." I felt panicked, almost like I was going to cry. I bit down on the inside of my cheek. I was just hung-over, I reminded myself. Extra-sensitive.

Lara uncrossed her legs and then crossed them again with the opposite knee.

"Well, I think it, like, depends. On the severity of the assault and the age of the victim."

*Victim. Victim. Victim.* I felt dizzy.

"The age?"

"Yeah, like it's different if it's a child versus an adult."

"And what, um, constitutes a child?" I tried to keep my breathing even.

"Um . . . like, up to thirteen, I guess? Fourteen? I know the age of consent or whatever is seventeen in most places, but by the time I was, like, fifteen, I acted like an adult. I think it's old enough to know what you're doing."

"Old enough? To be—"

"No! Of course not. I mean, like, old enough to be, like, more aware."

I was going to throw up.

"Can you pause it? I, um, I need a coffee."

I had already stood up. I booked it into the café, clenching my jaw and swallowing the spit starting to gather in my mouth. *Do not throw up here, Savannah. You can wait. You can wait. You can fucking wait.* The green VACANT sign was visible on the bathroom door and I pushed it open, barely locking it before I fell onto my knees and vomited into the toilet. Tears were streaming down my face. I tried not to look down. I didn't want to see the remnants of whatever I ate at two a.m. and the bagel I had just downed. After what felt like an hour, my stomach gave up and I was only dry heaving. I spit into the bowl and wiped my mouth. I pressed the lever and flushed. I pushed myself back away from the toilet and leaned against the bathroom door. The ground was sticky. I let out a sob.

•

THE LAST TIME I had cried like that was with Marie.

"Would you consider rape a trauma?"

That's what she had asked me.

Marie was a "wellness counselor" I was assigned to see for three mandatory sessions, second semester freshman year, after my RA found alcohol in my room. Twice. In the same week. The kicker was that the alcohol hadn't been mine either time. Julia and Victoria brought it over because I had a single and my room had become the designated pregame spot. But my RA was notoriously strict and said she had to take symptoms of alcoholism very seriously.

Marie was in her forties, I guessed, maybe early fifties. She was white, had tight brown ringlets, and she doodled abstract shapes in her notebook while we talked. She told me it helped her pay attention. One of the first things I noticed about Marie was that she cared about being comfortable. She always had a steaming-hot thermos. In the beginning I assumed it was coffee but learned later it was always herbal tea, mint or chamomile. She wore long cotton skirts and thick wool socks. When she smiled, soft creases formed around her mouth, which made me think she had done a lot of smiling thus far in her life. The three mandatory sessions turned into ten more voluntary ones, at her suggestion. I told her things I had never told anyone, things I didn't even think were worth telling anyone, and once I started talking, I realized there was so much I had to say. During our sixth session, I told her about the flashes. Images from that night at Izzie's that would interrupt my thoughts unexpectedly, unwelcome and terrifying every time. The blue room, the vodka, sometimes Thanksgiving weekend, the night Izzie showed up at my house with my stuff. She told me that flashbacks were often a sign of PTSD. I shook my head. I didn't have PTSD. That's what war veterans had. Women who had been kidnapped. People who had been stuck inside a burning building. People who had experienced serious trauma. I told her this.

"Would you consider rape a trauma?" she asked. I felt the air go still.

"Of course I do."

"Okay." Marie nodded.

*What are you saying, Marie?*

"You think, um." I stammered over the words. "Do you think I could call it that? What happened to me?"

Marie folded her hands in her lap. "I do think so, yes." She looked at me to gauge my reaction. I felt a surge of relief. Then doubt set in. I shook my head.

"But how could I not know that?"

"No one can know what your experience was except for you. If you say your experience was different now, because you have a greater understanding of it, then that's the truth. That's your truth."

"But how could I not know this was my experience? I thought it was something else. I thought it was something else up until right now. Is this what a repressed memory is?"

Marie was quiet.

"Maybe it is, in a way," she began. "How does it feel? To say that you were raped?" I gripped the edge of the couch. Each mention of the word was jarring. Wasn't "rape" a word for women who jogged too late at night? Bathroom stalls at run-down bars? Newspaper headlines that my mother read aloud to warn me?

It was a word I'd used so many times but never in relation to myself. *You were drunk, you wanted it, you begged for it like a little slut. You dreamed of him, led him on, you're just looking for excuses to feel better about yourself. And then you did it again.*

*Sober. No one at home would believe you for a second, let alone the people who were at that party.*

"I slept with him again." I looked Marie in the eye, watching her face for a sign of surprise.

"When did that happen?"

"Like, months later. When he came home for Thanksgiving break. And I texted him. A bunch. After the party. Not even texts, but sexts. Really fucking graphic sexts and naked pictures. Totally desperate. Just begging him to fuck me again."

Marie didn't seem fazed. I kept talking.

"So why would I do all that and have sex with him again after he, you know. Why would I do that again?"

"You tell me." Marie folded her hands in her lap.

"What?" I asked.

"You tell me why someone might sleep with their abuser again."

I considered this.

"I think I wanted to erase it. The first time. Like if I did it again, and I initiated it and I remembered it, then I could fix it."

"That sounds like some good problem solving." Marie nodded. "I imagine, however, it didn't have the desired result?"

I shook my head.

"I feel like if I ever said that he, um, raped me. Like, to anyone who was at the party with me that night or anyone who knew I slept with him over Thanksgiving break, they would tell me I was lying."

Marie nodded again. "And would that invalidate how you feel about what happened now?"

Right. How I feel. Me. Versus everybody else. How Izzie never stopped people from talking, even when it got really bad. In her eyes, and theirs, I had done a nasty, dirty, drunken thing.

"Savannah? What are you thinking about?"

*That this is not a good time for this to be happening. This
wasn't even my life anymore. I was so far from that time and that
party and that stupid blue comforter on the bed.*

"Savannah?"

"No. It wouldn't change how I feel now. Because no matter
how many times I tell myself that I'm lying, I still think about it
all the time. No matter how hard I try to forget it, I can't."

Marie leaned forward in her chair. When she spoke, her voice
was firm.

"I believe you, Savannah."

•

"YO, OTHER PEOPLE need to use this bathroom!" A voice
shouted from behind the door, followed by very aggressive
knocking.

"I HAVE MY PERIOD, OKAY?" I screamed through the door.

The knocking stopped.

I pulled my phone from my sweatshirt pocket and wiped the
snot leaking from my nose with my sleeve. Instinctively, I tapped
the first number on my favorites list.

Izzie answered on the second ring.

"You slut! You've been screening my calls. Did you get the Pinterest board I sent you for all the bridesmaids?"

Hearing her voice made me cry harder. I choked out a sob.

"Awwww, Savvy-girl, what's happening?"

"Iz—I . . ." It was all I could manage to say.

"I saw your story last night. You looked tequila drunk. Are you
having hangover heartbreak?"

How well she knew me, and how little, broke me. I couldn't
explain this to her.

"Mm-hmm." My throat was thick with phlegm.

"Savvy, this will pass. It always does. Pretend I'm there and we're eating shitty ramen in the bath, okay?"

"Okay." My voice sounded weak and small.

"Is anything else wrong?"

I took a few mangled breaths.

"No, um, just Sunday Scaries." I forced a little laugh.

"Okay. I love you. I'm getting a mani right now and the lady is looking at me weird. I have to go, okay?"

"I love you too."

I hung up.

I sat there for a while, silent, with my eyes closed. I wanted the call to have comforted me. I felt spit start to fill my mouth again, and I lunged for the toilet. I puked again, nothing but liquid this time, and as I pulled my chin away from the bowl, the sharp smell of vodka filled my nose. It smelled like Svedka. I thought of Zach holding my mouth to the bottle.

*No, no. Don't think about that. Don't fucking think about that.* I was crying so hard I couldn't see.

My phone buzzed and jolted me back to life. It was making a quacking sound, which meant it was Candace. She had programmed that sound as her text notification months ago. I wiped my eyes with the heels of my palms and reached for my phone. I rubbed my clean sleeve against the screen.

> Hope you're surviving. Tell miss
> Connecticut Cunt that if she's a bitch
> I'll stop going down on her before
> class.

I burst out into a laugh-sob.

It took all my willpower, but I pressed myself off the ground and walked over to the sink. I scrubbed my hands and my sleeve, not caring that I'd walk out of there with a soggy sweatshirt. I cupped water to my mouth and gargled. I blew my nose with scratchy paper towel and took a deep breath.

As I opened the door, I saw a line of people waiting for the bathroom. They glared at me. No one hates you more than the person waiting behind you at a public restroom. I glared back.

"All yours." I gestured to the door dramatically.

I saw Lara through the window, tapping at her phone. She looked annoyed.

I braced myself and walked out of the café and over to our table.

"Hey, I'm really sorry, but I'm not feeling well. Can we do this later this week?"

Lara looked confused for the second time that day. If she could tell I looked like death warmed over, she didn't say anything.

"Oh, um, sure. I guess. Just, like, text me."

"Okay."

I turned to go.

"Feel better!"

"Thanks," I mumbled, already halfway up the steps leading toward the quad.

I just needed to get back to my dorm to take a shower. I could smell the vomit that had dried on my sweatshirt and felt my stomach recoil. I was almost to the entrance of my building when I heard someone call my name.

"Sav!"

I closed my eyes for a moment and balled my hands into fists. I turned around. It was Matt.

"Hey." I gave a little wave.

He sprinted up to me.

"What's up, dude? I feel like I never see you on campus!"

Fuck. He was going to hug me.

Shockingly, his embrace didn't make me want to scream. It weirdly felt kind of nice. I prayed he couldn't smell the puke on my hair.

When he pulled back, he looked elated to see me. How was he always so fucking happy?

"How's the writing going?" he asked earnestly.

"You know, it's going." The only thing that was going was me, any second now. I needed to weasel my way out of this conversation.

"Good, that's so good, dude. Amazing to see you."

"You too." I tried to look sincere. "I have to run to meet a friend, but I hope you're well."

"Oh, for sure, for sure. I'm living the dream, as always. Have an awesome time with your friend. I'm sure we'll meet again, as they say."

Who? Who was they?

"Definitely. Okay, um, bye!" I waved again and made my escape. I pulled my phone out of my pocket and swiped to the front camera.

My hair was barely hanging on to my scrunchie, my eyes were so bloodshot it looked like I had just smoked an entire bong by myself, and the corners of my mouth were crusty. "Oh my god," I muttered aloud.

Back in my dorm, I thought about Marie again. I had told her I'd come back when classes resumed in the fall, but I'd never called. Besides, I had a feeling if I explained this wedding to her, she really wouldn't get it. What if she said that I didn't have to go? The thought of hearing those words out loud terrified me.

•

THAT NIGHT I spent hours looking through photos of Izzie and myself on my computer. My mom was always taking photos of us, making albums for our birthdays, endless snapshots of our life together. I did this sometimes, pored over the proof that we were best friends, that there wasn't a Savannah without an Izzie, not an Izzie without a Sav. *Sisters*, we said. *For life*. But as I scrolled through our high school years, watching myself grow more confident, lose the glasses, the baby fat, add some makeup, actually fill out the push-up bra, I grew more nervous. These photos were like a countdown: each one I clicked through inched me closer and closer to that night. When I landed on the photos from our sweet sixteen, I stopped. We had a huge, over-the-top party, and I loved it. I remembered it so clearly: getting our hair done, our nerves as we got ready, walking out to a stupid song that the DJ picked for us. The DJ my mom insisted on because he bleeped out all the curse words. For months I had dreamt about that party, and if everything had gone perfectly according to my wishes, I would have kissed someone at the end of the night. Maybe Alejandro from my science class, or Jeff—the only senior who accepted the invite. Anyone, really, would have been great. I didn't kiss anyone that night, but Izzie did, and that was exciting because that didn't happen very often. And sometimes it was enough, back then, when one of us got what we both wanted. We were never jealous of each other, though we were jealous of other girls. If Izzie got kissed, it somehow felt like I did too.

At the end of that week, when my mom uploaded photos from that night to Facebook, I got a message from Izzie's brother. He had never messaged me before. It was thrilling. And it was mine. He told me he was sorry he missed the party; he said it looked fun, even for a high school thing. He asked me if I had fun, and I said I did, and then I got a burst of confidence that came from having a screen between us, and I said, "yes, omg it was amazing. I wish I hooked up with someone, tho, lol. Your sister did, hahaha." And he said, "okay tmi, I don't ever want to think of my sister like that, lol." And when I didn't respond because I was mortified, I saw him start typing. I held my breath. "Crazy that no one kissed you tho. But high school teenage boys are fucking losers. You're really mature for your age so that's prob why." And just like that, everything changed. For the first time in my life, I went to bed keeping a secret from Izzie.

ON WEDNESDAY, VERA and Candace came over to do work. What work really consisted of, however, was eating microwave popcorn and bingeing YouTube videos about serial killers.

"I have to pee," I announced, rolling myself off my bed.

"If you need to masturbate we can just leave." Candace glanced up at me, completely serious.

"No, I am not going to the communal bathroom to masturbate."

"You say that as if it's weird?"

"Yes, Candace. I think that's very weird. I just have to pee."

"Whatever you say. Self-partnered sex is an essential part of intimacy."

I rolled my eyes.

In the bathroom I tapped through Instagram stories. Izzie's avatar always showed up first in my feed, and I always ignored it. They were usually harmless—pictures of her Starbucks order or boomerangs from whatever formal she had gone to the night before—but I knew she had stayed home a couple of extra days, and that meant she could be with her brother. I had him blocked on every form of social media, but sometimes I forgot to be vigilant about Izzie's stories. Every time I saw a photo of him it felt like I was being punched in the face.

Instead, I switched to my finsta and typed in Wesley's handle. I had figured it out a couple of weeks earlier and was overjoyed that they didn't have a private account. Much to my disappointment, they hadn't posted in two months, and the rest of their profile gave me zero insight into their life. All I could find were pictures of their childhood dog and a few photos of stacks of books they liked. I made a mental note to go to the library this weekend.

When I got back to my room Vera was at my desk. She turned to me, devious.

"Savannah, what are these pictures of you?"

My heart skipped a beat. What pictures was she talking about? She swiveled the screen toward me and started tapping through the photos of Izzie's and my sweet sixteen. Shit. I never fucking remembered to close my tabs.

"No, nope, no, no, thank you." I walked over to my desk and slammed my laptop shut.

"Come onnnn, let me see! Who even is that girl? Those look like engagement photos!"

"They are not."

"So what are they?"

"What are y'all even talking about?" Candace glanced over at us from where she was sitting, undoubtedly swiping through Tinder pictures.

"There are these photos of Savannah looking like a pageant queen, intertwined with some blond girl." Vera tried to pull my laptop back.

"It's nothing!" I shoved my computer under my pillow and sat on it.

"Wait, I want to see this. Scooch, Sav." Candace went to reach under my butt and tried to tickle me.

"Absolutely not!" I held on to the edge of my bed frame and refused to budge.

"Who is it? Your high school girlfriend?" Vera seemed to have lost interest, now sitting cross-legged on the floor and drawing what looked like a penis dripping blood in her sketchbook.

"You weren't out in high school, right?" Candace had pulled up my Facebook on her phone and was trying to find the album.

"It's hidden, Candy."

"Oh, come on, the suspense is killing me."

"So were you a child model, then?" Vera didn't look up from her sketch pad.

"No!"

"Then what?"

I chewed on my thumbnail.

"They'remysweetsixteenphotos."

"I'm sorry, *what*?" Vera had dropped her pencil to clasp her hand over her mouth.

"They. Are. My. Sweet. Sixteen. Photos."

"Savannah, please, for the love of gay god, let me see those pictures," Candace begged.

"You can't laugh."

"I will try my best," she half promised.

I dug the laptop out from under me. I shut my eyes and turned my screen.

"*No fucking way.*" Candace grabbed my laptop. "Savannah, oh my god. This is the best thing I've ever seen. You look like a sexy cherub!"

"Stop, please stop." I buried my face in my pillow. When I

peeked my eyes out, Candace and Vera were sitting together and scrolling through the photos.

"Vera looked up at me. "They're terrifying. I love them."

"Shut up."

"No, I'm truly in love with them. You must give me access to this album. I need to look at it every night before bed."

"Same." Candace nodded.

"Maybe for your birthdays." I crossed my arms.

"Savannah." Candace looked at me with very serious eyes. "Why did you need photos *before* your sweet sixteen?"

"I can't tell you."

"You must tell me."

"If you don't tell us I'll kill Candace." Vera was clicking her mechanical pencil very fast and pointing the lead toward Candace's neck.

"I'm a little turned on," Candace whispered.

"Focus, Candy," Vera whispered back.

"Savannah, Vera will murder me with her pencil if you don't tell us."

"I'm scared."

"She won't actually murder me."

"Yes, I will," Vera said, dead in the eyes.

"No, I'm not scared she's going to murder you. I'm scared to tell you."

"We love and support you and will keep your secret sexy sapphic child cherub photos safe." Candace put her hand over her heart.

I took a deep breath.

"Wehungthemonthewalls."

"Come again?" Candy's eyes were wide.

"Death approaches." Vera pressed the pencil to Candace's neck.

"WE HUNG THEM ON THE WALLS AT THE PARTY. THEY WERE EVERYWHERE. THEY WERE EVEN IN THE BATHROOM." I buried my head in my hands.

No one said anything. I peeked my eyes out from my hands and saw them both staring at me. Suddenly, Vera threw her head back and started cackling. "This is my new favorite thing about you."

"I agree. This is the cure to the sophomore slump."

I groaned.

"Who even is that girl?" Candace asked.

"Her name is Izzie." I pulled my computer into my lap and scrolled through the photos. We were in matching pink sparkly dresses. Izzie had done our makeup and my mom followed us around Izzie's backyard with her camera.

"Were you dating?"

"What? No? She was my, like, best friend. Growing up." Embarrassment coursed through me.

"I think they're sweet." Vera, who was wearing purple lipstick only on the center of her lips, and dagger earrings, was staring fondly at my computer screen. Candace and I both stared at her. She looked up at us.

"What? I have a heart! You look so young here, Sav. When I was sixteen, I thought I was the shit, like I knew everything. I look back now and realize I was such a baby."

"When I was sixteen I had to have my jaw wired shut for six months and got assigned a helper in my Spanish class to do oral presentations with. Her name was Diane, and I was so in love with her that I brought her Cheez-Its every day. I couldn't even fucking eat them," Candace said.

"Did she love you too?" I asked.

"I have no idea. I couldn't ever get up the nerve to ask her, even after my jaw was unwired."

"Too bad. I bet your oral presentations would have been amazing after that," I said.

Candace's mouth dropped open. Vera snorted.

"Fuck you. That was really good." Candace flipped me off.

"I know," I replied, a little too proud of myself.

"Okay, let's focus, though. You had a to be a little in love with this girl, Sav."

Fuck. Candace wasn't gonna let me off the hook.

"No, no, we were just really close. Like sisters."

"Uhhh, I don't know, I never took 'We're Expecting' photos with my sister." Candace looked suspicious.

"We met when we were five. She lived down the street. Same dance class. Same bus route. Built-in friends."

"Are y'all still friends?"

"What? Oh, yeah. She's, um. She's getting married, actually. So. Helping with that." Great. I had just opened up Pandora's box.

"She's getting married? Aren't y'all, like, liberal?" Candace asked.

"Yes."

"And she's our age?" Vera pressed.

"Yeah. Sophomore."

The more we talked about this, the more panicked I became. I didn't want Candace and Vera to see Izzie as a reflection of me, or even a part of me. We were different now, more different than I had ever thought, and I didn't know how to explain who she was to me in this space. With my cool, queer friends who hated the institution of marriage to begin with and questioned everything from patriarchal structures to what was in their deodorant.

"She fell in love with this guy, Ben, and he's a senior at her school. He's in ROTC, you know, like prepping to join the military? He could get sent anywhere, after he graduates, and they want to do this now, for the benefits and stuff."

Saying it out loud made it all seem stupid.

"Oh yeah. My cousin's doing that, actually. ROTC."

I glanced at Vera, surprised. I tried to picture her having a cousin joining the military, but the only image I could conjure up was a more masculine version of Vera wearing a camouflage muzzle and a gun made out of, like, hemp and pubic hair.

Vera's admission seemed to satisfy Candace's questions for now, though she still seemed skeptical.

"So you're the maid of honor?" Vera asked.

"Oh, no, I'm not. When I said helping, I just mean, like generally. She has a sister. A real one."

That was not true. Izzie only had brothers. But this was far too complicated for me to try to explain.

"Oh, got it. I was the maid of honor at my sister's wedding. It sucked. So much work and I had to wear a purple sparkly dress." Candace made a face like she was about to puke.

"Okay, *that* I want to see." Vera looked up from her phone.

"*Have* to see, pleeeeease!" I jumped at the chance to shift the conversation away from me.

Candace shook her head no, a solemn look on her face.

"Those photos are in a locked vault deep inside my small, sin-stricken heart and they will never again see the light of day."

I snorted. "Sure, until a pretty girl asks nicely and you promptly give her access to your heart and social security number."

"No comment," Candace replied.

"Wait, but I'm a pretty girl." Vera batted her eyes at Candace and started crawling toward her seductively. "I can ask nicely," she purred.

Candy put a hand up in front of Vera's face.

"No, no, you lost your chance at all this when you rejected me, V."

"Oh, come on, that was for the sake of *friendship*!" Vera sat back on her heels and rolled her eyes at Candace.

"But a rejection all the same."

"I'm hungry!" I tugged Vera's sleeve. "Let's eat, please?" Food was always a good escape route.

"Oh! Good idea. I've been meaning to ask one of the cooks if they'll let me use the convection oven. I want to bake a fake finger into a muffin tin for part of my thesis proposal."

Candace looked at Vera in horror. "You are so strange. Honestly, it's for the best that you rejected me." Vera stuck her ass out toward Candace, showing off the fishnets she was wearing underneath her oversized tee. Candace groaned.

"Can we smoke before we go?" I asked.

"Oh my god, I love when you want to smoke." Candace jumped up, fishing a squished joint out of one jean pocket and a lighter out of the other.

•

WE GOT TO the dining hall thirty minutes later, and I couldn't think about anything but food. I wanted french fries, ramen noodles, and a bowl of kale with salt and lemon. Munchies had no rhyme or reason; they just were. I was almost done gathering my feast, but the salad tongs by the kale were proving to be hard to use. I couldn't seem to squeeze them tight enough to actually pick up anything, and each time I failed I burst out laughing and dropped the tongs. This time they had scooted toward the back of the silver serving table and I had to hoist my body over the table to reach for them. They were dangerously close to falling, and my body was dangerously close to toppling into the salad.

"Can I, potentially, help you?"

My ears perked up. That voice was familiar. I turned my head and was met with very green eyes staring quizzically at me. Mine widened in response.

"I, um. I. The tongs." I gave up trying to explain and pointed to the runaway tongs.

"I see that. Well. I do think I have one idea," Wesley offered.

"We can't use our hands."

"What?"

"To pick up the salad," I whispered. "We can't use our hands."

"No, no. I don't think it would be appropriate to use our hands to serve the salad. I was thinking, um—" Wesley proceeded to walk around the table, where the tongs were teetering. I gasped. They had moved into forbidden territory. Students were not supposed to enter the kitchen.

"You're very brave," I whispered.

"I have been preparing my whole life for this," they whispered back.

They grabbed the tongs and ran back around the table, handing them to me, pretending to wipe sweat from their brow.

"I don't know how I can ever repay you."

"Hmm." They thought for a beat. "Ah! I know."

"What?" I stiffened. What if they were going to ask me out?

"I'm hosting an open mic this weekend. And I heard somewhere that a certain creative writing major had a knack for poetry?"

My cheeks grew hot.

"Oh, um—"

"Please?" They held their hands in prayer in front of their face, making puppy-dog eyes. Gorgeous green puppy-dog eyes.

"Do people really want to listen to poetry these days?" I stalled.

"Sav—"

*My name in their mouth, mynameintheirmouth.*

"I have seven different indie-folk singers signed up right now.

There's only so much acoustic guitar the people can bear. I really want to change it up."

"People love singer-songwriters!"

"They're all cis men."

"Oh." I bit my lip. That was a little much.

"Please?" they begged again.

"When is it?"

"Saturday night. My place."

Their place, they have a place, a place where they live and sleep. In a bed. Wesley has a bed and they sleep there. Maybe naked? God, I was high.

"It's okay if you're not comfortable—" they said.

"I'm in," I blurted.

"You are?" Their face lit up. "That's so awesome, Sav. I can't wait. Here, I'll give you the info. Can I, um—" They scrambled for something in their pocket. Phone. They were getting their phone. Because. The info. They needed to share it. I had a phone too.

"Yes! Text me!" I said very loudly.

"Okay!" They matched my tone.

They handed me their phone and I filled out my information, trying to type elegantly though my fingers suddenly felt very heavy and I noticed for the first time that my thumb looked like a pig in a blanket without the blanket.

"Sav, we lost you?" I felt hands squeeze my shoulders. It was Candy.

"Yo, Wesley! What's up?"

I immediately turned back to the salad station, ready to meet my nemesis again, but mostly just trying to avoid Candace noticing how nervous Wesley made me. I was too high to manage full sentences with Wesley and to ignore Candace's knowing glances. She still managed to reach behind her back and squeeze my butt. I jumped a little.

"You should totally come!" Wesley was inviting Candy to the mic.

"I'll be there. Can't miss my favorite poet doing her thing."

My heart fluttered a little. What had I gotten myself into?

"Cool. Let me know if you want to perform."

"My talents are, unfortunately, better suited for the bedroom. Trust that I would blow you away, though."

Wesley laughed awkwardly.

I almost kicked Candace. She loved to make people uncomfortable.

"See you on Friday. I'll text you the details." Wesley mimicked typing with their fingers.

"I'll text you back!"

*Why am I like this?*

"Oh, duh, and class. I'll see you in class?" Wes rolled their eyes at themself.

"Oh yeah, class!" I nodded.

"Awesome." Wesley's eyes crinkled. They waved and headed out the door. I turned toward Candace, whose mouth was poised and open until I pressed my hand over it.

"Nothing. You say nothing," I warned.

She held both hands up, admitting defeat.

I uncovered her mouth and raised my eyebrows.

"What is there to even say?" She feigned innocence.

"Exactly." I headed back to where Vera was sitting.

Vera was smiling at me devilishly.

"What?" I asked.

"I watched that entire interaction."

"Not you too," I groaned.

"The two of you turn into fucking teenagers around each other." Vera shook her head in disbelief. "It's like both of you have never flirted with anyone before. Which I know is not true, because I've seen you get past the dorm security guard *twice* without your ID."

She was right. With Wesley, all my confidence went out the window. I was just fumbling around in the dark. Everything I knew about flirting—which I thought I had mastered a long time ago—felt gross and performative. I didn't want to seduce Wesley or make them choose me. I didn't even know what I wanted from them. Besides, I knew the way they were seeing me wasn't really the way that I was. And if they knew the whole me, I doubted they would like that person.

"I don't know what you're talking about. We're just friends."

Candace scoffed and I glared at her, threatening my hand again.

"I said nothing. Nothing!" she exclaimed.

"Let's eat, please." I stuck my fork into my salad bowl, cramming kale into my mouth. I wondered if I was ever going to look at a pair of tongs again without losing feeling in my feet.

THE MORNING OF the open mic I canceled a FaceTime I had planned with Izzie. We usually did coffee dates on Friday mornings, but I lied and told her I needed to focus on a paper that was due later that day. Lately the calls had consisted of her bemoaning the drama of picking the perfect shade of rose gold for the bridesmaids dresses, and her fear that someone would have an allergic reaction to one of the dipping sauces that would be included at the Chinese and Malaysian fusion station at the wedding reception.

I wanted today to be perfect. I had woken up at six a.m., which only happened to me when I was so excited my body couldn't stand to be horizontal anymore. Sometime between our conversation in the dining hall and now, I had gotten it into my head that maybe Wesley really was interested in me. They had texted me an hour later, if that.

> Preserver of Salads here, is this the
> mobile device of one Savannah Henry?

I almost threw my phone across the room.

Wesley was funny. And smart. And kind. And they cared. The idea of dating them was something I couldn't think about for too long, I guess because the more I thought about why they were so great, the more I thought about all the reasons that I wasn't. It wasn't that I didn't like myself—I did, for the most part. But this year was proving to be complicated. Every time I got pulled into the vortex of Izzie's wedding, I felt this overwhelming sensation of being an imposter at school. It was like whiplash, going between two worlds, between two Savannahs.

There was no way I could date someone like Wesley. No way that someone so wholesome and with it and entirely unproblematic could ever understand what happened between Izzie and me, or why I had plans to go to this wedding, or who I was before coming to college. I tried to imagine explaining to Wesley how, at the end of senior year, I would show up at an underground nightclub and whisper into the ears of middle-aged men that I was only seventeen, just to see what they would do. I shuddered. I barely recognized that person; she felt like a distant memory. But maybe I would never have to tell any of this to them. Izzie's wedding wasn't far off at this point, and I really only had to make it through the bridal shower and a couple other events, and then I would be home free. Izzie and I could go back to seeing each other when we were home from school and could hang at the diner with no threat of her brother keeping me on high alert. The way our relationship had always thrived: coffee with way too much sugar, our own special language, and nobody else around. The wedding was the week after the school year ended, anyway. I didn't owe anyone my miserable backstory. All that mattered was the person I was now.

And all I had to do now was write a poem that would blow Wesley out of the fucking water and for once in my life I could be the prize that someone got to take home.

They had texted me again (!) the night before, at 6:53 p.m.

> Hey! I'm solidifying the lineup. Is it cool
> if your time slot is around 9pm? I know
> that's late and you might have
> somewhere else to go . . .

Wesley's text had made me jump, as if they were in the room with me and knew I was spending all this time thinking about them. I couldn't help but goofy-grin at my phone screen. No, I definitely had nowhere else I was going tomorrow night. I even had a small fantasy that I might stay late and help clean up. That Wesley would show me their room. Maybe we could order takeout and share a container of spring rolls. How many butterflies can you have in your belly before you need to have your stomach pumped at the hospital?

> 9 works for me. Great excuse not to
> go to a party I've been dreading.

Okay, I said I was done playing games, but I didn't need to come off as desperate.

Now I was sitting at my desk, staring at my notebook, willing the words to come. I knew I needed to write, but I also needed to figure out what I was going to wear. Both seemed equally important. I started tearing through my closet, unimpressed by everything. I texted Candace.

> I know it's early but if I bring you
> coffee can I come over and look
> through your closet for tonight?

> You're insane. Cold brew with almond
> milk.

I practically ran to Owen's and picked us up coffees. Fifteen minutes later I stopped at her door.

"Come in!"

When I walked through the door, I almost smacked into a person with a shaved head and huge gauges.

"Hi! Sorry!"

"Good morning!" Their voice was high-pitched and nasally.

"This is Axe. Axe is leaving," Candace called from her bed.

She had the covers pulled up to her shoulders. It didn't look like she was wearing a shirt. Or a bra.

"Bye, dude." Axe dipped behind me and shut the door.

"Who was that?"

"That was Axe."

"Did Axe stay over?"

"Axe sells me weed."

"Ah, got it." I glanced at my phone. It was only eight thirty a.m.

"Axe also stayed over."

"Right."

I plopped down on Candace's floor and grinned up at her.

"What's up, goofy?"

"Nothing! Just wanna borrow an outfit."

"What's wrong with your clothes? You can take whatever you want, but my stuff is way rattier than yours."

I was already by the dresser, scanning through her oversized skater tees.

"I just want to look cool."

"You always look cool!"

"I want to look cool in a gay way," I muttered.

"Sav, you can smell the bisexual on you from a million miles away. You don't need to wear a beanie for Wes to know you're gay."

I whipped my head around. "This is not about Wes!"

"This is one thousand percent about Wes."

"No, I just want to explore my style. Isn't that what college is for?"

"College is also for admitting when you have gigantic crushes on people who are clearly interested in you and going for it."

"We're friends. And they probably have a partner."

"Have you stalked to find out?"

"No, because we're friends." I paused. "But as a friend, I did happen to look, and it doesn't seem like it."

"Very friendly of you to know that!" Candace dug out a sweater from under her covers and put it on. Surprisingly, she was already wearing pants.

She came over to the dresser and started pulling out different shirts. I was deciding between two Carhartt beanies, but I wasn't sure if any color of neon would suit me.

"Here, try this." Candace shoved a band tee in my hand, and I pulled it on over my sports bra. She plunked the red beanie on my head. We both looked at my reflection in her mirror.

"I just look like a knockoff version of you."

Candace held back a laugh. "I don't think this is the look, babe."

I pulled off the hat and flopped on her bed. Candace's phone vibrated underneath my back. I dragged it out from under me. It was Vera FaceTiming. I answered.

She appeared on the screen wearing bright purple lipstick and had drawn spiderwebs spiraling out from under one eye. She looked completely unfazed to see me instead of Candy.

"What are you two doing?"

"How did you know I was with Candace?"

"I track you both," she said, matter-of-fact.

"You track us both at nine a.m.?"

"Murderers don't care what time of day it is."

"That's fair." I sat up and leaned against the wall. I flipped the front camera to back and showed Candace to Vera.

"Say hi, Candace."

"Hi, Candace."

"How was the sex?" Vera asked.

"What are you talking about?" Candace came to sit by me. I flipped the camera back.

"I'm just getting a vibe."

"What are you, psychic now? How do you know that?"

"I've always been psychic. But actually, it isn't a vibe. It's more like a dildo."

I burst out laughing. I hadn't noticed, but Candace had her strap-on hanging over her bedpost. She jumped up and ran to grab it.

"Oh, fuck you."

"That doesn't answer my question!" Vera called out.

Candace grumbled something under their breath. I pulled my phone closer to my face and pouted at Vera.

"I have nothing to wear."

"For what?" she asked.

"The open mic tonight."

"Oh, your lover's open mic."

"They are not my lover."

"Please, please let me dress you, Sav," Vera begged.

I imagined myself in one of Vera's outfits. Somehow, I did not think I could pull off a chain-link corset and assless chaps.

"That's so nice of you, V, but there's no way I would look good in your clothes."

"I have normal people clothes! I promise!"

"Like, *normal normal*? Or giraffe-print petticoat with mesh nipple tassels normal?" I asked.

"That was an iconic outfit so I'm not sure I understand your *tone*, but that's not the direction I was thinking for you, no."

"So what are you thinking?"

She didn't answer me. She disappeared from the screen and I could hear her stashing things in a bag. When she reappeared, she was breathless.

"I have to go. I promise it'll be perfect. I'll be over in twenty." She ended the call.

An hour later I stood in front of Candace's mirror again, but this time I couldn't stop smiling. Vera had come through on her promise. She had dressed me in a black V-neck slip that fell just below my knees, with a long slit up the leg. It hugged my waist ever so slightly and the way the straps looped around my shoulders, just tight enough, made my boobs look, well, phenomenal.

"Your tits look *unreal*," Candace called out to me from her desk.

"I'm such a proud slutty mommy," Vera fawned.

She had brought two gold necklaces, each with a small crystal pendant, to hang around my neck. One was longer than the other and dipped down through the V of the slip, so that the dress almost covered the tip of the crystal. She'd also draped a silky blazer around my shoulders, just to have something to walk into the party with, saving the dress as the big reveal. Miraculously, we had the same shoe size, and so now I was sporting thrifted Prada boots, dark purple, that she had found at the bottom of a thirty-five-dollar-and-under barrel at a Crossroads Trading Co. in Venice.

"I love it," I said, turning to Vera.

"They won't be able to stop staring," she replied.

I checked the time. Only seven more hours, two classes, and one killer poem to go before the mic.

•

WE ARRIVED AT Wes's apartment at eight p.m., after much debate. I didn't want to be late and miss other acts, but I also didn't want to seem overeager. I also didn't think Wesley was the kind of person who would clock showing up late as cooler or mysterious, and maybe showing up early would be more of the move. Why did it feel a hundred times harder to impress someone who was nice and nerdy than someone who was shitty and aloof? Eight o'clock was exactly thirty minutes late and felt appropriate. Wes was not the one to open the door to their apartment and I was so relieved that I hugged the person who greeted us instead. She introduced themself as Nieve, Wes's roommate. Nieve was so tall she seemed to levitate from the floor. She had olive skin, silver waist-length hair, and wore an emerald-green velvet jumpsuit. She had a name tag on that read "Nieve, she/her, Jordanian princess." She spoke only in a soft, gentle whisper and asked us very kindly if we would take our shoes off. I was a little disappointed that Wes wouldn't see the whole look, but maybe I could show them later. That thought made me inhale too fast and I managed to both hiccup and cough at the same time.

"Are you okay?" Candace nudged me.

"Fine, totally fine," I assured her.

"Do you think Nieve is single?" Vera asked. "She's, like, very, *Practical Magic* chic. It's hot."

"I'm hot," Candace reminded Vera.

"Of course you are, sugarplum," Vera cooed at Candace, and then went to go help Nieve greet more guests.

I saw Wesley out of the corner of my eye and quickly turned the other way, pretending to look out a window.

"What are you looking at?" Candace asked, way too loudly.

"Just orienting myself."

"That's a brick wall."

"I see that now. Let's go." I brought Candace to the kitchen and carefully unpacked the crackers we had brought onto a paper plate.

"I'm impressed with your plating."

It was Wes.

"They're crackers!"

*Obviously they are crackers.*

"Love crackers. Great crunch."

God, they were such a good sport. They looked so handsome I wanted to pass out.

"You're not wearing a backpack!"

*What in the fresh hell was wrong with me?*

Wes looked confused and then laughed.

"I try not to wear it in the apartment. I want to, of course, but gotta give myself some lumbar relief, you know?"

I could feel my cheeks burning.

"Thanks so much for inviting me."

Their face lit up.

"Oh, of course, are you kidding? Thank you for coming, honestly, you're saving me here."

"We'll see if that's true after I do my reading."

"I know it's gonna be great. Everything you do is great."

Oh.

Wesley's eyes got a little wide.

"I have to go check the mic!" They were flustered. I bit my cheek, trying not to smile.

"Definitely. Mic check one-two, one-two." I altered my voice but did not achieve the effect I intended.

"Exactly."

Wes spun around and walked toward the microphone in the opposite corner of the room.

"It's like watching a car crash so very slowly."

I had forgotten that Candace was behind me in the kitchen. She was eating cheese cubes on a toothpick, shaking her head at me in disbelief.

"Chew with your mouth closed."

"Oh fuck." Candace's face fell.

"What? I was kidding—"

"Sav. Whatever you do, do not turn around." They were speaking under their breath.

"Wait, why? You're scaring me."

"Just trust me, please."

I watched Candace's eyes following someone behind us. My heart raced.

"Oh, you fucker," Candace muttered under her breath.

"Who the fuck is it?"

Candace looked down.

"Savannah Henry, in the flesh!"

*Nova.*

I turned around.

*Goddamn it, you are so hot.*

Nova had cut her hair short, but a few front pieces fell and grazed her eyelids. She was serving *Titanic* Leo, every bisexual's downfall, and she had a new tattoo on her forearm of a scorpion. It was on the nose, but Nova could afford to be, she was just that hot.

"Hey." I tried to play it cool.

"The fit is good, Sav," she said, her eyes dropping down to the slit in my dress, giving me the most deliberate once-over she could manage.

*Don't you fucking "Sav" me.*

"Thanks. Did you need to get by?" I gestured to the drinks behind me. I wasn't gonna indulge in any small talk or eye-fucking.

"Sure," she said, not making any attempt to push by me. She didn't even move.

"Hey, I'm Candace."

If Nova knew who Candace was, she didn't let it register on her face.

"Nova." She gave Candy a nod.

"Nice of you to come support the local talent," Candace said, her voice suspiciously sweet.

"I'm playing tonight." There was an edge in Nova's voice.

"Oh, cool. Brave to try something new!"

I stifled a laugh.

"I'm in a band. Lead singer."

"Oh! Good for you! Have I heard any of your music? Have you been on *SNL* or *Ellen*?"

Nova's eyes narrowed.

"No."

"Bummer, I'm sure you'll get there, though! Cheers!" Candace took my hand and pushed past Nova, hard, purposefully bumping her shoulder. I could barely keep from laughing, and we tore down the hallway and into the nearest room.

"Oh my god," I said, shutting the door behind us.

Candace gave me a devilish look and shrugged.

"I've been waiting so long to fuck with them."

"Well, you were successful. I've never seen her look so pissed."

Candace laughed and sat down on the chair nearest to her. I looked around the room.

It was tidy and small, and there was an oil diffuser on a desk in the corner. I sniffed the air. Eucalyptus. I loved that smell. It made me think of my mom rubbing my chest with Vicks VapoRub when I was little and sick. Next to the desk was a bookshelf; the spines of the books were lined up according to color. I stepped closer and tilted my head to read a few titles. A vast collection of Toni Morrison novels put mine to shame. On the wall above the desk were album covers. I only recognized some: Muna and

Florence + the Machine and Frank Ocean. The rest were mysteries to me. And then there was a Taylor Swift album, which made the album selections officially perfect. In the corner of the room was a queen bed with a green duvet. And green pillows. And a green throw blanket. My heart started beating very fast.

"Candace," I whispered.

"Yeah, bud?" She was on her phone, no doubt swiping through Tinder.

"I think this is Wes's room!" My voice was frantic.

"No shit, literally everything in here is green. And peep the backpack." Candace pointed to the door, where on a hook hung the notorious massive backpack. I gasped.

"We have to leave!"

"Why?" Candace asked.

"Because it will seem so weird if we're in here."

"Relax, Wes is in the front row watching. It's like a maze getting out of that crowd. They won't be in here anytime soon. So, go ahead."

"Go ahead with what?"

Candace opened their arms wide to the room.

"You're in your crush's room. You have to snoop."

"Wes is not my crush!" I yelped. "And that would be so inappropriate."

Candace rolled her eyes.

"Fine. Don't snoop, then." She crossed her arms and looked at me with her eyebrows raised. I was quiet for a second.

"I'm not snooping. But I might look around. I like their style."

Candace nodded. "Great style."

I inched closer to Wes's dresser. Five rows. Nice. I touched it. Sturdy. I wondered if the drawers were easy to pull out. That was the mark of a good dresser. Everybody knew that. I just wanted to check. I grabbed hold of the knob of one of the drawers and pulled. It slid right open.

*Great choice in dressers, Wes.*

It was where they kept their shirts. Green after green after green shirt. I looked over at Candace, busy on their phone, and then glanced at the door. No sign of anyone. I tentatively touched one shirt and then slid my hand across the row. Soft. Must use fabric softener. Thinking about Wes doing their laundry made me so nervous I could have died. It felt intimate, thinking of them doing mundane tasks. Checking their mail. Ordering takeout. Tying a shoelace. Swiping their subway card. Getting ready for bed. Showering.

*Showering.*

I bent down to smell the shirts. I closed my eyes and breathed in deeply. It didn't smell like detergent. It was better. It smelled like them.

*What if I took one?*

No, that was ridiculous. I could not take one of Wes's shirts. That was creepy stalker vibes and I couldn't pull that off.

"Sav, what are you doing?"

I jumped, looking over at Candace. She pointed to my hand. I had pulled out a shirt.

"Oh my god. I don't know."

I quickly refolded the shirt the best I could and then went to put it back in the drawer. Just before I could, I noticed a Polaroid tucked under the row of clothes. I hesitated and then slid it out. There was a date on the back; it was marked from earlier this year. September. I turned it over. It was Wes and someone else, a femme person with round glasses and a pink bowl cut. They were kissing Wes's cheek. My heart sank.

"We should go," I said, replacing the photo and shoving the shirt back into the drawer.

Candace obliged and followed me out the door.

When I performed my poem that night, I couldn't look at Wes in the audience. I heard them, though, making affirming poetry noises, *hmms* and *woos* with snaps. I wanted to think it was cringey, but it wasn't, not even a little.

## 18

"I REALLY WANT a Gucci belt."

Izzie and I were FaceTiming. It was 9:30 p.m. on Thursday, and we had been talking for two hours. We hadn't had a call like this in weeks, and I felt guilty, so I stayed on extra-long. She was on Pinterest; I was half-heartedly editing a paper for my linguistics class. It was two days before my spring break, and this was the last paper I had to submit.

"What?" I asked.

"The one with the thick gold clasp? It's like three hundred dollars, but it's so cute."

"You're not gonna spend three hundred dollars on a belt, Iz, are you?"

"I don't know. I keep seeing them everywhere I go! They're taunting me!"

"The fact that you see Gucci everywhere you go tells me a lot about your 'everywhere.'"

"Oh, okay," Izzie scoffed. "Little Miss Liberal went to artsy college and no one can know about Daddy's money anymore!"

"Jesus, Izzie."

"I'm kidding! But you used to, like, love designer brands and you never wanted to talk about politics."

"What?"

"You're just, like, so political now. But you never wanted to talk about that stuff growing up. You said you didn't care about politics. I cared way more than you did."

"Well, that was a stupid thing of me to say. People change," I snapped at her.

The line got quiet.

"I think I know what belt you're talking about," I pressed on, lightening my tone.

"Does it have a big gold buckle?"

"Yeah, black leather."

"That's it! Who do you know who has one?"

"This girl in my class. Lara."

"Tell Lara she has amazing taste."

"I will."

*I definitely would not.*

"Oh crap, I have a pregame. I'll text you tomorrow. One week!"

"One week!"

Izzie hung up. My cheeks felt hot. I shoved open the window. Izzie was right, that I was political now. More political than I ever was before college. But something about talking to her made me feel sort of pretentious about it, regurgitating information I learned from rallies on campus, from overhearing conversations on the quad, from newsletters I received in my inbox, absentmindedly reading the titles before deleting. I wanted to prove to her, or mostly myself, that I was different now. And I felt like I was, when I wasn't talking to her, but something about hearing her voice and falling into our old rhythms made me feel like I was making it all up, that who I was with Izzie was the real me. Talking to Izzie had always been like pulling up a familiar cozy blanket, but recently it had started to feel newly constricting, like I shrunk it in the dryer and it felt sort of itchy. Izzie seemed to be under the impression that I had changed since getting to college, but what she didn't know is that it started happening way before. In the months when she and I weren't speaking. At school I was a shell of myself, doing what I needed to do to get through the day, the stares, the whispers. But after school and on the weekends, with nothing to do and no one to do things with, I began thinking about life after high school. I started reading again to fill my time, and the reading led to writing, and one day I decided to research colleges with creative writing majors. None of the schools I found were ones Izzie and I had ever talked about going to. But Izzie wasn't a promised part of my life anymore, I told myself. If she didn't want to be my friend, it was probably a good idea to look at different schools. Just in case.

•

"YOU'RE FROM NEW York too, yeah?" Reg asked, pushing her desk next to mine.

We were supposed to be talking about a short film we had just watched on the wage gap, but I was thrilled that Reg was being chatty.

"Yeah, um, outside the city, though. You?"

"Manhattan. Near Columbus Circle area, if you know it."

"Oh yeah. Near the park?" I tried to sound nonchalant.

"Yeah, kinda. I'm gonna be living in East Williamsburg this summer, though, with my cousin. I'm sick of Manhattan."

"I like Williamsburg!"

*Play it cooler, Savannah.*

"I mean, it's got cool stuff happening," I clarified. "I've been to concerts there. Brooklyn Bowl?"

Reg raised her eyebrow at me.

"What?" I asked.

"Hmm?" She smirked, playing it off like she didn't know what I was talking about.

"You look surprised!"

"Yeah, a little. No offense, but I can't picture you there."

"What? Why?!"

"Mm, I think you seem like . . . innocent? Like movies on the weekend, not mosh pits." She shrugged.

"Wait, are you saying that *you* like mosh pits?" I asked, incredulous.

Reg laughed. "I can fuck with a good mosh pit, yeah."

"Okay, well, I have not been known to mosh but I did get my first fake ID at fifteen."

"Oh yeah?"

"Yes! Fake at fifteen, snuck into the city at sixteen and—wait for it—by seventeen I was part of a super-secret underground bingo club that had prizes that could make cool girls in mosh pits blush."

Reg cackled with laughter. "Fuck me, then, I was wrong!"

"You were wrong," I said smugly.

"Well, I'm gonna need proof," Reg said, leaning back in her chair and crossing her arms.

"Like what?" I asked.

"I need some photo evidence to believe that double braids in front of me was playing dirty bingo in high school."

I touched one of my braids and glowered at her before reaching for my phone. I texted Izzie.

> Send me the pics of us at bingo!!
> The ones where we're on stage.

My phone buzzed within seconds. And there they were. A string of photos of me wearing basically no clothing, up on a stage with a humongous bingo-ball cage, Izzie and me cheering with our asses facing the crowd.

"Here," I said, triumphantly, sliding the phone across our desks.

"That's you?!" Reg said, glancing back up at me as if to make sure, and then swiping through the rest of the photos.

"Yeah, that's me! You can't tell?"

"I guess, yeah, now that I'm looking again. I don't know, something about you is different. Like your face has changed? Maybe 'cause you don't usually wear makeup or something."

"Oh yeah, my hair is straight," I deflected.

"Oh yeah." She zoomed in on my head.

"A lot of me was straight back then," I admitted.

"She's funny!" Reg clapped her hands together.

"Badass, though, Sav. I shouldn't have underestimated you. You still go to this thing?"

"It got shut down, actually." That was true, but I'd stopped going months before that happened.

"Very legit. Well, we gotta play bingo sometime, then."

Was Reg flirting with me?

"Definitely." I nodded.

"So no movies?"

"What?"

"Are you too cool for movies?"

I laughed. "No way, I love movies."

"Same. I do a movie night at my place with a group of my friends. You should come. Bring your crew." Reg nodded toward Vera and Candace, who were loudly arguing about whether it was icky for straight people to refer to their significant other as their partner.

"They seem weird, but cool," Reg said.

"That's the best kind of cool, I think."

"For sure." Reg chewed on her pen. She shook her head again. "What?!"

"Dirty bingo. I'm gonna remember that." She slid my phone back to me.

Reg turned to grab something out of her bag, and I looked down at the photos again. Was Reg right? Had my face changed? I zoomed in on my face. I was wearing a lot of makeup. Maybe it was the fake eyelashes. I opened my Instagram and tapped on the most recent photo I had posted: Candace, Vera, and me at the open mic. I zoomed in on my face again. Swiped back to the other photo. And then I saw it. It wasn't the hair or the lashes; it was my eyes. They were glazed over. Lifeless. It was senior year of high school, months after Izzie and I had made up. I remember being so relieved that she wanted to be my friend again. Now we could do senior year right, I thought. So everything we did had to be big enough and fun enough to distract us from the reality of what had happened between us, what had happened between me and her brother. All our new memories had to be the best ones. So, parties. So, boys. So, half-naked nights at fucked up bingo. If the Band-Aid was hot pink and shiny, no one would ask what was underneath.

"Take two more minutes to wrap up," Professor Tolino said, looking up briefly from her laptop.

"Guess we should actually talk about the film?" Reg asked.

"If we must."

## 19

I WAS AVOIDING Wes. I had sent a brief and friendly text back to them after they had thanked me for coming to the mic, had steered clear of the salad section in the dining hall, and was now sitting at the far end of the semicircle in GSS class.

The truth was that I hadn't been able to stop thinking about the Polaroid I had found in their room. Wes was so terminally off-line that I could not find a single indication—not even a soft launch—that they were dating the person with the pink bowl cut. And that lack of proof was excruciating, because it left me with a teensy, tiny morsel of hope that they were still single. And a shred of hope like that can make a bisexual crazy. I decided the best plan of action was to keep my distance until I knew for sure if they were together or not. Which is why it was important that I find out Wes's exact schedule. Like, for example, that they had work-study at the library on Tuesdays, Wednesdays, and Thursdays. I knew this because Vera told me. Well, Vera had told me that she saw Wesley on Wednesday evenings when she met with her Modern Wiccans Club.

"It's not a club. It's a coven!" Vera had exclaimed, glaring at

Candace. We were lounging in my dorm's common area, taking up two well-worn couches and ignoring dagger eyes from the chess club practicing nearby.

"I think it's more adorable if it's a club," Candace teased.

"It's not going to be adorable when I cast a spell that makes it impossible for your fingernails to get clean," Vera hissed, holding the back of Candy's hand in front of their face. Candace shrunk with fear.

"I'm staying out of this," I said, plugging my ears.

"Anyway," Vera went on, "Wes is there every Wednesday and is the cutest transmasc librarian I've ever seen."

"I've seen them there too, on Tuesdays, I think," Candace added. "But that was last semester, when I was hooking up with that history major. We would always meet there."

"And by meet you mean?" I asked.

"Fuck, obviously."

"Candace!" Vera and I had screamed, eliciting loud throat clearing from several chess club members.

"I did what I had to do to help a local scholar. It's what Dewey Decimal always intended. But the point is that I remember seeing Wes there."

So Vera had told me about Wednesdays, Candace mentioned Tuesdays, and I was the one who had figured out they also worked on Thursdays.

I wish I could say this realization came from a cute, spontaneous moment where we bumped into each other between the stacks, me with my nose tucked into a book and them returning a pile back to the shelves. A sweet and awkward encounter that would lead to us sitting cross-legged on the floor, trying to keep our voices down as we got lost in conversation. So lost that we wouldn't even notice the library emptying out. Alone and precariously close, we'd share a Clif Bar Wes had unearthed from their backpack. Before we knew it, the bar would be gone but our hunger still unsatisfied and then . . .

*In your dreams, Savannah.*

Yeah, no. That's not remotely close to what happened. Instead, I saw a flash of pink hair exiting the communications building one Thursday afternoon and I followed them. All the way to the library. Where I saw them stop by the help desk and say hello to someone wearing a green beanie.

*Wes.*

I should have left, but instead I camped out at a table in the corner of the library, my face hidden by a computer screen, and I watched them. I scoured their body language for sexual tension, but Wes didn't really seem like the kind of person who would go for a public butt grab. They made small talk for fifteen minutes, and then it looked it like Bowl Cut was leaving, slinging a black tote bag around their shoulder. This was the moment—a goodbye was pivotal intel—a kiss or lingering hug would tell me all I needed to know. I leaned backward in my chair to get a better look.

And then I fell.

Not a delicate little fall. A loud, crashing thud that made the entire library turn to look at me. Including Wes and their fuchsia-headed maybe-lover.

Someone at the computer next to me reached out their hand to me while I sat, stunned, splayed out on the floor. Everyone's eyes were on me. Had I died? Was this gay purgatory?

"Sav?" Wes called out, standing at their desk. I snapped back to reality, waving off the person offering to help me.

"I'mtotallyOKdon'tworryI'mSOfine! I spluttered, reassuring everyone in the library. "Chairs are very crazy, am I right? Ha ha!!"

Out of the corner of my eye I saw Wes walking toward me, giving a distracted wave to Bowl Cut as they turned to leave the library.

*Fuck.*

Before I could think, I grabbed my phone and pretended to pick up a phone call.

"Hello?" I whispered. "I'm so sorry I *can't* talk right now I'm at the *library*."

At this point Wes was in front of me, their green eyes visibly concerned.

*What the fuck are you doing, Savannah? Hang up. Hang up!*

"Okay, yes, of course I'm coming! I can't *believe* they did that to your dog!"

*Committing to the bit, are we?*

I waved to Wes and pointed to my phone with my free hand. "So sorry," I mouthed. "Got to go."

Their face scrunched with confusion and they gave me a weak thumbs-up. I gathered my things and stormed out of the library, my phone still pressed to my ear as I pushed open the double doors and ran out onto the quad.

"I *have* to go because I need to wallow in self-pity and check to see if my butt is bruised and I hope your dog fucking *dies*," I hissed into my phone before I crumpled onto the grass, pulled my sweater over my eyes, and let out a silent scream only my ego could hear.

# 20

I HAD ONE last class in the morning before I could leave for break. I would take the train home in the afternoon, and Izzie's shower was the next day. Vera, Candace, and I were in the dining hall, sharing a plate of fries.

"So you have your friend's bridal shower this week, right?" Candace turned to me. "What's her name again?"

I really didn't want to think about the shower. I really didn't want to think about Izzie.

"Izzie. And yeah, it's on Saturday."

"Are you excited?" Vera asked. She was filing her nails into sharp Vs. I tried not to think about how she managed having sex with them.

"Um, yeah, sort of. It'll be nice to be with her, but I don't really love all the people who are going. Izzie's friends from school aren't, like, my favorite group of people I've ever met."

"That sucks. What are they like?" Candace dunked a fry in mayo, then ketchup.

*Loud, white, and probably pro-life.*

I shrugged. "They're all in a sorority. They can be overwhelming."

"In theory, sororities sound amazing," Candace said, leaning back in their chair.

"Because in your theory you are somehow sleeping with the entire sorority?" Vera asked.

"Yes. In theory, I am."

"Some of them are nice." I poked at a soggy fry on my plate. Death by ketchup.

"How come Izzie did the whole sorority thing?" Candace asked.

"I think she just wanted to have a group of friends."

"But she likes it? All the weird rules and chapter meetings and dues and stuff?"

"Yeah." I nodded. "She does."

"Huh," Vera said, looking up from her nails. "It's funny to me to think you're friends with someone who is into all of that."

"Well, Izzie's different with me." I came back at her fast. My voice was sharp.

Vera looked taken aback. She nodded.

"Oh, yeah, I'm sure she is." Her voice was gentle.

It was true. Izzie was different with me. She dropped the whole sorority girl act and went back to being the goofy person she was at heart. But what I didn't say to Vera, the thing I really didn't want to admit, was that I was different with Izzie too.

"The best-best-best-friend thing," Candace interjected, mid-fry, "I never got that."

"I had it in middle school, with this girl Raya," Vera replied. "It was kind of fucked up."

My shoulders tensed. I pushed a fry around in the dregs of my ketchup.

"Why do you think that?" I asked.

"Um, it was really intense, I think. Too intense. And the whole thing kind of blew up. It actually really hurt. I still think about her sometimes."

"I'm sorry," I said.

"Yeah." Vera nodded. "Thanks. It's a lot to promise, you know? That you're gonna be in the same friendship for your whole life."

"We do that romantically, though," Candace said. "I mean, that's the basic idea, if you believe in marriage and stuff."

"Yeah, but that feels different," Vera argued. "You go into a romantic relationship knowing it can completely combust and leave you wrecked. You basically sign up for that. I feel like friends don't talk about that happening."

"You promise forever," I said quietly.

"Damn, my commitment issues are triggered even thinking about that," Candace said, finishing the last of their water bottle.

"I, um, went to therapy a couple times last year." I paused, looking to gauge their reactions. Both of them looked intrigued but not shocked.

"Yeah, she would say this one quote a lot, something like, 'We are never beholden to the person we were yesterday.'"

"Shit. That's deep," Candace said, crushing her empty bottle between her hands.

"I haven't quite internalized it," I admitted. "But in theory it sounds nice."

They both nodded.

"I mean, she's right, though. Forever is a long fucking time. And no one tells you that shit can end. Raya was, like, my friend soulmate. That was honestly worse than any romantic heartbreak I've gone through. It's heart murder. And not in the good way." Vera clawed Candace's thigh with one of her talons. Candace yelped and swatted her away.

"And that, my lovelies, is why we have more than one!" Vera

chirped, emptying the last of the ketchup packets onto her plate. She handed me another fry.

"More than one what?" Candace asked.

"Of everything. Friends. Lovers. Ketchup," Vera replied, and then licked a smearing of ketchup off her finger. "Right, Savvy?"

My shoulders softened.

"Totally," I agreed, and something clicked. I thought of Reg and the photo of her and her friends on Hinge. I looked at Vera and Candace, zoomed all the way out and saw the three of us together at the table. There it was, I thought. That ease. I imagined myself as a stranger walking by, thinking, "Wow, those three really found their people."

## 21

IN TRUE IZZIE style, her bridal party was outfitted according to a theme. And this theme was Garden Party. We were greeted by a very chipper man who was balancing a tower of sun hats, each one with a pink ribbon tied to the center and tiny rosebuds all along the brim. This was no doubt Izzie's Italian wedding planner, Alexi, whom she couldn't stop talking about. They had planned nearly everything over FaceTime because Alexi traveled between New York and Italy every other month. Izzie also had made a point of telling me he was "so fabulous" every time she mentioned him, even though I got that it was code for "he is very gay" the first time she said it.

"Ciao, bellas!" Alexi reached out to my mom and me with a sun hat in each hand, and I reluctantly plopped mine on my head. It was too tight; I could feel it digging into my forehead. I turned to my mom, who was nodding at Alexi and trying to return the hat.

"No, thank you."

"Signora, you must wear it! For the bride!" Alexi made a sweeping gesture to the right of the room, and we turned to find that Izzie was there, sitting atop what seemed to be a small grassy hill, at the bottom of which presents were stacked. Like a moat.

Jesus Christ.

I grabbed the hat meant for my mom and stacked it on top of the one already on my head.

Alexi pursed his lips. I shot him a wink.

"I'll make sure she puts it on later."

He didn't seem reassured.

I hooked my arm into my mother's elbow and tried to steer her away from the fake hill. I didn't want Izzie to see me yet.

"I am not putting that hat on."

"I know."

"It's very hot in here, isn't it?" she asked, her eyes wide, searching for the nearest window. It was not hot. She was constantly terrified of overheating.

"I'll have them turn on the AC. I'm sure the manager of the venue would love to adjust the temperature of the entire building for you!"

She nodded as if that were a perfectly reasonable request.

"Thank you."

"I'm not going to do that, Mom."

"Well, can't you ask Izzie—"

"Nope. Izzie is currently very busy."

She turned to look at Izzie on her hill.

"I see that."

"Come on, let's get this over with." I grabbed the gift we had brought from my mom's hand.

"Dad is so lucky he didn't have to come to this," I mumbled under my breath.

I tried to blend into the crowd and sneak our gift onto the present moat without her seeing me.

"Oh my god, Savvy's here!!"

Too late.

"Savvy!! Come up! Come up!"

Izzie was wildly gesturing for me to join her on her hill.

"Hi! It's okay! I'll see when you, um, come down!"

"Savannah Henry, get your cute butt up here!"

Oh my god. The sorority-girl sea parted so I could make my way closer to the hill. The present pile had gotten so high that there was no way I was going to be able to step over it on my own. This was ridiculous.

"Izzie, I can't—"

"Hey, here, let me help you." Someone touched my shoulder. I turned to see perhaps the only other person not wearing a peplum shirt holding out their hand to help boost me up. She was looking at me with the kind of energy you need in a top-secret emergency tampon exchange. I took her hand.

"Oh, thank you—sorry, this is ridiculous, she—" I whispered as she helped me leap over the presents littering the ground.

"I know. Izzie's day, Izzie's way, right? That's why we love her."

"Exactly."

She hoisted me up as best she could, and then Izzie took over and yanked me the rest of the way, pulling me into her arms. People were laughing and cheering around us. My armpits were sweating.

"Thank you, my sweet one!" Izzie called down to my new friend.

"Of course, cutie."

I was now crowded next to Izzie on top of what turned out to be a very real mound of moss. I could see there was dirt piling on the floor, and bits of branches and roots stuck out around the bottom.

"This is a little much, don't you think? Even for you." I raised my eyebrows at Izzie.

"I think it's very reasonable, actually. It was too cold to have the party out in the garden, so we brought the garden into the party!" Izzie smirked, pleased with herself.

We were standing shoulder to shoulder, absolutely at maximum hill capacity, and I was very aware that everyone in the room was staring at us.

"Well, what now?"

"Basically, I'm stuck up here until I finish opening presents. And now you are too." Izzie let out an evil laugh and crazy-smiled at me.

"Are you kidding me, Iz? You know I don't do well in crowds."

"It's barely a crowd! There are only fifty people here! And besides, this way we get to have bonding time."

It turned out that bonding time was basically just balling up wrapping paper and handing off already opened gifts to Izzie's mother. Izzie was given a small stool to sit on while I remained standing, shifting from foot to foot, trying to slyly kick away rocks that were starting to unearth themselves from the hill. I rolled a pebble directly into a golden chalice with only a bow on it and got a menacing look from one of Izzie's elderly second cousins. Izzie oohed and aahed at every gift, and often turned to me to say, "Oh my god, isn't this the best?" when she got an Instant Pot or yet another mug that read IT'S WINE O'CLOCK SOMEWHERE. My cheeks were starting to hurt from fake-smiling so hard. I caught my mother several times laughing into her ginger ale, especially when Izzie handed me silk pasties with the word BRIDE diamond-studded on each nipple and asked me to show them to the people crowded behind us. Finally, Izzie got to the last gift. It was small, a book maybe, and wrapped in a deep purple wrapping paper.

"I wonder what this could beeee!" Izzie shouted. She tore off the paper and I winced a little. Whoever had wrapped the present had done it expertly, carefully. Izzie tore the rest of the paper off and threw it my way as she pulled out a beautiful leather-bound notebook. Scripted into the cover were the words ABOVE ALL ELSE. Izzie looked confused.

"So pretty!" She looked over at me.

"I think they're for your vows," I whispered.

"I'm not doing vows," she whispered back.

She turned back to the room, smiling wide.

"I absolutely love this. It's so beautiful."

She opened the notebook, looking for a card. The pages were thick and creamy white. It really was beautiful.

"I think the card got lost in the wrapping paper!" It was my emergency tampon friend, doing a little wave toward the back of the crowd. Of course it was her gift.

"Oh my god, I'm so sorry! This is perfect. You're perfect! Sav, can you hunt down the card?"

"Um, sure." I looked down at the wrapping paper piled in a huge mess on the floor. I now had a path to get down the hill, but it wasn't going to be graceful. I looked at my mom, pleading. She rushed over and did her best to help me down. I grabbed her with one hand and clutched my hats with the other, both of us nearly falling over in the process. Luckily no one was staring this time; they were all busy taking pictures of Izzie, who was now posing atop her stool.

I knelt by the pile of wrapping paper, looking around for a crumple of purple among the pastel.

"Hey, this is no big deal. I'll write her a new card this week and get it to her. You don't have to muck around in all this." It was my new friend again.

"I feel so bad! Your present was amazing."

"Truly, do not worry about it. I feel like you probably need a drink? Or, like, four?"

I laughed. "You know what I want, weirdly? A Shirley Temple."

"Oh my god, those are the fucking best. Let's go."

We snuck away from the group and made it to the bar.

"Two Shirley Temples, please!" she called over to the bartender, who looked very unhappy to be wearing a sun hat. I felt their pain and then realized that mine were giving me a headache.

"I'm going to take these off now and you cannot say anything about the huge indent I'm going to have on my forehead."

"Absolutely. Won't even look at your head for the rest of this conversation."

I peeled the hats off my head and chucked them onto the nearest table.

"I feel like a new woman." I breathed a sigh of relief.

The bartender slid our Shirley Temples over to us.

"Cheers to that." She handed me my drink and we clinked. I watched her take an eager sip.

"Oh my god, so good."

"So good," I agreed. "I haven't had one of these since, like, well, honestly, since last year. Something about being home makes me crave them. Izzie and I used to down them like shots."

"That's amazing. I feel like I'm ten again but not, like, bored at the table with my parents droning on."

"Yes, exactly. Wait, I love your tattoo." I noticed she had a snake winding down from her shoulder to her elbow. But instead of typical snakeskin, it had tiny flowers covering its body.

"Oh, thank you! I got it a couple years ago. It's an Adam and Eve thing. Like, what if the snake was a softie after all?"

"That's fucking awesome." This girl was so cool.

"Do you have any?"

"Not yet. I really want one." I thought of what I'd told Wesley back in January.

"It's worth it. But I must warn you, once you get one you can't stop. I have, like, seven, but they are, um, not visible, ha ha. And I totally did that thing you're absolutely not supposed to do, which is get a matching tattoo with your boyfriend."

"You didn't."

"I really did."

"Is he *the one?*"

"He better be. Otherwise I'm gonna have this dumb tattoo of his name for the rest of my life." She turned the inside of her wrist toward me and my heart stopped. I couldn't take my eyes off it.

"I know, I know, it's terrible."

I looked up at her and shook my head, trying to steady myself.

"Oh, no, um. It's nice. I, uh. You know what, I really have to pee."

She looked at me, concerned.

"You okay? Your face is kind of pale."

"Yes! I'm fine! Do you know where—" I pointed vaguely behind me.

"Yeah, it's, um, out that door and toward the right. Are you sure you're—"

"Totally. Fine. Thanks!"

I grabbed my drink and beelined for my mother, who was talking to one of Izzie's aunts.

I clutched her wrist and she turned to look behind her.

"We need to go, Mom, now."

"What's wrong, sweetie?" She looked scared.

"I, um, feel sick. Please, I need to go home." I was basically hyperventilating.

"Okay, okay! Let me get our coats. Go to the car." She grabbed her keys from her purse and I practically ripped them from her hand, bounding toward the exit.

"Sav? Savvy!" I heard Izzie call behind me.

I rushed toward the lobby.

"Signora! Signora!" Alexi was running down the hall.

"What?!" I whipped my head around to look at him.

"Your gift!" He was holding a small bonsai tree.

I looked at him, dumbfounded. He was holding it so tenderly.

"Um, okay. Thank you."

I took the tree from him, turned around, and walked out the door. It was like time had stopped. The parking lot was deserted, just a sea of empty Lexus SUVs and a lone green Mini Cooper that belonged to someone clearly unconcerned about their shitty parking skills. I had no recollection of where we had parked. I reached my arm out, stiff, and pressed the unlock button on the keys. I heard a distant click on my right and walked aimlessly toward the sound. One by one, I started yanking on the doors of the parked cars, not even bothering to peek into the windows to at least try to decipher which one was my mother's.

"Sweetie! We're parked in the back of the lot—that is not our car!" My mom was trotting toward me, her heels teetering on the gravel.

"Don't run, Mom, it's fine."

She reached me, breathless, and handed me my puffer coat. It was only then that I realized I was freezing and slid it over my shoulders, zipping it up to my neck.

"You rushed out of there so quickly! What happened?"

My eyes filled with tears, but I quickly brushed them away. I handed her the keys.

"Can we get in the car, please?"

She started walking ahead of me and I followed.

"We left at the right time." She half turned her head back toward me. "When I walked into the hallway, I saw Izzie's brother walking in."

I stopped in my tracks.

"Which brother?"

My mom opened the car door and turned back to me, quizzical as to why I had stopped. She got into the front seat.

"The one I don't like," she said, disdain in her voice, before shutting the door.

I swallowed hard. Had I walked past him? Had he seen me? No, he would have said hi. He always tried to say hi. God, what if I hadn't left when I did? He would have walked right up to the bar, kissed his girlfriend on the cheek, and pretended he and I were buds from way back when. I wanted to puke.

"Sweetie!" My mom's voice was muffled by the window, which she was also rapping her knuckles against.

"Coming," I mumbled.

"What is going on with you?"

I crumpled into the seat next to her. "I just felt really overwhelmed. And, um, light-headed."

My mom reached out and rested her hand against my head. I closed my eyes, willing away tears again.

"No fever, but you're probably just exhausted. I told you that room was too hot." She clicked her tongue in disapproval. She rummaged around in her purse and pulled out a small bottle of water and a bottle of aspirin. "Here, take this. We'll go home and just rest."

"Thank you." I popped the aspirin into my mouth and took a gulp of the water.

My mother was peering at me from the corner of her eye. She seemed to have no intention of driving.

"Why does it matter which brother?" she asked.

Fuck. She knew. I mean, she didn't *know* but she knew. In the infuriating way that moms sometimes just know.

"It's just, uh, awkward between us."

"Really? Why?"

"You know, just, like. Our history, I guess."

"But you've spent quite a bit of time with him since then, haven't you?"

"No, I haven't," I snapped.

"Not the two of you, alone. I meant when you go over to Izzie's house. When her mother throws those parties." The way she said "*those parties*" summed up about every feeling my mother had about Izzie's mom.

"It's always been awkward, Mom."

"Oh, okay. I didn't know that. Sorry."

"It's fine. Can we go?"

My mother paused for a moment, just looking at me.

I turned away, pretending to look out the window.

"I always thought he was a creep. I know you liked each other, so I never said anything, but he should have been dating girls his own age."

Dating. Right. I had told her we were dating.

"Yeah."

I leaned my head against the window. It was cold. It felt good.

I heard her start the engine.

When we got home, I collapsed into bed. It was only seven p.m., but it was so dark out, and all I wanted to do was watch Netflix on my computer and drown out the nightmare that had been this afternoon. I climbed between the new sheets that had replaced mine when I graduated high school. They were fancy, some kind of satin. They made me feel like everything was washed clean after I left. I stretched my legs wide, charting the width of the twin bed with my toes. My throat was tight. I couldn't even manage to open my laptop before my eyes started closing. But the second they did, I saw the map. It's this thing that started happening when I came home. This topographical map unfolded in my head, and this time it marked the mile between my bedroom and the blue room. The map measured everything in my hometown by the distance I was from that room.

Ever since I had gone to therapy, coming home was different. Each time I did, it was like the memories of that night became more vivid. Like the more I trusted myself that I had been assaulted, the more I was reminded of it. It was stronger than trust, even. It was more like a promise. Like I was promising my younger self, the person who used to sleep in this bed, that I believed her. That she was right, that what happened in that room didn't feel okay because it wasn't. So now I felt choked between promises: the ancient one I made to Izzie when I swore forever, and this new one, the one to myself, as fresh as these sheets, as if the wound he opened in me was not from years ago but just today.

# 22

I WOKE UP the next morning and had approximately thirty seconds of peace before I remembered the previous day. Thirty seconds in my bed, light streaming through my window, and the sound of my mom's wedge heels climbing down the staircase, going to feed the dog. And then came a sinking feeling, and then I remembered all of it. The hats, the hill, the tattoo. That he had been there. That I had missed him, just barely, and the fact was that it was only a matter of time before I saw him again. Had no choice but to see him again.

I rolled over to face the wall, guiding my hand alongside the wrought-iron frame of my bed, which was built like a day bed. There was a spot on the wall where I had written "FUCK" in all capital letters. It was after the anonymous texts started happening, calling me a whore. Instead of responding, I had taken a Sharpie to the wall. It made me feel better.

I heard the doorbell ring and startled. It wasn't even nine a.m., and no one ever rang our doorbell anyway. Except. Fuck. It was Izzie. Izzie always rang the doorbell. It was how I could be sure it was her. Any second now my mother would run up the back steps and tell me she was not dressed and the house wasn't tidy enough for guests and Izzie couldn't come in right now.

Right on cue, I heard her shoes race up the stairs.

"Savannah." She flung the door to my room open. I careened my head backward, staring at her.

"I didn't invite her over."

"My house is a mess."

"Our earth is melting. Does it matter in the long run?"

"Yes." She glared at me.

"Okay, okay." I sighed. "I'm going. We'll go drive somewhere. Close the door, I'm naked."

She didn't move.

The doorbell rang again. My mom shook her head in disapproval.

"Hurry up." She slammed the door behind her.

I felt for my phone under my pillow and saw three missed calls from Izzie. I texted her.

I just woke up.

My mom is pissed you're here
without warning

I tried calling you first!

I was sleeping. Just wait in the car
pls. I'll be down soon

Diner?

I mean, pancakes couldn't hurt.

**Yes please.**

KK. Hurry butthead

I sat up and swung my legs around, letting my feet land on the carpet. I didn't get up right away. Instead, I looked over at the mirror in the corner of my room, a standalone. From where I was sitting, I could see just a sliver of my mouth and chin, but mostly my boobs and belly, which was a round folded pouch completely covering my vagina. I took a breath and straightened up, watching my skin stretch and elongate, the pouch turning into a soft layer of flesh sheathing my rib cage and my navel. I could see my belly button again, and the upper part of my pubic hair. I had seen my body at every age in this mirror. When I begged for tits. When I shaved my pussy for the first time and stared at it, stroking the soft skin, pretending my hand was someone else's, judging if it was actually soft enough to want to touch it.

I pressed my feet into the floor and rose, walking over to the closet in pursuit of something I forgot I owned, knowing full well that the remnants of my childhood closet were atrocious. I did this when I came home on breaks, even though I always brought a suitcase from school. As if one day I'd open a drawer and find something worth remembering, some part of me I'd left behind and might decide to want again. I pulled open the door and took inventory. A brown pair of Uggs, stained with road salt, no doubt crusty on the inside from wearing them without socks. A cardigan my great-aunt bought me for Christmas three years ago that I had never even tried on. A corduroy skirt that would definitely no longer fit, two different sneakers without their mates, and my prom dresses. I reached out to finger the hem of the dark blue one, the one I wore my junior year. A dress far too pretty to have given Devon Whelan a blow job in the back of his car after prom. I was

Devon Whelan's prom pity ask, after everything, after Izzie had turned everyone against me and then welcomed me back into the fold. The dress came loose from the hanger and fell. I scrambled to grab it, and when I stood back up, my sweet sixteen dress was staring back at me in all its pink sequined glory.

Savannahhhhh

Coming

I put on a T-shirt and pulled the three-year-old cardigan over it. My leggings were draped over the hamper, and I could see the crotch was white and sort of flaky from dried discharge, but I grabbed them anyway and slid them on. I picked up my shoes and ran down the stairs, snagging my jacket along the way, and made for the front door.

"I put money in your pocket."

I paused. My dad was sitting in his armchair, reading the newspaper.

"Thanks, Pops. I'm just going to the diner."

He nodded and shooed me away, not looking up from the paper.

I ran out onto the driveway barefoot and immediately regretted it. It was chilly out. I jumped into Izzie's passenger seat.

"Put your fucking shoes on, you lunatic."

"I know, I know. Let me just put my feet on the heater first."

Izzie rolled her eyes and started the car. She looked like an entirely different person than the one she was yesterday. Her hair was in a low ponytail and I could see a glaze of dry shampoo around her hairline. She was wearing sweats and a raggedy sweater that I knew was once her mom's, from college. She looked like a person I actually knew.

It was like a billion Sundays we'd already had, just us looking like shit going to the diner.

"You left early yesterday." Izzie was leaning forward and squinting at the road.

"Where are your driving glasses?" I asked.

"I don't need them. I actually think my eyesight has gotten better."

"That's not how that works."

"You're avoiding the question."

"I felt really sick. I was, like, overheating, and my head was killing me. I felt like I was going to pass out."

"I knew it was too fucking hot in there. I told Alexi—whatever, why didn't you say goodbye? Are you feeling okay now?"

"I'm sorry, you were surrounded by people. I just had to get out of there. And then I got home and passed out."

"Okay."

Izzie looked like she wanted to say something, but she didn't.

"I'm glad you feel better now. And that we can have you and me time. Yesterday was insane. Even for me."

"I'm not gonna say I told you so."

"Saying you're not gonna say I told you is the same thing as saying I told you so, bitch."

"You said it! Not me!"

Izzie laughed and flipped me off. I wiggled my feet against the heater. We didn't talk for a bit. It was the good kind of silence. I didn't want it to be so easy between us; it felt dangerous to admit that I did. But it was Izzie. The person I had spent nearly all my time with. Sometimes in silence, sometimes in constant chatter, on the phone all hours of the night, watching the same TV show and not speaking at all but laughing at all the same parts.

"I have a crazy idea," she said, eyes wide.

"What?" I asked.

"Let's get Dunkin'."

I snorted.

"Why is that crazy?"

"Because we'll, like, bring the Dunkin' into the diner with us. The coffee sucks there. And the Dunkin' by your house makes me nostalgic."

It was our pit stop before school started, every day our senior year. It made us late to class, but we didn't care. I, especially, did not care. That year was purgatory.

"Me too."

"Can we?"

Izzie looked at me with hopeful eyes. Like we were nine and she wanted to know if I could ask my dad to buy us ice cream.

I laughed.

"Yes, of course."

Izzie veered into the parking lot. We got out of the car, and when she saw me, she stopped abruptly and cupped her hand over her mouth.

"What the fuck are you wearing, Sav?"

I looked at her blankly, and then down at my hodgepodge of an outfit.

I shrugged.

"It's eclectic?"

"You look like a hobo."

I grimaced.

"Iz, you can't say shit like that."

She rolled her eyes again and waved her hand like I was over-reacting and started walking toward the door. I thought of Vera and what she would say if she heard Izzie say that, and my stomach dropped a little.

"Are you coming?" Izzie turned to look at me.

"Yeah."

We paid for our coffee and got back in the car. Izzie connected her phone to the charger and tapped on a playlist, blasting Taylor Swift oldies. I clenched my teeth. She started singing along, screaming off pitch and giggling.

At the chorus she grabbed my knee and shook my leg.

"Come on, Savvy, I know you know the words better than I do."

It was true. I knew every word. We listened to it every day the summer we were sixteen. I reached out to the dash and cranked the volume all the way down.

"Hey! Party pooper!"

"I'm sorry, my head is still kind of hurting," I lied.

She looked sad.

"Oh, okay. I might have some Advil in the console."

"Thanks, Iz," I said, not making a move to look for the bottle.

We pulled up to the diner, crowded with cars, like it always was on a Sunday. Izzie parked and then we joined the small line outside the entrance. It was all young girls, high school age, also in their slippers and hoodies, crowded together around a phone and laughing hysterically as they swiped through photos from the night before.

"Oh my god, you were so fucked upppp!" one of them cackled. She had smudged purple eyeshadow, likely left over from the night before. She was nudging the person next to her, who had her hair tied up in a pink satin scrunchie, and who looked a little uncomfortable.

"What did I do?"

"You don't remember?!"

My fingernails dug into the skin of my palm inside my pocket, bracing myself for this girl, who looked like she was about to cry, no doubt because the carousel of things she could have done was spinning in her head. I whirled around and faced Izzie instead, and started speaking loudly.

"So how was the rest of the shower?"

"Well, not to make you jealous, but the chocolate fountain was wheeled out like ten minutes after you left."

I tried not to strain my ears to listen to the conversation behind me. All the other girls had joined in laughing and I felt the second-hand shame of Pink Scrunchie searing through the back of my sweater.

"Milk or dark?" I asked.

"Dark. I'm not an amateur," Izzie scoffed.

"Did they have to cover you in a giant bib? Your dress, which was beautiful by the way, did not look like it could withstand a chocolate fountain."

"Sav, you underestimate me again. Couldn't risk it. I had an outfit change planned."

"Ah." I nodded.

Izzie burst out laughing.

"I'm kidding! I just tucked a bunch of napkins into my tits and basically drank from the thing. It was so good, oh my god."

Izzie couldn't exist without chocolate. When we were little, she would down whole candy bars after dinner, sneak extra fudge onto her sundae, lick way more of the brownie batter out of the bowl than was FDA approved. Izzie had the sweet tooth; I liked everything salty. Which, of course, is always the best flavor combination. We just worked.

The girls ahead of us in line stepped through the diner's entrance, and a very annoyed hostess waved us in after them. We were marched over to a corner window and menus were thrust into our hands.

"Oh thank god, a booth." Izzie slid in.

"There's no other way."

"No other way. Holy fuck, I'm so thirsty." Izzie reached for the ice water on the table and gulped fast.

"Izzie—slow down—you're gonna get—"

"Fuuuuuckkkkk!" Izzie pulled away from her straw and reached for her temples.

"Brain freeze."

"Precisely."

"I always do that."

"You always do that."

"I had way too many Izzie Fizzies yesterday. Did you have one? Weren't they amazing?"

"So good." I nodded.

Izzie rubbed her forehead. Then she leaned forward and rested her chin on her palm.

"Tell me everything."

My knee started bouncing under the table. I knew she wasn't referring to yesterday, but that's the only thing that I could think about. I started picking a hole in the thigh of my leggings under the table.

"You know, school. Busy. I'm in this one class that's way more intense than I thought it would be. I'm supposed to be working on this proposal for a project right now; it's due like a week after I get back. I have to present on a topic I'm passionate about, but I keep getting bogged down about what to choose, and I just feel like maybe I'm not actually passionate about anything, and everyone in my class—"

"Sav?"

I was rambling.

"You're rambling."

"Sorry." I paused. "Hungry."

"Same." Izzie gave a little wave to the server nearest to us. She practically sprinted toward us, extremely flustered, and pulled out a small notepad.

"Hi!" Izzie smiled up at her.

She seemed taken aback.

"Hi?"

"How are you?" Izzie gestured to the room around us. "It's so busy today, oh my god."

The girl looked stunned. As if this was the first person to ask her how she was today, or the first one all week. "Honestly, it's so stressful. Sundays are nightmares here."

"I can't even imagine. We're gonna be your easiest table, I promise. We know this menu better than we know each other. Well, almost as well as we know each other." Izzie winked at me.

Our server's demeanor had changed. All because of Izzie. Izzie with the sweet tooth. Izzie, the joy magnet.

"Sav?" Izzie and the server were looking at me.

"Yeah?"

"Food. Usual?"

"Oh, yeah. Yes."

"Great."

"Pancakes, please. Two chocolate, two blueberry. Side of scrambled eggs and sausage, and a bowl of strawberries. And one OJ! All to share!"

Our waitress ran back into the brunch madness and I felt a wash of overwhelm that for the next hour it would just be Izzie and me, sitting in one place, with very few distractions. We hadn't been alone together like this in a long time.

I reached for the paper wrapper covering my straw and started to meticulously peel pieces from it, grateful to have something to focus my eyes on that wasn't the person across from me.

"Savvy, what's up?"

"Hmm?" I asked, pretending there wasn't already a lump in my throat.

"You're being weird. Stop with the wrapper. How are you? What's happening at school?"

I glanced up at her quickly and then grabbed my water cup, taking a long sip instead of responding.

"You know, what I told you already. That class and stuff, the project."

"How are your friends? Candace, and who's that beautiful girl I've seen in your stories? Like, very cool but also potentially dangerous? Her handle is killbillandallmen?"

I laughed. "That would be Vera."

"Vera. Is she nice? What's she like?"

Izzie's phone buzzed. She turned it facedown and slid it to the other side of the table.

"She's great. From LA. Amazing artist and also a witch."

"Stop. I'm obsessed with witches. Remember how many times I rewatched *Charmed*?"

"Except that episode where they took out that person's eyeballs."

Izzie yelped. "Sav. Don't. I'll have nightmares."

"She's also polyamorous and has two boyfriends."

"Okay, so Vera is basically a queen among us?"

"She's pretty perfect."

"I think in another life I'd be polyamorous."

"Why in another life?"

"Oh, I'm too fucked up in this one. My daddy issues couldn't handle it. But in another world where my dad wasn't a sexist asshole and didn't comment on my body and my mother's body for my entire life? I'd be free to roam, baby."

I winced a little. Izzie's dad sucked.

"How is he? With the wedding and stuff?" I felt guilty I hadn't asked.

"Horrible. Complains about everything. Everything's too expensive, and he didn't raise me to be a child bride, and I better be going to bridal bootcamp if I want to wear such a fitted wedding dress, or how he doesn't want his grandkids to be military brats."

"Izzie."

She shook her head and shrugged. "Did you expect anything less?"

"I guess not. It's just so unfair, Iz, I'm sorry."

Izzie teared up a little.

"It's fine. I just try and focus on the day, and Ben, and making everything perfect."

"Yeah. That's good."

We were both quiet for a moment.

"Have you thought about, um, what I said over the summer? Trying therapy?"

Izzie looked up at me and sort of blinked a couple of times.

"No, Savannah, I haven't."

"Why? You said you were already thinking about it, even before I asked."

"I changed my mind. I realized I just needed more support from, like, the people around me."

That felt like a dig.

She shrugged. "My dad isn't gonna change."

"Right, that's probably true. But your relationship to him might. He just makes you so upset, and I think some tools could help—"

"Didn't you go because you had to? Because that RA caught you drinking?"

"Yeah, but it ended up being really helpful. I wish I had gone earlier." I looked down at a few water droplets that had glommed together on the table. I poked at it.

"Like in high school?"

"Yeah. I think it would have been good. With everything that happened."

Izzie was silent for a second. I looked up at her, caught her eye. We never said any of this shit out loud.

"Right," she said, not breaking my gaze. Then she blurted, "I've really needed you."

"What?"

"Like, I know you're not my maid of honor. But you're still my best friend. And you're the only one who knows, like actually knows, what my family is like."

Izzie's brother flashed through my head.

"I'm sorry you feel that way."

"I feel like you're judging me."

*I was.*

My breath quickened.

"What? Why?"

"I don't know, Sav. You're just, like, living this life at school, and I know it's really different than, like, what I'm doing, but I feel like you think your life is better?"

"I don't think that!"

"I've asked you a bunch of times if I could visit you."

"You can! I just thought, you have the wedding and you're in the middle of school, I feel like there's time, you know, after Ben leaves."

Izzie nodded.

"Yeah, that's true."

"Look, Izzie. I'm just trying to be present at school. It took me a while to find a group of friends, and I'm still not convinced the group I found likes me. It was easy for you with rush and stuff, and it is really different than what we grew up with. I'm just trying to fit in. Sometimes I feel like an imposter; everyone is just so cool and creative—"

"You're cool and creative!" Izzie yelled.

I laughed. "Thank you, but—"

"No, it's true! I always brag about you. You're so creative and you worked so hard to get into school. Everyone should be dying to be your friend. I'll call them all, I'll tell them. They don't know what they're missing out on."

"That's really sweet, Iz."

"So you're not mad at me?"

"No, no." I shook my head. "Really."

"Okay, good. Because I miss you. And once this wedding stuff is over it'll be summer, and we can just hang out by the pool together the whole time. Get crispy."

"Totally."

"Good. 'Cause I need my best friend." Izzie slapped the table, demanding it.

"I know."

"And you're gonna do great on that project. I know it." She beamed at me.

Seconds later our food arrived, covering the entire table. Izzie started opening the butter packets and dumping maple syrup all over the pancakes, and the eggs were so hot they were steaming in my face, and all of it seemed like too much. It was so much food, so much to eat. I realized then that I really wasn't hungry.

# 23

## Sixteen

IT WAS THE end of Thanksgiving break. I was in my oldest nightgown, threadbare and full of holes, poking at the remains of the sushi takeout my dad had brought home, like he did every Sunday, and avoiding my English homework. I was eating it in my room, on the floor, the contents of my backpack fanned around me. I couldn't even open my English textbook. I just kept looking at my phone. Your brother hadn't texted me all day, not since he dropped me back at home the night before. Every time I looked at our text thread my stomach dropped, but that was probably just part of love. It was just the next level of butterflies.

I was the first one to text your brother after the barbecue in July. He had gone back to school early, only a few days after. The first time I texted I was almost as drunk as I had been at the barbecue. I sent it at 12:06 in the morning.

> Did I feel as good as you
> imagined?

He didn't respond for seventeen hours.

better

After that I texted him every time I was drunk.

> No one my age can fuck me like
> you

He texted back three days later.

> i know

> I made myself cum thinking about
> you

No response.

> I can't stop thinking about you
> inside me

No response.

Three days before Thanksgiving break, I sent him a photo of
me kneeling naked in front of my mirror, my spare hand squeezing
my tits together. That one worked.

> ur gonna sneak out saturday so i can
> fuck you

·

"SAVANNAH!" MY MOM called me from downstairs. My
body flashed with rage, a feeling I was entirely used to. In health
class we were given a "Psychology of Teenagers" handout that
explained that teens want to destroy their parents. Like they want

to try to literally kill them. But only because they're trying to see if they can withstand that destruction. Teenagers want proof that their parents really won't go anywhere, no matter how hard they try to murder them.

"What?" I asked, barely loud enough for her to hear.

"Some car is outside, Savannah."

*Who the fuck would be here on a Sunday?*

"Did you invite someone here?" She was two seconds away from freaking, I could tell. As much as I wanted to kill her, I didn't doubt she could still kill me first.

"Coming, I'm coming." I shoved my sushi aside and rushed down the stairs. There was a blue sedan outside. I didn't recognize it. Someone got out of the passenger side, but I couldn't make out their features in the dark.

The person was carrying something, a huge box. I hit the switch by the door, turning on the driveway lights. It was you.

My body felt cold. My hands were icy.

I didn't open the door right away. I didn't want to. I wanted you to get right back into the car, go home, text me before bed about your outfit for tomorrow.

You got closer and you looked weird. Your face was blank. You stared at me, saying nothing. You were in front of the door now, and I still hadn't opened it.

"Savannah, why is she here? You know she needs to call first." My mom stood by the entrance to the kitchen, grabbing at my dog's collar to stop him from bounding toward the door. He loved you.

"I don't know." I didn't turn back to talk to her. You and I had locked eyes.

"Open the door." I read your lips. I couldn't do it.

"Tell her she needs to go home. You'll see each other at school in the morning. It's not appropriate to drop in like this without warning."

I didn't answer.

"Savannah. Now."

I opened the door. You pushed inside and shoved the box into my arms.

"What's going on?" My throat was dry.

"You know what's fucking going on."

"I don't! Why did you bring this here?"

I looked down at the box, realizing then that it was all my shit that I kept at your house. My extra pajamas, a photo album from our sweet sixteen, the teddy bear I kept on your bed. A sports bra I was always forgetting to take home, the lace G-string I kept at yours because I was terrified of my mom finding it.

"Because I don't want it anymore." You spoke slowly.

"Why? What's going on?"

*She knows.*

"I thought about burning it, you know, but it doesn't even deserve that much energy."

My dog was yelping now, whining for you.

"Savannah." My mother's voice was stern.

Izzie looked behind me, at her. I heard my dad's footsteps come up the stairs.

"Izzie!" I didn't turn around. My hands were starting to shake.

"Hey!" you said brightly. Fake nice.

"Sorry to intrude. Just wanted to come over and let you both know something."

"Sure. Go ahead," my dad said, walking closer to us. I clenched my teeth.

Izzie continued to smile, cocking her head to one side while she looked behind me at my dad.

"Well, I just wanted to tell you both that your daughter? Your perfect little girl? She's actually a slut who slept with her best friend's brother."

I froze.

*This isn't happening.*

No one spoke. Izzie looked at me and her fake smile dropped. She didn't blink. I knew it was because, if she did, tears would fall. Instead, she turned around and walked back out to the car.

I couldn't move.

My mom let go of the dog. He galloped toward the door and clawed at the wood.

"Savannah?" My mother's voice was quiet.

"I'm going to bed now," I said, careful not to let my voice break.

I turned toward the stairs and didn't look back at my parents.

# 24

"DO YOU REALLY need to go back early?"

My mom and I were in the car, parked outside the train station.

"Yes." I nodded, answering her question for the third time that day.

"I'm so stressed about this project and I can't focus here. The wi-fi sucks."

I had repeated the lie so many times that now I believed it.

She looked sad, and I tried to ignore the twist of guilt in my throat.

"Okay, well, we're early. It's cold, so will you stay in the car until you have to go?"

"I'm fine, Mom." I wanted to stay in the car. But if she kept looking at me like that I would cry.

"Are you mad at me?" She looked at me earnestly. Her eyes were wide, searching my face, almost like a little kid asking why they can't stay at the playground longer. "You seem so distant."

"No." My voice was firm. "I told you, I'm stressed."

I busied myself looking for a tissue in the glove box, blowing my nose louder than I needed to.

"Do you want a mint?" I glanced over at her, a half-empty roll of Life Savers on her open palm.

"Okay."

She hurried to dislodge one from the pack and handed it to me. I knew this was more than an offering; it was a plea to stay. As if mints were enough to make me throw my hands up and say, "*Hey, let's just go back home.*"

"Did something happen with Izzie?" Her words were careful, tentative.

"Besides the fact that she's a Stepford wife in training?" I shot back.

"So something did happen?" she pressed.

I sighed. "No, everything is fine."

"You know she's always been a little like that. Her mother is—" She cut herself off. "Well, you know how she is. I shouldn't judge her. It's just the way she likes to be."

"I guess."

"You know"—she hesitated—"there was a time that you talked that way too. It wasn't that long ago."

I felt my teeth grit together.

"I hate when you do that."

"What did I say?"

"It's like you try and remind me of the person you thought I wanted to be. I didn't actually want that." I started picking at a hangnail.

"Savannah, I'm only going off what you said to me. I'm glad you don't actually want that life."

"I was a teenager. You believed everything I said at, like, seventeen years old? I was a kid." I heard my voice rise slightly.

"A pretty stubborn, convincing kid," she said, giving me a knowing look.

"Well, it wasn't."

"Wasn't what?"

"It wasn't true!" I exclaimed. "I lied. All the time. And you should have—"

I felt myself getting emotional. I clamped my mouth shut again.

"I should have what?"

I shook my head.

"Like, you just, you never noticed how sad I was?" I turned to look at her.

"Of course I knew you were sad. You missed Izzie, and she said those awful things. Those kids in your school were idiots. But you shut me out."

"You should have tried harder," I mumbled under my breath.

"What?" she asked.

"Nothing. I need to go."

"I'm sorry you're feeling so upset."

"It's fine. I'm stressed. I keep telling you that."

I grabbed my coat from the back seat and got out of the car, walking around to the trunk. I rapped my knuckles on the car and heard a click. I pushed the trunk door up and reached for my overnight bag. My mother turned in her seat and looked back at me.

"I love you, Savannah. Always."

"I know, Mom. I love you too." My voice had more of an edge to it than I intended.

I slung my bag over my shoulder and shut the door.

Fifteen minutes later, when I'd settled in and was catching up in the group chat, my mom texted.

> Was there something else you were
> sad about that I didn't know of?

I ignored the text.

•

WHEN I GOT back to school, I had the inexplicable desire to
be stupid. I wanted to get drunk, text people I shouldn't, do something just for the story. I didn't want to think. About myself, about
Izzie, about my mother, about him. No one I knew was on campus.
Candace had weaseled her way onto a birthright trip, less because
she wanted to learn about her Jewish heritage and more because
a girl she had gone to summer camp with helped organize it and
posted about a last-minute spot opening. The girl had come out
recently and had been asking Candace for "advice." One of Vera's
boyfriends had a house in Monaco and she had gone to visit, be-
grudgingly, because she didn't want to be associated with "rich
people bullshit" or contributing to tourism. She said it was capitalism's fucked up little sister. She did, however, ask for my opinion
between two bikinis she had "scrounged up" in the back of her
closet. I told her that although I did really like the leather one
studded with (possibly real?) teeth, the one with the decapitated
Barbie-head print might be slightly better for the first time meeting her boyfriend's parents.

I had peeked at Wesley's Instagram, even feeling bold enough
to tap on their story, but it gave me no insight into whether they
were back at school yet. It was an infographic on how to use multiple pronouns in conversation. I debated clap-reacting but my
hands got sweaty and I worried I'd choose the heart-eyes reaction
or shocked-eyes reaction instead and instantly felt embarrassed,
so I decided against it.

When I got to my dorm, I got right in the shower, trying to
wash off the mess of the last couple of days. Scenes of the bridal
shower replayed in my head, and the look on my mom's face when
I checked to see if she had driven away from the train parking lot

yet. She hadn't, and she looked frozen there, and sad. I wondered how long she had stayed after the train had left. I grabbed an exfoliating mask from my shower caddy and scrubbed my face with it. It stung a little, but I didn't care. I couldn't get my mind to stop racing. I was so antsy. What the fuck was I going to do for the next couple of days? *Or whom?* I rolled my eyes at myself. And then I thought of Matt.

"Now, that would be really stupid," I muttered out loud.

I reached for my conditioner and squeezed a bunch into my hand and stared at it. Then I propped my leg up against the wall and started to lather my calf, then my thigh. I grabbed my razor out of my shower caddy and paused.

"Well, here goes nothing," I said, and began to shave six months of hair from my legs. I felt guilty, almost. Like every feminist in the world was watching me in disappointment. I shook my head. *Fuck it,* I thought, these rules were exhausting. I just wanted to slip into this old ritual. I knew how to get my body ready for a man. I was good at this. *You're good at being straight,* I thought.

I shaved my legs, then my armpits, then any stray nipple hairs I found. I trimmed off as much pubic hair as I could before sliding my razor over my vagina. I hadn't seen myself bare in years. My skin felt slick as I checked to see if any hair remained, the feeling both foreign and totally familiar. I washed inside myself with soap, even though you weren't supposed to, because you weren't supposed to. When I got out of the shower, I blow-dried my hair, taking care to make it pin straight and shiny, and then I curled the ends. I put my makeup on, the way Izzie taught me: primer, foundation, then concealer. I covered all signs of redness from crying earlier and any blemishes I had. Bronzer, applied in the shape of a 3 with a makeup brush. Blush on my cheekbones. Highlighter over the blush, and in the corner of my eyes, on the bridge of my nose, and a touch on my Cupid's bow. A little bronzer on my lids. Mascara, two coats, a tiny swipe of the wand on the lower lashes. I bit down on my lips to make them swell up, and then coated them with a gloss. I sprayed my naked body with an old bottle of Marc Jacobs perfume I had tucked away in one of my suitcases, misting it into the air and walking through it. An extra mist a few inches from my vagina. It stung. I dug around my dresser for my only wire bra and a black lacy thong. I surveyed my body in the mirror. I was surprised. It wasn't that I didn't recognize myself. It was the opposite. This was the way I looked, every day, for a very long time. *Yes,* I thought. *I know exactly how to be this girl.*

I dressed simply, a tight black pair of jeans and a soft oversized beige sweater, slightly cropped so you could see a sliver of my abdomen. I walked over to my desk and unplugged my phone from the charger. I scrolled through my texts for an unsaved number, but I had no luck.

"Ugh." I groaned. I was going to have to DM him. *No,* I thought, *I'm going to have to Snap him.* I sighed and opened the app, turning toward the window so light would flood my face. I took the right selfie on the third try: slight smirk on my mouth, eyes wide enough to seem innocent, just enough of my outfit to suggest I wanted him to see what I looked like, and my hand positioned in a wave.

Where are you? I typed, and then I sent the Snap into the ether.

*And now we wait.* I sat down on my bed, pulling my legs into my chest. I inspected underneath my fingernails. They were a little dirty, but that was one thing I did not have to care about tonight. I chewed the jagged edge of my thumbnail. My phone screen lit up. I shook my head in feigned disbelief.

He had sent me a photo back. I quickly opened it, ready to cringe, but it was just a photo of a window looking out onto the quad. I could see a stack of Solo cups on top of his microwave, and a massive canister of protein powder next to it. He was in his room.

Just chillin here? Are you back on campus? I swiped over to the chat, deciding he had seen more than enough to be interested.

Came back early! Lonely:(

He started typing right away.

Come over. I have popcorn!

Without warning, I smiled. Matt had popcorn? I didn't expect that Matt would have popcorn, or offer it to me, or use an exclamation point.

I like popcorn.

Dope. Radner, room 502.

I bit down on my lip, feeling my heart start to beat a little faster in my chest. Did I really want to go see Matt? Was this a complete idiot move?

"Fuck it," I said aloud, for the second time that afternoon. I grabbed my jacket and my bag and headed toward the door. I paused for a second and then ran back to my desk. I opened the drawer and felt for the back of it. My handed landed on a slippery piece of plastic. *Bingo*, I thought and shoved the condom in my bag.

# 25

MATT HAD SMALL hands. He had to be six one, at least, and as far as I could tell, everything but his hands was very proportional. Small dicks I could handle; small hands made me want to scream and run.

*It's fucked up that you care about this. You're just nitpicking. If Matt weren't cis, you wouldn't care.*

Matt squeezed my palm. We were sitting in his bed, popcorn on my lap, watching *Superbad*. Holding hands. We passed a wine bottle between us. I could tell it was really old, probably remnants of a night-before-spring-break party. Matt didn't seem like the wine type; someone else had probably left it in his room. We were now nearing the end of the bottle.

"Oh man, I love this part," Matt said, laughing and squeezing my hand.

*My hands are the same size as his. Abort abort abort.*

Instead, I squeezed back.

I loved this part too, McLovin in the liquor store.

"Damn, I forgot this movie is kind of fucked up, though." Matt paused his computer for a second.

*No shit. The ancient proverb reads: Where there is Judd Apatow, there is also rampant misogyny.*

"Uh-huh," I said, stuffing my mouth with more popcorn, quickly unlacing my fingers from his.

"Like, the whole reason they want the alcohol is to get girls drunk so they'll fuck them?" Matt looked like he was having an aneurysm. He waited for me to acknowledge his enlightenment.

"Yeah, it's pretty bad. You could even say it's . . . super bad." I added finger guns for good measure. Wes's signature.

"I can't believe I watched this as a kid. It definitely fucked with my mind." Matt leaned back against the wall. He did not acknowledge my joke. Or, worse, he didn't get it. I took a long gulp of the shitty wine.

Were we really doing this? The whole point of watching this movie with Matt was because I couldn't watch it with any of my other friends at school. Admitting to liking Judd Apatow and his crew of nerdy predators would be feminist social suicide, which was also a term I could never say out loud.

"Do you think it fucked with you too?"

"Probably." I took the last sip and slid the wine bottle onto the dresser next to me.

I reached out to the laptop and closed it. I turned to Matt, bit my lip, and ran my fingers through my hair. My cheeks felt warm, buzzy.

"So, were you gonna make a move or . . ."

Matt's existential crisis came to a quick end, and he leaned in to kiss me.

*Too much tongue!*

I pulled back and took hold of his chin.

"I like less tongue, okay?"

"And I like a girl who knows what she wants."

*Don't you dare roll your eyes, Savannah.*

I lay down against his pillows and pulled him on top of me. The kissing was much better now. How old was Matt? Senior? I calculated in my head: He had probably had two to three serious girlfriends and fucked around twenty. Forty if he had gone on a spring break trip more than once. That was enough to make him decent at sex, right? Were we going to have sex? The condom made me pretty sure we were going to have sex. If I brought a prop, I was going to use it.

"Can I go down on you?" Matt whispered.

*Nope.*

There was no way I'd come from him eating me out. Even if he had fucked forty girls, I doubted his pussy-licking prowess and, besides, it just wasn't something I liked that much. It took Nova at least five times to make me come like that, and god knows no boy in high school ever did. And I really didn't want the image of Matt looking up at me while he licked my pussy. Just thinking about it made me gag.

"I want you to fuck me," I said, a little whine in my throat, innocent eyes and my boobs pressed up against him. I felt him get hard against my thigh.

"You sure?" He looked at me quizzically.

"Mm-hmm." I pulled my sweater off. This seemed to be enough of a distraction from his questions considering the way he lunged for my tits with both hands.

Both really, really small hands.

"I have a condom!" I pushed him off and grabbed my bag off the floor, sifting through it. I heard Matt laugh.

"I have some of those too, you know."

"Right. Well, I didn't have any wine to bring, so . . ."

Matt grinned. We settled back into things, meaning Matt settled back into my boobs, sucking on them this time, while I gripped the condom in one hand and looked out the window. Men sucking on nipples made me think of them as babies and I found it both funny and kind of pathetic. I stifled a laugh. Fuck, was I drunk?

"You have perfect tits," Matt said, his mouth still full of me.

"Thanks." I avoided looking down. I lifted his head with my free hand and brought his mouth back to mine. Then I scooted out from under him and climbed on top of his legs.

"Hold this," I instructed, handing him the condom.

I unbuttoned his jeans and tugged them down. Reaching into his boxers, I found a perfectly normal-sized dick. Proportionate. But then I made the mistake of thinking about his stupid tiny hand wrapped around it and I visibly shuddered, quickly recovering by pretending to moan.

I did the whole sexy condom-putting-on thing, deftly and secretly wiping excess condom lube on his sheets, and then slid him inside me.

His past girlfriends plus miscellaneous hookups had taught him well. He rubbed my clit while we fucked and did most of the heavy thrusting. I made noises like they do in porn, and bit my lips, and showed him how flexible I was even though I actually wasn't. My right hip would regret this later. He told me I was sexy, beautiful, making him insane, so hard for me.

But then he wanted to fuck me from behind. And for some stupid reason, I let him.

"Your ass looks so good like this," he said, hands clamped around my hips, little nubby nails digging into me.

"You're holding me too tightly."

"Can't handle a little pain?" he asked, his voice goading and lower than I liked.

And before I could blink, Matt's hands were replaced with *his*, *his* dick so far inside me, too far, and my head smushed against an old, flat pillow that smelled like cafeteria soup. My body was shaking and he was slamming himself into me over, and over, and I kept telling myself, *this is what you wanted, this is how you fix this.*

"Get out, get out, get out of me!" I crumpled onto the bed, one of my arms giving out and awkwardly lodging itself underneath me. My ass was still in the air, butthole available for all to see.

"What the fuck?"

"Sorry, no, I'm not sorry—I—hold on—" I unfurled myself and reached for the nearest article of clothing I could find, his sports jersey, and scrambled to put it on. I turned to face him.

"Sorry, I have to go."

"Right now?" Matt looked bewildered, his eyes glancing down at his still-hard dick.

"Yeah, I, uh. Yeah, this wasn't what I—I shouldn't have come over." I was gathering my shit, not bothering to button my pants or put my shoes on fully. I bundled my coat and piled my bag on top of it. I didn't even want to think about what my hair looked like.

"Sav, did I—? Are you okay?" He stood up and I backed away, starting to open the door.

"Yeah, no, not a you thing. I have to, um. I'm sorry. I'll, um, Snap you."

On the way out of the lobby I deleted the app from my phone.

·

AT FOUR IN the morning, I found Izzie's brother's girlfriend's Instagram. It was public. I slid down to the floor, a bottle of tequila Vera had left in my room at my side, and I leaned against the foot of my bed. I took one drunken finger to my screen and started scrolling. She did pottery. Of vaginas. Photo after photo of ceramic vulvas, hairy and shaven and innies and outies and long, drooping labias and teeny-tiny pussies that would tuck perfectly into a G-string. Vagina after vagina after vagina until, ten scrolls down, a picture of them. Of him. I sucked in my breath and my body became still. They were smiling. It was a sunny day in the park—Central Park, said the location tag—and she was holding up a half a grapefruit. Massive, purply-red, bursting with juice, and a tiny nub at the top, a perfect clitoris. "Life imitates art;)," read the caption.

My knees magnetized to my chest; the knobby parts dug into my skin. I pulled them tighter and tighter until it was hard to breathe. I didn't let tears fall.

I clicked the follow button.

It was so early, and Wednesday, and there was no fucking way she was awake, but I still refreshed my feed over and over again, willing a tiny red icon to appear on my screen. I held my breath until my lungs felt like they were going to burst.

When I breathed out, as if on cue, the red icon appeared on my screen. I cried out and the sound was a mix between elation and sorrow. A minute later, I received a message from her.

> Hiiii fellow night owl
>
> I'm so happy you found me!
>
> I lost you the other day, what
> happened to you?!?

And then my phone died.

# 26

## Sixteen

YOU DIDN'T TAG me in the story, so I didn't get that it was about me right away.

My dad drove me to school that day. I couldn't bear to face you on the bus. In the car, he didn't ask me if it was true, what you said about me sleeping with your brother. He didn't ask me anything at all. My mom had knocked on my bedroom door around eleven, whispering my name. I stifled my sob against my pillow and pretended to be asleep.

I had turned off my phone the night before when you didn't call me back. I texted you over and over again but got nothing in return.

I'm so sorry Izzie

Please answer

I can explain this

Iz please

We're sisters

I turned my phone on as we entered the school driveway. I held my breath before checking my messages. You hadn't replied. You never posted on socials, so I opened Instagram as a distraction and tapped on the first story I saw. Apparently, Aiden from history class had seen the newest Marvel movie, then he had a whole pizza to himself, and then he threw up. I sighed and quickly tapped through the five consecutive slides of him hurling, but I stopped at his most recent post. I lurched forward in my seat. On a blank white slide, written in red all caps, was the phrase "*HIDE YOUR BROTHERS.*" Nothing else.

*What?*

I frantically swiped to the next story. Julia Romero, the only freshman on the dance team.

She posted it too.

*This isn't fucking happening.*

Luke Herman. Steven Freed. Annie Cohen. Andrea Wong. Leslie Oppenheim.

People I had known since elementary school. Seniors I followed who didn't even know my name. A girl who transferred out of our school in ninth grade.

And on and on and on.

"*HIDE YOUR BROTHERS*" filled my screen. My fingers clawed at my inner thigh. This couldn't be happening. How was this happening?

My fingers shook as I typed your name into the search bar. Before I even tapped on your profile, I saw that you had posted on your story. You never posted on your story.

I held my breath as I tapped on the glowing circle around your picture. And there it was, in bright red text: If you think what Sav Henry did was fucked up, screen shot the next slide. I gasped and tapped forward, losing all feeling in my feet. My brain short-circuited.

Hide

Your

Brothers

Everyone knew.

## 27

THE FOLLOWING WEEKS back were a blur. Getting back into classes felt hard, like I was wading through mud. I just couldn't seem to focus. I needed to start planning my presentation for class—we had to submit an outline by the end of the week—and I still couldn't think of anything I was passionate enough about to present on. My work was piling up and every time I looked at my phone Izzie was calling, or texting, or emailing me. She wanted to go over every detail of the wedding, and I just couldn't. Every time she mentioned it, I was filled with dread.

Today, Izzie wanted to see pictures of my dress. Which I hadn't bought. Which I hadn't even thought about buying. Well, I had thought about it, if avoiding thinking about it counted as thinking about it. It needed to be blue, she said, but not royal blue because that's what the men were wearing. Women could do robin's egg, periwinkle, even get away with a hint of lavender. I thought it was stupid to have a dress code for a wedding. And not just because blue wasn't my color.

I was scouring the internet now, looking for something that didn't resemble a prom dress or give off Republican vibes. I knew

I could ask Vera to help, but I didn't want to risk another conversation about Izzie. Besides, Vera would pick out something fantastic that would probably terrify Izzie's southern relatives.

I found a dress I sort of liked, a green-blue slip dress with a low, swooping back. The color was technically seafoam green.

Green made me think of Wes.

If Wes wanted to have an all-green dress code at our wedding, I would be okay with that.

I wondered if Wes wanted to get married, if they even believed in it. As much as I understood that the institution was a hoax, and that queer people only got the right to marry like five minutes ago, I still wanted to get married. And I really wanted a wedding. The whole stupid thing, large cake and all. I didn't want it Izzie's way, but I did want it my way.

A ceremony by the beach, no shoes, a live band. Vows and speeches and everyone staying in one big house. A seafood buffet and a whole three days of activities leading up. No gendered invites, no awkwardness between guests, real connections made and late-night skinny-dipping. Hits from the 2000s at the end of the night and everyone in their pajamas for the last five songs. A wedding for all of us. A vow to community.

I sent the link to the dress to Izzie.

> Omigod I love it. Perfect for you. I'd
> say no to anyone else, because we
> both know that's more green than it is
> blue, but you're my person and I'll
> allow it.

I wondered what he would be wearing. If she had gone to his suit fitting. If his girlfriend was sharing links of her dress too. Maybe Izzie was saying some variation of what she was telling me,

"You're my sister now, obvi, you can wear whatever color you want." I wonder if he fucked her slowly, his girlfriend, if he asked if it felt good and could he do anything differently. And after the wedding, when they fell back into the bed in their hotel suite down the hall from Izzie's, would they drunkenly dream about their own wedding together? I hadn't responded to her DM. I left it unread.

I didn't text Izzie back. I slammed my laptop shut.

Instead, I called Nova.

She picked up on the third ring.

"Where are you?" she asked, her voice low and smug.

*Don't tell her. Don't do this.*

"My dorm."

"Same one as last year?"

"Yeah."

"I'll meet you out front in twenty."

"Okay."

An hour later, I was on my knees, my mouth pressing against Nova's pussy as my fingers dug into her thighs. She was petting my hair, groaning my name, saying she missed my tongue. I pulled back from her clit, cocooning two fingers inside her, as she pulled my hair from the nape of my neck so that my chin swung upward. I moved in and out of her while she stared at me, digging her thumb into my mouth as I furiously sucked on it.

"Let me make you come," she panted, trying to wrench me away from her pussy.

"Not yet," I replied, my voice steady, firm.

"Who are you?" she moaned as my fingers traveled farther inside her.

"Come for me," I whispered, and she did, throwing her body back flat on the bed and groaning into her pillow. I pulled out from inside her and wiped my hand on my thigh.

"Fuck me from behind," I said.

"Fuck yes." She launched herself from the bed, her body coming back to life. She pulled me on top of her and then rolled me over, dragging my hips back so I was on my hands and knees. I looked back at her.

"You have to look at me the whole time," I told her. "You can't take your eyes off of mine."

She nodded and felt for my clit with one hand, as the other started fucking me. My breath quickened, but neither of us spoke. I pushed her fingers away from my clit and replaced them with my own, my eyes never moving from hers. The waves rippled through me, climbing taller and taller, my orgasm a riptide clawing under the surface.

"Yes, baby," she said. "Keep touching yourself."

"Shut up," I said. "This is for me. Not for you."

She nodded.

"Say it," I demanded.

"This is for you, baby," she panted.

"All for me."

"All for you, Sav."

"For me, for me, for me!" I screamed as the riptide pulled me, as the wave crashed, as I came all over Nova's fingers. My body slumped onto the bed, and Nova fell beside me, breathing hard. We didn't talk for a while. I stared at the ceiling. Those same glowing stars.

"You good, Sav?" Nova asked me quietly, pushing her hair back from her face and propping up on one elbow, her body turned in toward mine. I didn't look at her.

Instead, I wept.

I lay on my back, naked, and let rivers swim down my temples and into my ears, my hair, onto the brown duvet. I cried with my mouth open, no sound.

Nova lay on her back too. She hummed. Something low, quiet. Something that felt like the pulse of the room, of our bodies, of my tears. We didn't touch, save for her pointer finger resting against my hand. My palms lay open by my sides.

Eventually, I stopped crying. It had either been five minutes or an hour.

I looked over at Nova.

"I missed you," she said.

"Me too," I replied, even though it didn't feel true anymore.

Later, we ate microwave ramen noodles on her floor and she painted her toenails black. We fell asleep watching *Planet Earth*, and in the morning she drove me home.

"I'll see you next weekend?"

"Yeah," I told her. "Definitely."

The guilt set in as soon as I got out of the car. A guilt I knew like the back of my hand. The same guilt I felt when I looked at Izzie three years ago when she woke me up the morning after that horrible party.

"Did you fuck my brother?" she had asked me, her voice sharp. One of her cheeks was indented with the pattern of the baby blanket she still curled up with to sleep.

"No," I lied, the word shooting out of my mouth.

"You didn't?"

I looked at her and shook my head.

"I would never," I said. "I would never do that to you."

•

AT THE END of GSS on Tuesday, Professor Tolino stopped me before I left class.

"Savannah?"

"Yes?"

"Come chat with me for a second."

*Oh no.*

I walked over to her desk.

"Should I, um?" I gestured to a chair.

"Yes! Of course!"

"Cool." I awkwardly ran over to the chair, scooting it over to where her desk was.

We both sat down.

"Hi," I said.

"Hello."

There was silence for a few seconds, and then Professor Tolino propped her elbows up on the desk and rested her chin on her palms.

"You've been quiet the past couple of classes."

I chewed on my lip.

"Oh," I said. "I guess?"

"Before break I noticed that you were feeling a bit bolder. I saw real growth from the beginning of the semester. A sureness in your voice, no?"

"Um, yeah."

"I must admit I was a little disappointed with your outline for your final project."

"I'm sorry," I responded, not knowing what else to say.

My outline sucked. She was right to be disappointed. The only thing I had come up with was a PowerPoint presentation on the wage gap.

"It's an important topic, but would you say you're really passionate about it?"

"I mean, not really."

"What's shifted with you, do you think?" She clasped her hands together on the desk.

I looked out the window. Really bitchy of Mother Earth to make a beautiful day when you feel like total shit.

"I'm having some issues with people at home. Where I grew up."

"Okay." Professor Tolino nodded. "I'm sorry to hear that."

"Thanks." My foot was restless. I kept kicking my heel into the metal leg of my chair.

"I think you have very important things to say, Savannah."

*Don't cry, don't cry, don't cry.*

"Thank you."

"You're welcome."

It got quiet again. I looked down at my lap.

"Doesn't this stuff get to you?" I asked.

She leaned her head to one side, inquisitive. "What do you mean?"

"I mean, when we talk about—" I took a deep breath. "Rape. When we talk about rape. It's a lot."

Professor Tolino nodded fast. "It certainly is. Is it hard for you?"

"Yeah," I said, the word flying from my lips. "I was raped. In high school."

*What the fuck am I doing?*

"I'm so sorry, Savannah." Her face softened.

"Thanks."

"Sometimes I think it doesn't count."

"I think a lot of us feel that way."

*Us.*

Why was I telling her all this?

"And I have to go to this wedding. And he'll be there."

Professor Tolino leaned back in her chair and whistled.

"Well, that fucking sucks, doesn't it?"

I had never heard her curse before. I kind of loved it.

"Yeah. I don't talk about it. Ever. Even though I know what it was. But I'm so fucking scared sometimes, that if I say it out loud, someone's going to tell me I'm wrong. Because it was someone close to me. Someone that I liked. Had feelings for. And we were drinking. And Lara said this, like, in one of our first classes, and it just haunts me. How some people drink, and do things, with people that they have feelings for. And they don't wake up and regret it or hate themselves and feel like they want to die. They think it's funny. I don't understand that."

"Hmm." Professor Tolino looked up at the ceiling for a moment. We sat in silence. Eventually, her eyes came back to me.

"The more I teach, the more I learn how different students, and all people, really, file information. What I mean to say is, we each have this file cabinet full of shit, but what I might file as important, another person might file as complete junk. Does that make any sense?"

"Yeah, it does."

"And you know," she said quietly, "sometimes people go back into the junk drawer, eventually. And sometimes they don't."

"Right."

"I don't want to minimize the things you're sifting through, Sav. But these things also have a place in this class, if you want them to. The nuances of your dilemmas do not only belong to you, do you understand?"

I nodded.

"All I mean to say is that you have a powerful voice. And it's apparent when it's absent."

"Thank you."

"You're very welcome."

I slid the chair back to its place and lifted my bag up over my shoulder. Professor Tolino had taken a stack of papers from her purse and was beginning to grade them. I made my way to the door.

"Oh, Savannah?"

"Yeah?" I looked back at her.

"Take a look at that wedding invite again. Maybe it could go in a different folder." She shrugged her shoulders.

"Maybe," I said.

"Have a good night."

"You too," I said, and headed toward the quad.

## 28

# Seventeen

"I STILL DON'T get how she forgave you."

Aiden was the kind of person who always was smiling no matter what he was talking about. He also had no eyebrows.

"What?" I asked, my hands sucking into fists under the tablecloth.

"What you did? With her brother?"

I glanced around to see if anyone was looking. We were at this kid Duncan's graduation party. He'd been a classmate since elementary school. It was sunny and I was wearing a new dress and it had been months since anyone had broached this topic with me. You had forgiven me almost a full year ago.

Aiden was supposed to be a nice boy. He was pale and freckly and wore light blue button-ups and got straight As. He was polite, he blushed a lot, and as far as I knew he hadn't had sex yet. He was the kind of boy I told myself I should try to like. Good, and nice, and smart. That's why I stupidly let my guard down when I sat next to him at the table.

Aiden was staring at me, waiting for my eyes to meet his again. He cracked his knuckles. I looked up. He was still smiling.

"That shit was unforgivable."

I could tell that he wanted me to agree, to hike up my dress and show him the scarlet letter between my legs. He wanted me to look sad and guilty and disgusted with myself, and then leave smug with his slut shaming. At home, he'd zoom in on my most recent bikini picture on Instagram and jack off thinking about my sins.

I blinked at him, still sort of stunned he of all people was capable of being so vicious.

"Do you really believe that?" I asked.

"Yeah," he said, the corner of his mouth twisting into a snarl.

I shrugged. "People have sex. It happens."

I got up before he could say anything else. I went to look for you to take me home.

I had started to like myself again when I got the acceptance letter from college. When I could see the way out of this hellhole. After you posted on Instagram, it took three months before the anonymous threats stopped. Another two months before people stopped whispering "hide your brothers" in the hallway. And it wasn't until the end of junior year that people started inviting me to parties again, and that only happened because you took me back in the spring.

"Savvy, I didn't think things would go so far," you explained, sitting across from me on your bed. I hadn't been over to your house since I slept with your brother again, the time I did it on purpose as though it could undo what happened before.

"I know," I said, and I meant it.

"I was really fucking mad at you. I still am kind of mad."

I nodded. "You don't have to forgive me."

"I don't think I can, like, fully. Like, I love you and I miss you so much, but you lied to me, you did the one thing I asked you not to do." You looked down at your lap.

"I know. I know I betrayed you."

"Yeah."

"It's okay if you don't want to be friends anymore." I bit my lip, trying not to cry. "I just wanted to see, one more time, if there was a chance to start over."

"I mean, I want to."

My eyes widened. "Really?"

"Yeah. Life sucks without you. This has been the worst school year ever. I feel like I have no one to talk to."

*At least people talk to you at all.*

Having the whole school turn on me gave you something you had never had before: true popularity. Everyone knew who you were, and everyone was on your side. You went to parties we'd never have been invited to before, ate at the lunch table with seniors, joined the prom committee, and left with the popular kids when they went out for lunch during a free period.

But I knew you were sad. I could see it in your posture; your shoulders were slumped forward. Your hair was a little dull, which meant you weren't washing it as much. When we'd pass each other in the hallway, silent and avoiding eye contact, I could feel that your heart was as broken as mine. We had been friends for so long, I could feel you like I could feel myself.

"Yeah. I mean, same. It's been awful."

"I just want my best friend back."

"Same, Iz. That's all I want."

And it was. I was willing to forget everything that had happened, *wanted* to forget everything that happened, as long as we could be together again. Surviving high school without your person was excruciating, and I would do anything to make things go back to normal.

And they did. Sort of.

You and I resumed being inseparable. Sleepovers on the

weekends, college apps, prom dresses, spring break, phone calls every night, double features at the movies. We never talked about your brother. It went without saying that I wouldn't come over to your house during the holidays, and if anyone brought it up in front of us at school, we'd change the subject or walk away. It was like nothing ever happened.

Except that I still thought about it all the time, thought about that night all the time, and every so often would struggle to re-mind myself why what I had done was so awful and bad. *You betrayed your best friend, Savannah. And, somehow, she forgave you. Just be grateful.*

I wish it clicked sooner for me that I didn't want to sleep with your brother the night of the barbecue. I wish I understood that even if I had wanted to sleep with him, that wouldn't have been bad either. The only bad thing I did was lie to a friend.

I was a child. I was just a little girl.

## 29

"THERE'S A GUY in my history class who says he knows you," Vera said, cranking up the volume on the car radio. Rihanna started blaring through the speakers.

"Who is it?" I asked.

"What?" she yelled, pointing at the radio and bopping her head to the beat.

"WHO IS IT?" I yelled back at her.

"HIS NAME IS MATT!"

*Oh fuck.*

I had managed to mostly forget about our tragic encounter over spring break. I hadn't seen him on campus, and I had skipped out on karaoke night twice just in case he and his sporty boy band went back for more beer.

I gave Vera a noncommittal shrug, hoping Rihanna's siren call would make her drop the subject. She shot me a look and turned the music down.

"How do you know him?" she asked.

"I don't, I don't think."

"Do not hold out on gossip, Savannah Henry."

"I'm not! I really don't think I know a Matt."

"Okay, well, he's got the most orange aura I have ever seen. Does that ring a bell?"

"Oh yes, it's all coming back to me now!" I pretended to smack my forehead. "How could I forget about his aura?!"

"Okay, fine. He's Pete Davidson tall with a Prince Harry complexion and says 'living the dream' every three to five sentences."

"Sounds annoying?" I said. She glared at me. I knew Vera well enough to know that she wasn't going to stop until I admitted I knew Matt.

"Oh wait!" I snapped my fingers. "I think I know who you're talking about. That Matt. I do know him. We worked together over the summer."

Vera nodded with satisfaction. "How was the sex?"

"Vera! What are you talking about?"

She rolled her eyes. "I don't know when you and Candace are going to realize that I am telesapphic. I can sense these things. So how was it?" There was no point trying to hide from her now.

"It was complicated."

"You did fuck him! I knew it!"

I slumped in my seat. "I did and it was a mistake."

"Oh no. Sav—did he hurt you? I'm so sorry, I didn't mean to—"

"No, no." I stopped her. "I actually think I probably hurt him. I left him, kind of, like, mid . . . moment." Vera's eyes widened.

"Okay, wait. Hold on. I'm gonna pull in here." Vera signaled left and drove into the parking lot of a CVS. She parked, undid her seat belt, and turned to face me. Resting her knee on the console, she leaned over and unbuckled my seat belt too.

"Okay. Rewind. Go back to the beginning."

I told her about coming back from break early. I explained that I had had a weird time at Izzie's bridal shower. How I just wanted to get back to campus and feel like myself again.

"But instead of just, like, waiting for you all to get back and hanging out at the dorm, I was an idiot and reached out to him." I sighed.

"Wait, wait. You're not an idiot. Going home is a fucking trip, feral sorority girl bridal shower or not. It's okay to want to do something to counteract that, even if it isn't the best thing."

I looked at her, saw such a softness on her face. I wondered what it would have been like if someone had comforted me like this when I was in high school. Took the stakes down. Talked it out with me.

"I just wanted something familiar. Or at least I thought I did. What I do know, however, is that I fully unplugged his dick from my vagina and ran out the door." Vera squealed with laughter. I let out a giggle.

"Okay, but can I ask why? What happened?"

"Uh, we, like, switched positions at one point and it didn't feel good. Like, right. It didn't feel right."

She nodded. "Been there. Yes, totally."

"I cringe even thinking about it now, V."

She reached out and grabbed my hand. "I get it. I do. I feel like people make it sound so easy to have these open-communication moments during sex where you take a break and breathe and reconnect or whatever, but it is so hard in the moment. Especially with a fucking stranger."

"Exactly."

"Look, when I go home I turn into the worst version of myself. My family doesn't know I'm polyamorous yet, because it took so long to get to a place where my queerness was even acknowledged. I start to, like, romanticize monogamy because my parents think marriage is this godly thing."

"I can't imagine you in a wedding dress," I admitted.

"If I ever get married, I'm wearing a full snakeskin bodysuit.

And doing a seance at the reception. Instead of the reception, actually."

"Oh, obviously." I laughed.

"You're still hung on up on this, yeah?" V poked my shoulder.

I chewed the inside of my cheek, thinking. "I'm just debating whether or not I should say something. Apologize."

"It's up to you. I don't know if you need to apologize for being triggered."

I tried to put myself in Matt's position. What would I do if someone hurricane-stormed out of the room mid-penetration? Guys had pulled way worse shit. But still.

"Vera," I whispered. "I don't think I respect men."

Vera burst out laughing.

"But I like them! I can even love them!"

"Yes. Also yes." She clapped, giddy. "We call that little epiphany a fluid-femme milestone. Welcome!" She grabbed my hands and smacked them together so I would join her. I feigned sobbing as I clapped.

"You're figuring it all out, Sav. You have to cut yourself some slack. Seriously. Hooking up with this guy is just intel. Even if it was cringey."

I nodded, trying my best to imagine a reality where I would ever figure anything out. Vera buckled her belt again and started to reverse out of the parking lot. Before turning onto the street that led back to campus, she looked over at me and slid her sunglasses halfway down her nose. "I have to be honest about one thing, though." Her voice was stern.

I winced. "What?"

"Downloading Snapchat for a cis guy might be the most biphobic thing you've ever done."

"Noooooooooo!" I screamed.

She cackled and reached for the radio knob, turned the volume all the way up, and sped out onto the road.

The next day, Candace wanted to go to a party. I didn't really want to go, but I was feeling guilty as fuck for not telling her about Nova. We were still talking. I mean, we were doing more than talking. I had never meant for things to go on with her for so long. I just wanted to have that one hookup after break, but I blinked and suddenly it was the end of April.

"How do you know these people again?" I asked Candace as we walked through a ground-floor apartment and toward a back patio.

"Roula was in my psych class last semester. This is her apartment. She's graduating early and going back to Lebanon, so this is a goodbye thing."

"Got it."

Candace hesitated before pushing open the sliding door that led outside.

"What's up?" she asked, looking at me for a prolonged second.

"What?"

"You seem off? I don't know, you seem like you're not home lately."

"I'm here!" I smiled wanly.

Candy nudged me with her shoulder. "You know you can tell me whatever, whenever, right?"

"I know!" I forced a lightness into my voice.

"You don't need to keep it all up here all the time," they said, tapping her forehead. "I know your brain is always moving a mile a minute, but I promise I can keep up." My throat felt tight, and I swallowed hard.

"Thank you. I know that. Really. But I'm good! Let's go get you a drink and find your new crush of the month," I teased.

Candace opened the door and spoke over her shoulder as we walked through. "You know, I actually think I'm looking for something a little less month to month."

"Nooooo!" I said, incredulous.

"It might be good to get out of the sublet game, maybe sign a lease. Could be nice."

"Could be really nice," I said, trying not to sound too excited.

"I can tell what you're doing. Don't get too attached, okay? Don't get ahead of yourself. We're talking short-term rental here."

I laughed. "Please don't use real estate metaphors when you flirt tonight, okay?"

"I don't know, Sav, I gotta brag about these utilities." She gestured to her body. I rolled my eyes.

"What about you? Should we find you a cutie as an early birthday present?"

*God, my fucking birthday.* I kept forgetting. It was this weekend. If I had my way, I'd be doing nothing. I had no birthday energy this year. But Vera, surprisingly, loved birthdays. She had convinced me to do a thing at Fir Bar, and then Candace got into the whole thing, so I ended up giving in. Maybe I would feel better by then. It could be fun.

"Neither. I'm good for tonight. Happy to be your wing-woman."

"Okay, suit yourself. I'll be right back, going to get drinks." Candace cocked her head over to where the bar was.

"Diet Coke, please?"

"You got it, gorgeous." She walked off toward the back of the patio.

I surveyed the yard. It was enclosed by a wooden fence and decorated with fairy lights. A bright warm glow cast through the space, making even cheap Solo cups shimmer as the last glimpses of the sun faded from the sky. There was a tall blond boy at the grill, arguing with a stocky lesbian wearing one of those aprons with a chiseled body on it, except hers was bright green and I think it was supposed to be a Teenage Mutant Ninja Turtle. They were gesturing wildly at the grill, but all I could make out from their argument was "this shit is gonna taste like lighter fluid" and "my eyebrow literally just singed off." The whole yard smelled like burgers now, which made me think of barbecues at Izzie's, which made me think of him. I felt my vagina clench, which only ever happened if he flashed through my mind in a moment I least expected.

"Fuck you for ruining burgers," I muttered.

"You want a burger?" Candace was back with a beer and a Diet Coke.

"Oh no, I'm okay. I don't really like them. I used to."

"You'll like them again once you taste mine. You don't want one from over there anyway." She pointed to the grill. "I saw a girl take a bite from her hot dog and spit it out. She said it tasted like straight-up gasoline."

"Yeah, no, I definitely don't want one."

Candace checked her phone. "Vera's coming. Are you gonna text Wes?"

I shook my head no. I couldn't be around Wes like this.

"They're probably busy."

"Busy is never as interesting as making out."

"True, but Wes most likely already has someone to make out with."

"Unless they don't."

"Have you seen anyone you could sign a lease with?" I changed the subject.

Candace rolled their eyes at me.

"I know you're evading, but I will allow it because I did see someone very cute."

I looked around the yard, trying to clock someone who was Candace's type. My eyes landed on a person behind the bar who looked vaguely familiar. A femme with a pixie cut and huge teeth, kind of like a cartoon.

"Bartender?" I asked.

"Damn, you're good! You remember her from karaoke? Her name's Gracie."

Oh shit, right. Karaoke night. She was the same bartender who made Candy get down from the table. The same night Candace found out about Nova. Nova, the whole reason Candace couldn't date anyone for more than a month. Nova, who had texted me three times since we had arrived at this party, telling me she was thinking of me sitting on her face.

*Fuck.*

"Sav?" Candace waved their hand in front of my face.

"What? Sorry. Got distracted for a second."

They gave me another suspicious look.

"I'm fine! You should go talk to her!"

"I already got drinks from her. I don't want her to think I can drink a beer that fast, even if I did win the record for longest keg stand in high school."

"That is the straightest thing you've ever told me."

"I could blow your hetero world, baby."

I looked back over at the bar. Gracie looked totally over-whelmed; people were swarming her. She could barely move fast enough. I nudged Candace, pointing toward the bar.

"She needs help, don't you think?"

"You're a genius. Take this." Candace handed me their beer and jogged over to the drink table. They dipped under the table and popped up on the other side, picking up a vodka bottle in one hand and a liter of Coke in the other. She started pouring drinks, pointing to folks on the perimeter of the crowd to get their order, and then, as the crowd got quieter, Candace glanced over at Gracie and winked. I shook my head and laughed. They were impossible not to love.

I glanced down at the leftover beer in my hand. It was still half-full. I had promised myself to cool it on the alcohol after Matt's, but it wasn't like I was gonna get drunk from half a beer. I took a sip and wrinkled my nose. Too sour, but I'd drink it anyway. I checked my phone again. Another text from Nova.

Let me pick you up from this party

Can't hang out. Here with friends

Your friends don't make you come like
I do

That much was true. I bit my lip. I looked back at the bar. The crowd had dissipated and now Candace and Gracie were just talking. I saw Candy take one of Gracie's hands and start to trace the lines on it. I rolled my eyes. I probably would not be seeing her for the rest of the night. I checked my phone again.

Do they???

No, they don't. Dropping a pin now

Be there in 7 minutes.

I would miss Vera, but she was notoriously late, and I probably would have gone home soon anyway, I reasoned with myself.

"Sav?"

"Yeah?" I turned around, half expecting it be Vera, but it

wasn't. It was Wes. Wes was alone, at a party where I was also alone, and I had to leave in four minutes. Gay god was not on my side tonight.

"Hi! How are you?" I tried to make my voice sound light, carefree.

"I'm good! How are you? How do you know Roula? How's your project coming?"

I opened my mouth and then closed it.

"That was too many questions, wasn't it?" Wes cracked their knuckles nervously.

"No, no, I got this." I took a breath for dramatic effect. "Okay, question one: I'm good! Question two: I don't know Roula, Candace does, and I came here with Candace, but I've lost her to a very pretty bartender. Question three: I haven't started, I'm totally avoiding it. How are you, how do you know Roula, how's your project going?"

Wes was impressed. "Better now, she lived on my floor freshman year, and I'm also totally avoiding it."

My phone started ringing. I furiously turned the volume down. Nova could wait.

"We should do work in the library together," I blurted.

"Definitely!" Wes nodded, but they looked a little distracted. *Dumb dumb dummy move.*

"I'm, uh, busy this week but maybe next week?" They shifted their feet nervously.

*Boulder to my soul, soul officially crushed.*

"Yeah! Sure! No worries!" My phone started ringing again. "I actually, um, have to go. I'll see you in class!" I pushed past them before they could respond and headed to the front door. I saw Nova parked right in front. She rolled down the window.

"Need a ride?"

I looked behind me to make sure no one was looking.

"I was gonna walk, but . . ."

Nova flipped me off and then opened the door to get out. My heart started racing.

"You don't have to get out! I'm coming now."

"Relax, I have to pee. Show me the bathroom?"

*Don't panic don't panic.*

"Hello?" Nova gestured to the front door.

"My dorm is so close! It's crowded in there. Can you just wait till we get to mine?"

"Sav, I don't want to go to your dorm." She said it like it was a dirty word. "We're going to my apartment. I'm just going to use the bathroom here. Come on."

I nodded. We started walking to the door. It was going to be fine. The bathroom was nowhere near the backyard, and unless Wes and Candace both had to pee, no one was going to see us. When we got inside, I grabbed Nova's hand and gunned for the bathroom. I locked us both inside.

"Can't even wait till we get home, baby?" Nova snuck her hands around me and leaned in to kiss me. I pushed against her shoulders to pull her face away from mine.

"No, *baby*, I just want to wash my hands before I fuck you."

Nova narrowed her eyes at me.

"Since when do you fuck me?"

"Since classifying ourselves as strictly tops or bottoms is about as useful as the gender binary. Go pee." I marched her over to the toilet. She acquiesced and sat down. I checked the lock again.

"It's locked already. What's up with you? Are you stressed?"

"I'm fine," I snapped back. "Just want to leave."

I looked in the mirror. I was pale. I rubbed at my cheeks.

"You're perfect." Nova zipped up her pants and sidled over to me again. She leaned against me from behind and bent me over so she could wash her hands. I looked at our reflection. Nova wiped her hands on her jeans and then pulled my ass into her as I steadied myself on the sink with my hands.

"We have to go," I said to her in the mirror. She yanked my hair a little, smirking.

"Then, let's go," she whispered.

I opened the door and collided with a sheath of blue hair. It was Vera.

*Okay, officially panicking now.*

"Sav!" She pulled me in for a hug. "I thought maybe you left!"

"I did! Um, I mean, I am. I'm leaving now." Vera glanced behind me and a look of recognition clicked onto her face.

"Oh, okay. Well, I'll see you tomorrow, then?"

I nodded fast. "Yeah, definitely! Have fun!" I grabbed for Nova's hand behind me and started yanking her into the hallway. The door was in my line of sight.

Three, two, one.

We were outside.

*Thank god.*

"Sav?"

*Nopleasenopleaseno.*

Candace was also outside.

"Hi, um, I'm gonna leave now." My words came out in a squeak.

Candace started moving toward me, squinting. It was totally dark now and I could tell she hadn't seen whom I was with.

"Okay, dude, I'll see you at home. You okay?"

"I'm fine." My voice was small.

Candace reached me, approaching the light of the streetlamp. Her eyes moved beyond my face and landed where I knew Nova was standing. She dropped the cigarette in her hand.

"What is she doing here?" She searched my face for answers.

"I came to pick her up," Nova called out from behind me.

Candace's eyes flashed with anger.

"I wasn't fucking talking to you."

"Candace," I whispered. She looked back at me.

"You're seeing her now?"

"No, not really, we're just. I don't know. Hanging out. It's nothing."

"It's nothing?" Nova was standing next to me now.

I shot her a look. "Please get in the car. I'll be right there." She looked like she was going to argue with me. I pleaded with her with my eyes. She sighed and unlocked the car.

Candace was standing with their arms crossed. I'd never seen her look so angry.

"I can explain. She reached out over break and I saw her. I don't even know why, I'm just in a really weird moment right now—"

Candace held up her hands, stopping me.

"You've been seeing her since *break*?"

*Shit.*

"I mean, barely, but yeah. I'm sorry, I should have—"

"You know what, Sav? You're sneaky. I've been asking you for weeks what's up and it's this? I thought something was seriously wrong. I've been fucking worried. And it ends up being that you're fucking Nova behind my back?"

"I'm not—that's not—"

"Save it. I can't talk to you right now." Candace stepped on her burning cigarette with her boot and walked away.

This wasn't happening, was it? I had never imagined that Candace and I would have anything to fight about. God, how fucking stupid was I? She was right. I was a sneaky fucking bitch. Just like I was with Izzie. I was lying to myself. I hadn't changed at all.

A car horn beeped behind me and I jumped. I whirled around and saw Nova hanging out the window.

"Are you coming?" She pulled up to where I was standing on the sidewalk.

I blinked back tears and circled the car, getting into the passenger seat. Wordlessly, we started driving. At the end of the block, Nova's foot slammed the brakes. Two people were crossing the street in the dark. Nova shone her headlights on them, and I noticed the pink bowl cut first. Every part of my body froze.

It was the person from the Polaroid. Holding hands with Wes. The two ran across the street, laughing.

*Proof.*

As if this night could get any worse.

Nova sighed and put her foot back on the gas.

"Wait. I need you to take me home." My voice was firm.

She stopped the car again and looked over at me. "Uh, why? I thought you were coming over."

"I can't. We shouldn't be doing this. I just need to get back to the dorms."

"Why, because of Candace? She's got to get over this Nat thing. We're not even together anymore."

My face felt hot and anger gripped at my chest.

"That doesn't matter. Nat broke her heart and you broke mine. I can't see you anymore, okay? It isn't fair to her and it isn't fair to me."

Nova leaned her head back on her seat and sighed.

"You texted me, Sav."

"Yeah, I did." I nodded. "And I shouldn't have. I was drunk and it was stupid. But you know what? You did a lot of things you didn't mean to when we met."

"What, so this is revenge?"

"No." I sighed. "It's not."

"Then what is it?" she asked, grit in her voice.

"A mistake. Take me home."

"Fine." She drove.

We spent the ride in silence. I stared out the window, away from Nova, and tried not to think about the way Candace's face fell when she saw us together. I couldn't lose Candace. I couldn't lose one of the only people in my life who made me feel entirely safe. When we pulled up to campus, I had Nova drop me off by the quad. I could walk the rest of the way to my dorm. I paused before opening the door.

"I'm sorry for reaching out when I shouldn't have. That wasn't my best move."

Her eyes softened a little. "Yeah, thanks."

I leaned in and kissed her on the cheek, and then got out of the car. As she pulled away, I heard Fletcher blare from her speakers. I walked onto the quad and felt the grass compress under my feet. I leaned down and untied my shoes, slipping them off and then my socks. I pressed my toes into the earth and closed my eyes, breathing deeply.

*What is my fucking life right now?*

And then I heard someone crying. I opened my eyes and searched for where the sound was coming from. In the distance, I could see someone leaning against a tree. I picked up my shoes and started walking. As I got closer, I could make out long blond hair. It reminded me of Izzie's.

Wait, I knew someone else with hair like Izzie's. But—no—she wouldn't be—

The blond crying person turned around and I could just make out their face. *Lara.*

A very messy, drunken, crying Lara, but Lara all the same. Her lipstick was smudged and her eyeliner was running. She had a beer in her hand that was on the verge of tipping over.

"Lara?" I tentatively approached her.

"Oh my god, *Savannah*!" Lara threw her arms around me. She smelled like cigarettes and Jell-O shots.

"Hey!" She had gone slightly limp in our embrace. I tried to steady her without pushing.

"How's your night going?" I asked.

She was slugging back her beer, some of it dribbling out of the bottle and onto her chin.

"It's soooo good. Do you want some?" She basically shoved the drink into my hand.

"Sure, thank you." I pretended to take a sip and very much did not hand it back to her.

"Actually, like, my night fucking suuuuucks." I had never heard her curse before.

Lara slumped against the tree and let her head droop low.

"What happened?"

"I can't tell you, definitely not you."

"Why not me?"

"Because you don't like me." She pouted her lips.

Well, I didn't want to lie to her. She was right, for the most part.

"I think we're really different, that's all."

"Well, that's a fancy way of saying that you, you don't . . ." She swallowed the last few words of what she was about to say because her phone started ringing. She reached into her bag, the same one from that day at Owen's, and I could see the contact calling her had a million pink emoji hearts next to the name. Lara tried to swipe the phone open but couldn't seem to do it.

"Um, here, let me." I awkwardly reached out my pointer finger and swiped her phone open for her. The person calling was named Ryan.

"Where are you?" A stern, low voice came through the phone. I didn't know if Lara realized she had put him on speaker.

"Fuck you," Lara slurred into the phone.

"Lara, where are you? You can't just dip from a party like that."

"I'm not telling you. You're an . . . asshole. Asshole."

"It's not gonna look good if you're crying in the middle of campus again. You made me look like an idiot last time."

Lara spoke into the phone very quietly, mumbling the words. I barely could make out what she was saying.

"Well, maybe you shouldn't hit me."

Fuck. This couldn't be her boyfriend. Was Ryan the promise ring? The fancy date night?

"You're being dramatic, I didn't—"

"You did! You know you did! You're, like, you're, like, gaslighting me!" She was basically shouting into her phone now.

"Here we go with that again. You are overreacting."

I was seething. I couldn't listen to this idiot any longer.

"No, she's not." I grabbed Lara's phone from her.

"Who is that? Lara? Where are you?"

"She's safe. Leave her alone."

I clicked the phone off and slid it into my pocket. Lara had her arms crossed over her body and was sniffling a little, stumbling even while standing still. I couldn't leave her here.

"Come on, my dorm's close." I reached for her hand.

"He's, he sounds bad, but he . . ." She trailed off again.

"Hey, we don't need to talk about that right now. Let's just go inside."

Lara looked around as if she had just realized we were standing in the middle of the quad at two in the morning. She turned back to me and stared at my hand for a moment, before reaching out to grab it. Fifteen minutes later, Lara Wentworth was sitting on my futon, wearing a sweatshirt I had from summer camp and a pair of my fuzzy socks. Candace was not going to believe this.

"Do you want a snack?"

Lara looked up, eyes wide.

"Do you have any string cheese?"

Ope. Okay.

"Uh, weirdly, I do."

She clapped her hands, genuinely thrilled by my response. I opened the mini-fridge, grabbed four pieces of string cheese, and handed her two, keeping the rest for myself. I handed her my water bottle too. She swallowed a big gulp. I sat down on the floor across from her, my back against the wall. I learned once that if you wanted to make someone feel safe, you should position yourself closer to the ground than them. I watched her peel apart her string cheese and tried to think of what to say.

"How come you and Wesley aren't dating yet?" she asked, ripping off a chunk of cheese.

My mouth dropped open.

"What? I mean, we're not. It's not like that between us. What?"

She scoffed and waggled her string cheese at me.

"They, like, love you."

"I don't know about that; we don't really know each other outside of—"

"You love them too. It's, like, very obvious. In class. You both stare at each other when the other person isn't looking." A cheese string was hanging out of her mouth.

"Oh." I didn't know what else to say, and I couldn't wipe the stupid grin off my face.

"They're cute." She said this as if it was a math equation she had just solved.

"Yes, they are." I narrowed my eyes at her.

"Does that mean I'm gay? If I think that?"

Oh boy.

"Maybe now is not the time to contemplate your sexuality?"

Lara shrugged in agreement.

"Do you want more cheese?"

Lara jumped up, staring at the wrappers already in her hand, as if they had just appeared.

"I'm dairy-free!"

She looked like I had caught her in a terrible lie.

"Uh . . . not . . . anymore?"

Lara stood still for a moment, and then burst out laughing. I couldn't help but laugh with her. *What the fuck is happening?*

"NOT ANYMORE!!" she screamed at the ceiling, and then promptly sat back down on the futon.

"Lara?"

"Ya?" She cocked her head to the side and looked at me, the same way she did when Professor Tolino called on her in class.

"What happened tonight?"

She blew air out of her mouth and leaned back against the wall, pulling one of my little pillows into her lap.

"We fight."

I nodded. "A lot?"

"No. I mean, like, the normal? I don't know. My parents fight, I guess, so I thought . . . I don't know." She was fiddling with a loose thread on the cushion.

"I followed him here. We met in high school," she said eventually.

"You must really care about him."

She nodded, her head a little wobbly. "He's the best. And his family, they're, like, so great. And we want the same things. We love bulldogs. Oh my god, can I show you this bulldog Instagram I follow?" She started to dig around for her phone. I had forgotten that I still had it.

"Here." I scooted across the rug and handed it to her. She

looked confused at first, like she didn't know how I had gotten hold of her phone, and then recognition washed over her face. She took the phone limply in her hand, staring down at it.

"He's just different when he drinks."

"Yeah."

"He says it just makes him, like, really want me."

I cringed, but I tried to hide it.

"Do you feel that way too?"

"What, like do I want my boyfriend? Of course, why would I be dating—" Her voice was on edge now.

"Sorry, no, that's not what I meant. I mean, like, when you're drunk together, do you feel the same way?"

"No," she said it so fast that it almost shocked me. I think it shocked her too.

"Oh."

"But we love each other." She looked at me as if she was asking a question.

"Of course."

"He gave me this the day he graduated high school." She dangled her hand in front of me. There it was, that fucking ring.

"It's really pretty."

Tears started to well up in her eyes. I looked away, trying to give her space. A thousand thoughts were running through my head.

"You know you can love someone and still feel uncomfortable with things they do?"

She bit her lip. I knew she was trying to keep from sobbing. She nodded.

"I'm really sorry, Lara," I whispered.

Her phone rang again, this time it was one of her sorority sisters looking for her. I helped text her my dorm info, and Lara's friend showed up shortly after to bring her home. When I helped her up to leave, Lara hugged me. The embrace was real, not at all a formality, her head nestling into my shoulder as she sighed out a long breath. When she pulled away, she reached for my hand and pressed her crumpled-up string cheese wrappers into it, like they were a gift.

·

THAT NIGHT I had dreams about a snow day. I was dressed in snow pants and snow boots and wore a bulky coat. My ears and hair were tucked into a fleece hat and I had enormous red mittens on. I was trudging the mile from my house to Izzie's, pressing my feet into fresh powder, snow falling directly onto my eyelashes. I talked out loud to myself. "We'll have hot chocolate and go sledding and watch *Legally Blonde* again, and then we can make soup, and hopefully by then school will call again and tell us that there'll be another snow day tomorrow, and we can have a sleepover, and do it all over again the next day."

I was talking to Izzie, but Izzie wasn't there. I was walking to her house. I was preparing the plan before I got to her house. We needed a snow day plan. I was winded and I could feel sweat gathering under my armpits. My fingers were freezing but that made no sense since I had the red mittens on. I looked down at my hand and one mitten was gone. I whirled around and looked for it in the snow. I thought it would be easy to see a bright red mitten in the middle of the fresh white snow. But it wasn't there. And my hand was getting really cold. And then Izzie was there, standing ten feet away or so, even though she was supposed to be waiting for me at her house.

"Help me find my mitten, Iz!" I called out.

Izzie just stood there, unmoving.

"I can't find it! It's bright red. Help me find it!"

She didn't move.

"Izzie, what are you doing? Can you hear me?" I cupped my hands against my mouth and called out to her again.

She started walking toward me, her face unmoving, and in the way that only dreams can do, she went from walking toward me to standing inches from my face.

"I know what you did," she said.

Now we were in the foyer of my parents' home. I was standing in my pajamas and Izzie was there too, just outside the front door, holding a large box with every single thing of mine that I kept at her house. And she was crying. She was furious. She looked over at my parents, who were very confused, and her voice came out steely and low.

"Your daughter? Your perfect little girl? She's actually a slut who slept with her best friend's brother."

And now my mother is looking at me and my father is looking away.

And then I am in the blue room. It is the middle of the night. It is hot and two people are on the bed, Izzie's old bed, and one person is on top of the other. It is a man and a girl. The man is naked and the girl is almost naked, and her eyes are closed, and one of her hands is splayed out, limp, near the pillow. The man is grunting and moving his body very fast and the girl opens her eyes. She gasps and jolts upward.

"Where is the condom?" she demands.

"We already used one," he says, still inside her.

"What are you talking about?" She is full of panic.

"I already came," he says, as if it all should make sense now. Them on the bed, her almost naked, him panting on top of her, and no condom on his penis.

And then Izzie is beside me, and she is watching it all. "See?" I say. "I never wanted to. I never wanted this."

I wake up with one hand trapped underneath my chest. I fling it free and pins and needles explode inside it.

"Fuck."

I sit up and try and hang the arm down off the bed, using my other hand to push the blood down into my fingers. I know it will wear off in minutes, and that I'll close my eyes and go back to sleep, but in this moment it feels like my hand will be buzzing in stiff discomfort forever, and I cannot imagine it ever going back to normal.

## 30

I WENT TO Student Health to see Marie. If she was surprised to see me, she didn't let on.

"Savannah, it's so lovely to see you." Her voice was warm. The little crinkles that formed around her eyes when she smiled had become more defined, and seeing them flooded me with comfort. I had missed my sessions with her.

"I'm sorry I didn't come back when I said I would." My knee began to bob up and down, fast. "I think I've been avoiding you," I admitted.

Marie looked delighted. "Do tell."

"Oh god. I don't even know where to start. First, I'm bisexual now. Well, I always have been, but I'm out now. I don't need to process that. Well, I do, I think we all do. Bisexuals, I mean, not you—well, I don't want to assume your sexuality, sorry." I was practically panting now. "Wow, okay, I'm out of practice. Hold on." I kicked off my shoes, gulped from my water bottle, and took a breath. Marie sat patiently, hands clasped in her lap.

"Okay," I said, collecting myself. "I think I might have ruined my relationship with my friend Candace. And I really don't want that to be true."

"Why don't you catch me up a little?" Marie asked.

I told Marie about Nova, about Nat, about meeting Candace right when I was at my most heartbroken. I told her about texting with Nova again after spring break, her picking me up from the party, running into Candy outside.

"And I don't know what to say to her. Because I did something I said I wouldn't."

"Why?" Marie asked.

"Why what?"

"Why did you see Nova again after you said you wouldn't? What changed?"

I thought about it. Traced my mind back to the last time I felt good, normal. Being in the dining hall with V and Candace, before break. And then an onslaught of mess and chaos. The shower, the girlfriend with the snake tattoo, the diner with Izzie. The night with Matt. The wedding just months away.

"I don't know. I feel kind of, like, separate from myself right now. Like I lost myself, if that makes sense."

Marie nodded. "It does, sure. Does Candace know that? That you feel so lost?"

I bit my lip. "No." I shook my head. "No one does."

Marie's eyebrows rose slightly.

"Do you think they might feel differently about your relationship with Nova if they knew how you felt?"

"Maybe. But my friends don't know—I mean my school friends—they, um, they don't know about everything that happened"—I gestured aimlessly—"in high school."

"Is that important to share?" Marie asked. "Is it part of that lost feeling?"

"I think so, yes." I hesitated. "My friend from growing up, Izzie? She's getting married."

"Oh?"

I looked down at my lap. There was a faint tan line where my denim shorts met my thigh. "Her brother will be there. And I'm going." I looked up at Marie, expecting disdain, horror. But her face remained neutral.

"That sounds complicated."

Without thinking, I laughed. I couldn't help it. "That's a very good way to put it."

"That's a lot to hold alone, Sav. But it sounds to me, after what you've told me about your friends, there's a world in which you might not have to."

That night I sat on my bed for a while, willing myself to get up and put on real clothes, willing myself to do anything at all but sit around and feel bad for myself. When we were younger and I'd get like this, Izzie would roll her eyes and drag me out the door. To get food, to go shopping, to do whatever. Sometimes it made me feel better. Most of the time, it just helped me pretend I felt better. *Just like you do now*, I thought. *Pretend*.

I got a text from Vera asking me if I wanted her to come over and help me pick out an outfit for the party tomorrow. I didn't respond. I knew it wasn't a pity ask, but it still felt like one. Candace and I hadn't talked in three days. I had called her a few times, but she didn't pick up. It felt cheap to text her, so I didn't. I kept thinking about what Marie had said, but it felt impossible to consider Candace holding me when I couldn't even get ahold of them. In class on Monday Professor Tolino kept using the word "strapped" to describe underserved communities and Candace didn't crack a smile once, no matter how many times I tried to catch her eye. In our group text, she had only like-reacted to all the details for tomorrow. She didn't send even a single cowboy emoji. I stared at the ceiling. Birthdays were overrated.

Vera texted me again.

> I tried to warn you!!!!

I sat up.

> What????

There was a knock on my door. Confused, I got up to open it, praying it was Candace ready to talk things out.

"SURPRISE, BITCH!"

*You've got to be kidding.*

Izzie was standing in the hallway of my dorm with a giant purple teddy bear in her arms and a paisley weekender bag slung over one shoulder. And behind her, Vera cowered guiltily.

"Izzie—what are you—?"

"I wanted to be with you for your birthday, silly! Your best friend only turns twenty once, right?"

Vera half-heartedly nodded and gave a limp thumbs-up.

"Well, I actually have to leave *on* your birthday; I have a mandatory chapter meeting that afternoon. But I'm here for the party tomorrow!!!"

"Oh, okay . . ." I was dumbfounded.

"Let me through, bitch." She stuffed the teddy into my chest and pushed past me, swinging her bag onto my bed and then taking piles of clothes out of it. How fucking long did she think she was staying?

"Psst." Vera was poking my shoulder. I turned back to the hallway.

"I'm so sorry," she whispered.

"How did this even happen?"

"Vera was such a doll picking me up from the airport," Izzie called out. "I remember you saying V had a car. So I totally slid into her DMs. Our little covert op was such a success!"

I whirled around to face Vera again, my entire face one big question mark.

"I'm so sorry, Sav, she was so convincing. I thought since you've been having such a um, hard, I don't know, I was totally off here—" Vera looked pale. Well, paler than usual. I could tell she was genuinely sorry. I knew how Izzie was when she had a plan.

"Hey," I reached out and squeezed her hand. "It's okay. Thank you, V. This is really great."

Before she could respond, Izzie seat belted her arms around me.

"I'm so happy to be here. I'm going to make this your best birthday ever, Sav. Even better than Cancún." She squeezed my boob.

I slowly un-velcroed her hands from my skin.

I stared at Vera, willing myself not to break right then and there.

"Nothing could ever beat Cancún." I sounded like a robot.

Cancún was horrible, actually. I got sun poisoning the first day and spent the next two days, including my birthday, in a feverish stupor. Izzie had a great time, though.

I took a breath. "This is awesome, Iz. Are you hungry? Should we—"

"Oh my god, I'm legitimately starving! Let me just change!"

Before she even finished speaking, Izzie had half her clothes off.

"Iz," I hissed, "the door is still open."

Izzie glanced over at the door.

"Then close it? Vera, come in."

"You can't take your clothes off in front of someone without asking if it's okay."

Izzie snorted. "We're all girls here, Savvy. Right, Vera?"

"I'm honored that you feel so comfortable with me."

"See?" Izzie was smug. And very naked.

"Oh, obviously. We totally bonded in the car. Besides, Savannah, since when are you such a prude?"

"I'm not—I just. People need to feel comfortable and—"

"Okay, I'm ready!" Izzie had pulled on a green sundress and slipped her sandals back on. "Isn't this so cute?"

I nodded, officially in full robot mode.

"Do I need a jacket?" Izzie asked.

"The dining hall is close by."

"Oh boo! Let's go somewhere where we can drink. Hello, it's your birthday weekend!"

"Sav doesn't really drink." Vera was looking at me questioningly.

Izzie laughed.

"Sav was the one who pressured *me* to drink when we were, like, twelve. You're coming, right, V? I'll pay for the Ubers." Izzie whipped her phone out of her pocket and handed it to me. I looked at Vera, who shrugged.

"You don't have to come with us," I whispered as Izzie bounded ahead of us down the hall.

Vera shrugged. "Honestly, this girl's kind of a trip. And besides, she's your person from home. I want to know her."

Fuck. That was so nice. And so not what I wanted her to say. A wave of nausea hit me. When Izzie was just an idea, a photo on my computer, I could make her make sense. Make us make sense. But with 3D Izzie here, I couldn't control the story. I had no idea what she was going to say, or when she was going to say it. Izzie was a fucking ticking time bomb.

"You're the best, V."

When the elevator doors opened downstairs, my body collided with Candace's.

*Fuck me.*

"Uh, hey." She looked confused.

"Oh my god, the infamous Candy!" Izzie wrapped Candace in what appeared to be a death-trap hug.

"You must be Izzie," came Candace's muffled voice from inside Izzie's shoulder.

Izzie pulled back and giggled. "That's me!"

Any signs of confusion had wiped off Candace's face, and now they were back to ever-cool and confident Candy.

"Welcome to our humble, gay, and very problematic American institution! Don't mind the socialists; they're loud but harmless."

"I knew I would love you. We're going to dinner and birthday drinks for Savvy. She said you were studying, and *I said* you needed a break, and *I* was obviously right."

Candace's eyes briefly landed on mine, but they didn't miss a beat.

"I really should get back to studying. Big test tomorrow."

*Just shut me inside of an industrial freezer now.*

"No, no, I simply won't allow it! And look, Uber's here. No arguments." Izzie grabbed Candace's hand and opened the door for her.

"I guess I'll just fail, then," she said, scooting into the far side of the car.

In the car, Izzie asked the driver to turn up the music and then proceeded to yell over it and barrage Vera with questions about her boyfriends.

"I prefer to call them my partners!" Vera shouted.

"Totally! I use that with my fiancé all the time. My fiancé loves it too. Language is so important." Izzie grinned at me, and I squirmed in my seat. I didn't like it when she played the part of amazing ally. I didn't like thinking about the way she talked about my queerness when I wasn't around. Her *gay* best friend. My *best friend* is *gay*.

When we got to Farmhouse, I was relieved that no one else I knew was there. I don't know what I would have done if Wesley had been sitting in the corner booth. Well, that wasn't true. I would have told Izzie that I saw a dog trapped in a car in the parking lot. She volunteered at an animal shelter every Monday afternoon every year of high school.

Thankfully, Wes was nowhere in sight, and the restaurant was pretty empty for a Thursday night.

"There's nobody here," I mumbled to myself.

"Raymond Lafaro is on campus tonight doing stand-up."

"Oh my god, what time? My fiancé loves him!" Izzie squealed.

"Who is Raymond Lafaro?" I asked.

"He's a rampant misogynist" / "He's so hilarious!" Vera and Izzie said at the same time.

"Oh well, agree to disagree, I guess!" Izzie didn't even flinch and turned to chat with the hostess, pointing to a table toward the back that she liked.

"He hosts this podcast. Basically, straight couples call in and complain about their sex life, and he makes fun of them and gives shitty advice that usually ends in 'Sorry, *ladies, it's just what makes a man happy!*'"

"Fuck, that sounds awful. Wait, so why are so many people on our campus there?"

"H-Club is holding a protest. A lot of people went," V explained.

H-Club stood for Heathens Club. It was started in the sixties by a bunch of feminists who had been called heathens by the administration for rejecting patriarchal norms and spending a lot of time naked on the quad together. Eventually, it evolved into a community organizing effort. They held protests every couple of weeks, everything from sleeping in the library for fifteen days until *Huckleberry Finn* was removed from the shelves to demanding we no longer outsource eggs in the dining hall and instead have our own chicken coop on campus. The eggs had actually been tasting a lot better, but I wasn't sure if that was just the placebo effect of ethical eating.

"How haven't I heard about this?" I asked, dumbfounded.

"Their Instagram got shadow-banned this week because they're doing a sex ed series, and I guess the algorithm can't handle cock rings. But they've been canvassing at Owen's for the last week." Vera tapped on H-Club's story, which showed them camped out at Owen's earlier in the day, handing out fliers.

"Oh yeah, I haven't really been going." I looked down awkwardly. Owen's was Candace's main study spot.

"Did I hear someone say cock rings? I love cock rings!" Izzie was back from the hostess stand.

"Our table awaits," she sang, lacing her fingers in mine and pulling me toward the back of the restaurant.

Dinner was fine. Which was surprising. I kept waiting for Izzie to say something horrific, but she mostly just talked about the wedding and told us about her wedding cake baker from hell, who tried to convince her that anything but vanilla cake would signal to the guests that she was a whore.

"But you hate vanilla!"

"I know! She said vanilla is virginal. Chocolate at your wedding is sinful." Izzie rolled her eyes.

"That's the South for you," Candace said dryly.

"Are you from the South?" Izzie asked.

"No, but my mom is. Tennessee. Not the cool part."

"I went to Tennessee once," Vera chimed in. "For a debate tournament. It felt very, how do you say . . . homophobic?"

"Ding-ding-ding," Candace said, pointing her thumb at Vera.

"Does your mom know you're gay?" Izzie asked.

"Oh, she knows. Sleepovers every weekend senior year may have tipped her off," Candace said.

"Is she supportive?" Izzie spoke through a mouthful of spinach.

"Nope. She says she loves me but doesn't agree with my lifestyle."

"That sucks. I'm really sorry." Izzie's voice was quiet. Sincere.

Vera pointed her fork at Candace. "My dad sent me to live with my grandmother in Korea for a year because he saw lesbian porn on my computer."

My eyes widened. "Oh my god, were you okay?"

Vera shooed me with her hand. "Don't worry, it was great. I mean, my relationship with my dad sucks. But my grandmother doesn't give a shit. I went to an all-girls international school. I was in heaven."

Izzie laughed and ate another forkful of her salad. "Well, my mom told me she would disown me if I ever came out as a lesbian, so. This dressing is really good."

Candace glanced over at me quickly, then back to Izzie.

"Oof. Must be tough for Sav."

Izzie looked up from her salad bowl.

"Oh, um, well, I haven't really—" Izzie looked over at me desperately.

"Oh, yeah, she doesn't know. Should we get dessert or—"

"Yeah, she doesn't know until she, like, needs to know. You know?" Izzie was smiling again.

"No, I don't know?" Candace's lips were pursed.

"I could have dessert!" Vera scrambled for a menu.

Izzie leaned in as if she had some hot goss to share.

"It's just like, well, Sav's *bi*, you know? So if she marries a girl, then we'd obviously tell her. But if she . . ." Her voice trailed off.

"Alex, can I get 'Biphobia' for one thousand?"

"Wait, ha ha, what? I'm not—" Izzie's smile was waning.

"Drop it, Candy," my voice was sharp.

"Oh, come on, it was right there!" Candace gave me a look.

"Let it go."

I could tell she was about to say something, but she took a breath instead.

"Right. The cheesecake is good here."

·

ONCE WE WERE back at my dorm, I knew I needed to escape, even if it was just for twenty minutes.

"Shoot, Iz, I forgot to print an assignment that I need for tomorrow. I have to run to the library."

"Don't you have a printer right there?" she asked, pointing to my desk, where the ancient HP contraption I had stolen from my dad had grown dusty.

"It stopped working like five months ago." I was grateful I didn't have to lie.

"Gotcha. Okay, I'm going to shower, and then we can do pj's and watch a movie?"

"Definitely." The thought of sleeping in bed together filled me with dread. I knew I wouldn't be able to sleep.

"Be back soon."

Izzie waved me away as she plucked a towel from my closet and fished around in my shower caddy. Of course she didn't bring any of her own toiletries. I held in a sigh.

I took the stairs out of the building, too overwhelmed to wait for the elevator. When I finally got out to the quad, I was relieved to find that the weather had cooled and there was a breeze in the air. I took a deep breath and closed my eyes. It was so quiet. And I really needed quiet. Thank god for Raymond Lafaro, I guess.

My phone buzzed in my pocket. It was Vera.

> I'm sorry again, I really should have told you. But I had a good time!! Hope you're feeling better. I know this isn't the birthday weekend you wanted, but I think the party will be really fun.

I stopped on the sidewalk for a second, trying to think of what to say.

> It's really okay. Normal people would love nothing more than to be surprised by their friend for their birthday. I need to work on being normal, lol. Tomorrow will be really good. Love you

I stuffed my phone back in my sweatshirt and rounded the corner that took me the long way to the library, which was an absolute mistake, because it passed the auditorium. Just as the show got out. Along the perimeter of the building there was a horde of H-Club members and other protesters, holding massive signs and chanting.

*Hey hey, ho ho*
*Toxic assholes have got to go!*

The words rang out in the night air, and now the path to the library was blocked by very angry bodies.

"Fuck."

"Savannah!" I squinted; someone in the crowd was waving to me. My heart did a little cartwheel. It was Wes. I yanked my hair out of its massive top knot, praying their eyesight was as bad as mine.

They were waving about as hard as a human could wave, but it didn't look like a "come here!" wave, just a lateral wave. The classic kind. I waved back, frozen in my spot on the grass. I really didn't know where to go from here, and I did not want to approach H-Club in their agitated state. Even if Wesley was waving at me.

I saw them lean in toward the ear of a very petite, angelic-looking person who was holding a sign bigger than their own body and wearing bright pink sneakers. I groaned under my breath. Pink Bowl Cut. They nodded eagerly and seemed to shoo Wesley away. Where were they being shooed toward? They started running. Very fast. Backpack bucking against their shoulders. Toward me.

Wesley was out of breath by the time they got to me. I guess I could have met them halfway, but the thought of them seeing me run gave me pre-embarrassment. Also, I didn't want to give them the impression that we were having a cinematic, mega-romantic run-toward-each-other-in-a-field kind of moment. Because I was pretty sure it was just a running-toward-a-friend-in-a-field kind of moment.

"Hi!" they panted.

"Hey!"

"I didn't see you inside. Where were you camped out?"

"Oh, I wasn't here at all. I actually didn't know about the protest. A friend surprised me from out of town."

"That's amazing!" They took a big gulp from their Hydro Flask.

"For my birthday," I blurted.

Wes choked on their water.

"Oh my god, sorry, I didn't mean to—" I reached out instinctively and put my hand on their shoulder. It was a little damp. I wanted to smell my hand so badly, but I resisted. My hand placement was unhelpful, but I left it there anyway. I counted to ten in my head, not wanting them to think I removed my hand because they were sweating.

"Totally . . . fine . . . no . . . worries!" Wes had their hands on their knees, was bent over, and their words were interspersed with hacking coughs.

"Put your hands up!" I shouted.

They turned to me, still hunched over, confused.

"What?" They coughed again.

"Like this!" I threw my hands into the air above my head.

They stood up, still spluttering, and mirrored me. Almost immediately, they stopped coughing.

"I think you just saved my life?" A little bit of saliva glimmered on their chin.

"Happy to," I said.

They caught their breath. "So I think you said something about it being your birthday, right before I thoroughly forgot how to drink water and embarrassed myself in front of the girl I like."

All the breath inside me left my body.

*Did they just?*

"Tomorrow," I croaked.

"Tomorrow!"

"Wait, no. Sorry. It's on Sunday. My birthday I mean. But I'm having a thing—"

"Tomorrow?"

"Yes."

Our arms were still raised above our heads.

"Yeah, it's just a small thing at Fir Bar with some people if you want to come, um, you could?"

"I definitely could."

"Oh. Great!"

Wes glanced up at our arms.

"We probably could stop doing this now."

"Right, totally." I nodded and let my arms flop by my sides, slapping against my hips.

*Queen of Grace, Savannah.*

"Wes! We're heading out!" Both of our heads turned to see Pink Bowl Cut calling to Wesley. They turned back toward me.

"Gotta run. But. Tomorrow?"

"Tomorrow."

"Cool."

When they walked away, my fingers were tingling.

I practically skipped back to my dorm. Their words echoed in my head: *the girl I like, the girl I like, the girl I like.* The girl they like. Is me. Bold fucking move, Wes. Pink Bowl Cut flashed through my mind, but I ignored the thought. I really needed a win tonight. And this was a monumental win.

I made a pit stop at the convenience store before going home. I bought sour gummies, Izzie's favorite. Tonight was almost over, and we'd get through tomorrow, and then she'd be back to sorority land on Sunday morning. The crossover episode nobody asked for would be over. And I could have a normal, quiet birthday.

I heard Izzie snoring before I even opened the door. She was passed out on my bed, her phone still in her hand. Relief washed over me. Sleep was an even better option. I gently took her phone out of her clenched hand, and before I could set it on my dresser, her lock screen lit up. I swallowed hard. It was a photo from the bridal shower, of Izzie and her family. Standing behind her, in a navy-blue suit and tie, with his hand palming her shoulder, was her brother. And next to him, head resting on his shoulder, was her. The girlfriend. A stupid-happy look on her face, with an arm linked in his. Her other arm was relaxed against her hip, the snake tattoo winding down it. Without thinking, I slammed the phone face-down on the dresser. Izzie's eyes opened a little. She blinked.

"I fell asleep," she whispered.

"Yeah, that's fine, babe," I whispered back.

She scooted over to the wall, making space for me. I climbed into bed, trying to leave a sliver of space between our bodies. Within a minute, Izzie's snores resumed. I stared at her back for a long time, willing sleep to come.

## 31

# Sixteen
## July 12 — Evening

"YOU SAID YOU can drink, right?"

"Yes, I can fucking drink!" I tried to look equal parts offended and bored.

"All right, big girl." Your brother's best friend, Zach, was on the couch, and he opened his arms wide and spoke to the room around us. "Let's fucking see it in action!"

He gestured for me to sit beside him on the couch, and he made a big show of surveying the table in front of us. After a moment, he reached for the entire liter bottle of Svedka on the coffee table. He raised it high and then slowly brought the bottle close to my face. I tried to take it from him, but he jerked it away, shaking his head. He tipped the bottle toward my lips, then pulled it away again.

"Come on, don't be annoying," I said.

He pressed the bottle to my lips, too hard, and my head tipped back, unable to control his pour of vodka into my mouth. I could barely keep my throat open, it burned so badly, and it was all I could do not to choke and sputter. I refused to admit defeat, so I closed my eyes and guzzled. I needed to look cool, even if I was swallowing shoe polish. Tears were forming at the corners of my eyes and my nose felt like it was going to drip. I had no idea how much I was drinking. He didn't let up on his pour, the bottle pushing my upper lip into my teeth. I could hear people behind me cheering. Your brother stopped him.

"Okay, guy, we get it now! Pull it, dude."

The bottle was pulled from my lips so forcefully that liquid spilled down the front of my dress. I lurched forward, trying to find anything I could chase the poison down with, but the only thing left on the table was leftover sticky red cups, half-full and stained with red lipstick. My throat burned; my tongue was on fire. I tasted metallic in my mouth; the inside of my lip was bleeding. I swallowed hard and told myself I would be fine in a couple of minutes. I could take it. I turned away from the crowd around me and wiped my eyes and nose, and then tried to wipe the liquor from my dress. When I turned back, Zach was already gone, sauntering over to some girls trying to play a different song on the speakers.

I felt a pair of hands on my shoulders.

"That was fucking awesome. You're such a champ."

His breath was hot. His lips brushed against my earlobe. My lower belly tightened, and my underwear felt hot under my dress. My throat didn't hurt so badly anymore.

I turned to look at him, his face inches from mine.

"Told you I could take it."

He squeezed my shoulders a little and winked at me as he walked away. As if that whole interaction had been a dream. As if all the vodka had been pointless. I wanted to grab his wrist, claw my fingernails into his skin. *Stay with me*, I thought. *Show everyone that you're picking me*. I watched him as he returned to Older Girl, who was leaning against the door to the garden. She had changed into low-rise jeans and a black tank top, a smear of pink lip gloss across her mouth. She interlocked her hands with both of his, making giant fists. She tried to push against him, pressing all her body weight into him. He barely moved. She laughed, a real laugh this time, and stuck her tongue out at him. I felt dizzy.

Someone grabbed my hand. I turned to find you yanking me up off the couch.

"What the fuck, I leave for two seconds and you're an alcoholic?"

The room spun around me. Your eyelids were so sparkly.

"I'm fiiiiine, bitch. Don't be so dramatic."

It was hard to talk. The words felt thick coming out of my mouth, like I was chewing taffy.

"You're fucking wasted."

I laughed hysterically and threw my arms around your neck.

"Your turn, slut," I whispered.

I could tell you were angry, but I kept laughing. Eventually you couldn't resist and fell into a fit of giggles with me.

"You're so dumb."

I snuck a half-empty cup off the table and wiggled it in front of your face."

"Whose is that?"

"Who fucking cares!" I jumped up and down.

You plugged your nose and gulped from the cup.

"CHUG! CHUG! CHUGGGGG!" I screamed.

Your hand slapped over my mouth. I licked it. You didn't flinch.

You tipped your cup all the way back, grimacing through the last big sip.

"THAT'S MY BEST FRIEND." The words came out muffled and somehow more amplified, your hand still glued to my mouth. You rolled your eyes and took your hand away, wiping it on your dress. I could tell the alcohol was softening you too, your eyes a little glazed now.

"That's my besssst fuckingggg friend," I slurred to a stranger near us. He had bright red hair and was wearing a green polo.

"You look like Chrisssstmas," I purred, reaching for his hair.

The guy looked down at his shirt and rolled his eyes.

"That's your best ginger joke, huh?"

You cackled. You had a thing for redheads.

"Christmas is actually my favorite holiday."

"Yes! Yes, we love Christmas!" I was now doing a loose interpretation of a Christmas jig.

"Y'all are nuts." The ginger was looking at you, not me, and had a sheepish grin on his face.

"How old are you, Mr. Christmas?" I slurred.

"Seventeen. I go to Regis Prep."

"Smarty-pants." You nudged him with your elbow.

"Ha. Yeah, I guess. My brother is friends with yours, from school." He gestured to an older, much hairier redhead who was wrestling a very small, but evidently very strong, boy wearing only a pair of plaid boxers.

"So gay." The ginger rolled his eyes.

"You should not—you shouldn't . . . say . . . that." I pointed my finger in his face.

"We have to pee! Let's go!" You grabbed my arm and we bounded for the bathroom.

"Ow. Your nailsssss. You're hurtingggg me, bitch."

You slammed the bathroom door behind us, yanking your pants down as you sat on the toilet.

"He's *so* cute, right?" You were thrilled.

Boys didn't flirt with you a lot then. Which was stupid and unfair but one of those things decided in the sixth grade by a hierarchy of greasy, sweaty, prepubescent boys, and somehow it was

etched in stone, permanent until graduation lifted all of high
school's curses and reality could be restored. You were tall and
blond and beautiful, skinny in the impossibly gangly way that
only a teenage metabolism could achieve, but it took forever for
your boobs and your ass and your period to show up. These things
plagued you and so they plagued me too.

"You just gotta kishem! Take him to the bathroom and kishem!
I can go get him! And bringem here to you, and you can make out!
Make out on the sink, that would be ssoooo hot. I'll go! I'll go
right now." I reached for the door.

"No, no, no, no." You grabbed the doorknob.

"Come onnnn!"

We both fought for the handle. You locked eyes with me.

"Please don't, okay? You can't do that! Please. I don't even
know if I want to kiss him yet." There was real panic in your
voice.

"Okay! Okay okay. I won't," I relented.

We were quiet for a moment. I tried not to let my body sway.

"What if he doesn't want me like that?" Your voice was very
small.

"STOP." I grabbed your chin and turned your face toward
mine.

"You're perfect. YOU are the most, the most perfect person I
know. You're so pretty and sooo hot and the most, the most beautiful girl in the whole world."

You laughed and reached out to steady me. Your eyes looked
wet, but it could have been from your eyeshadow.

"I feel the same way about you. Jeremy is really lucky."

I gulped. The sound of his name jolted me into a momentary
sobriety. I didn't want to think about him or what had happened
behind the tennis court earlier. I was relieved he had left to go to
his aunt's birthday dinner. He had texted me three times since

leaving but I kept ignoring my phone. I wanted to get back to the family room.

"Let's go," I whispered, squeezing both your hands in mine.

"I'm so nervous."

I bent my knees so our faces were the same height. I pressed my nose against yours.

"I'll be there the whole time. In a not creepy way."

"Your breath stinks."

"GOOD, 'CAUSE I'M DRUNK, BITCH!"

"I need to catch up."

I pushed open the door and we stumbled into the hallway. My vision blurred again. The family room seemed so far away. A tunnel appeared in front of me, and I suddenly felt scared. Like I wanted to skip the rest of the party and get in my pj's and eat your dad's Entenmann's doughnuts. Like I wanted to wrap scarves around our heads and pretend to be old ladies on Chatroulette, slamming the computer shut and screaming bloody murder when some creep inevitably took out his dick.

I thought about telling you that. But when I turned to look at you, I could tell you were so excited in a way you seldom got to be. There was nothing more exciting than a boy who might like you.

You pushed me forward and the tunnel evaporated. And then I was in the room, had crossed the threshold, and your brother was sitting on the sofa, palming a beer, looking right at me. He glanced at the empty seat next to him. I walked toward him, trying not to stumble, trying to make him love me in those few steps. I managed to get all the way there in a straight line, and now was in the space where his legs had splayed open. Neither of us moved or spoke or even blinked, I don't think, until he silently handed me his beer and pressed himself off the couch. I felt fingers slowly clasp mine, our hands hidden between our bodies. He looked behind his shoulder, placing you in the room. You were playing beer pong with the ginger and laughing. You missed a shot and he pretended to be exasperated. You looked so happy. "Let's go," your brother said, pulling me toward the door.

Once again, the tunnel reappeared, but I still don't remember going through it.

## 32

WE GOT TO the bar at eight forty-five the next night. The day had gone by surprisingly fast, which I was grateful for. I borrowed Vera's car and showed Izzie the sights, of which there were very few, but she was thrilled to take photos against a bright red barn a few miles from campus, and even happier when we went to the one juice bar in town. She took a nap before dinner, and I went to Vera's with outfit options. I managed to escape mandatory birthday shots by claiming that we would have our fill at the bar, and before I knew it, we were walking through the doors of Fir.

I was bombarded with hugs from V, who ushered us over to a little table behind the dance floor. Balloons were tied to all the chairs. They were all black, which wouldn't normally be my pick, but Vera looked so excited she might puke, and I couldn't help but grin.

"This is so cute, V."

She hugged me again.

Someone tapped me on the shoulder. I turned to see Candace.

"Hey, birthday dude."

"Hey, that's me."

"Look, we got things to talk about, but it's your birthday, so. We can figure it out later."

"That sounds really good."

"Cool." Candace pulled me in for a hug. I blinked away the tears that sprang to my eyes.

"Is that THEM?" Izzie was shouting at me and pointing across the room.

"This fucking girl," Candy muttered under her breath.

"Please help me," I whispered.

I knew Izzie was looking for Wes, but it was Reg whom her eyes had landed on. Reg was shimmying her way across the bar toward us.

Candace leaned over to Izzie.

"Hot tip, hot stuff. Androgyny is not analogous with identity. You can be femme and be a they/them. And Reg is a good ol' she/her."

Izzie's eyes looked like lightbulbs had been stuffed inside them.

"Totally! I get that. I totally get that."

Reg had made it through the crowd, over to me, and was thrusting a small parcel in my hand, yellow wrapping paper with twine tied around it.

"Hey, birthday human. Got you something."

I beamed.

"Go for it," she said. I unwrapped the gift. It was the illustration I had seen her drawing in class earlier in the semester. I squealed. Confirmed: ass eating.

"I saw you staring at it, perv."

"I won't deny it. Thank you, this is my newest prized possession."

"Hiiiiii! I'm Izzie!"

Izzie's voice, three octaves higher than it needed to be, cut through the noise of the crowd. Our mushy moment had been blitz-attacked and I noticed that Izzie's drink was considerably less full than it had been ten minutes ago. Reg looked up at Izzie and then looked back at me, then looked back at Izzie, and did not respond for a full five seconds.

"Reg, this is my friend Izzie. She's visiting." I interrupted the silence.

"Best friend," Izzie chided.

I stifled an eye roll.

"Best friend."

Izzie thrust her hand in Reg's, and the action made Reg come back to life.

"Hey, what's up?"

"So nice to meet you, Reg. Any friend of Savvy's is a friend of mine." Izzie's eyes were shining the way they did when she was drunk.

Before she could answer the question, Izzie's phone lit up in her free hand.

"Oh my god, I'm so sorry, this is my fiancé calling, I have to answer." Izzie held up a finger to us as she answered the phone, mouthing "Just a minute," and hurried toward the door for better service.

Reg looked over at me and blinked twice. "You're telling me that's *not* the blond girl from GSS class?"

I burst out laughing.

"No, but, uh, that is." I pointed behind Reg and she turned. We both watched Lara walk through the door.

"She looks different," Reg said.

And she did. Lara was wearing the most casual outfit I'd ever seen her in, worn-in blue jeans and a white T-shirt. She didn't have any makeup on, and she looked happy. Free, somehow. I squinted at her hand. Her nails weren't painted and the ring was gone.

"She broke up with him," I muttered under my breath.

Lara was headed to the bar, where a slew of her sorority sisters were waiting for her. But then she caught my eye and hesitated. She gave me a quick wave. I waved back.

Reg whistled quietly. "She looks good."

My eyes widened and I whipped my head to look at Reg.

"What?" She shrugged. "She pisses me off *and* she's kinda cute. I'm allowed to be complicated, Miss Dirty Bingo." She winked.

"Fair."

I felt a hand on my shoulder. And then:

"I hear it's your birthday."

Instant melt.

Wesley was wearing green on green again: an olive-green tee and mossy-green corduroys. They were also holding a bright pink drink, which should have screamed Lilly Pulitzer against their ensemble, but my brain computed it as cool, hot, very cool, very hot.

"This is for you," they said, handing me the drink.

"Oh—I—thank you. So much." I stared down at it for a moment, and it must have been a moment too long, because Wes jolted back into speaking.

"There's no alcohol in it. It's a Shirley Temple. Because you said you liked them—in your . . ." Their cheeks nearly matched the color of the drink.

"My poem?"

"Poem."

I couldn't stop my teeth from bursting through my lips. I couldn't believe they remembered that.

"I can't believe you remembered that."

"What? Of course I did! Are you kidding? I remember the whole thing."

I was having trouble concentrating on anything they were saying. All I could think was *maybe we could kiss now*, even though this was probably not the moment. I had been running through our conversation last night all day. I was second-guessing myself now. I kept thinking about Pink Bowl Cut. Weren't they still together? What if Wes was polyamorous and thought I was too? I couldn't do that after Nova. I wasn't cool or evolved enough for that. I still hadn't mastered the whole monogamy thing. I steadied myself. What were they saying? The important thing was that they were here, right? The heat had made their hair frizz a little, giving them a half an inch more height, but my rare choice of heels—at Izzie's convincing—made me tower over them.

"Sav was never very good at keeping a promise."

My head lurched toward the sound of Izzie's voice, and I saw that she had cornered Candace, Vera, and Reg. She was leaning forward the way she did when she was gossiping, the corner of her mouth slightly upturned, as if to say, "Now I gotcha."

"I have to go!" I blurted at Wes.

"Oh, okay! Right, of course, it's your birthday party and here I am keeping you all to myself—"

"I love when you keep me! I mean, no—sorry, that's not what I meant. I just. That friend I was telling you about, she's really on one tonight and there's damage control to be done. Can you, would you, um . . ."

"I'll be here."

"Thank you." The words came out like an exhale.

I ran over to where Izzie was standing.

"She had, like, no self-control in high school," Izzie was dishing to Vera.

"Do any teenagers have self-control? Isn't that, like, the definition of adolescence?" Vera asked, shooting me a look.

"Yes," I said. "One hundred percent."

"Okay, sure, but get Sav drunk and she would really throw you a wild card." Izzie was gulping her drink now.

"And that's why I don't drink very much anymore, Iz."

"One time she got so drunk that she fucked my brother." Izzie laughed as she said it, like it was the most hilarious thing in the world. My throat felt like it had been lit on fire. I looked at Candace, desperate for help. They took the cue.

"Well, all right, keep it in the family, I guess!" Candace reached for Izzie's empty drink. "Let me get you a refill, Iz." She took a step behind Izzie but made no move toward the bar.

"We don't need to go down memory lane right now, do we?" I tried to keep my voice light.

"I think we dooooo!" Izzie sang, lurching her elbows forward onto the hightop table. I avoided her gaze.

Vera jumped in. "It's Sav's birthday, so all conversation requests from her must be obeyed. No awkward hometown stories allowed." She squeezed my hand under the table. "Birthday rules."

"Thank you."

Behind Vera, I saw some more people approaching the table. *Thank fucking god.*

"Look, V!" I yelled. "Your partners are here!"

There was nothing like the entrance of a mind-numbingly gorgeous polycule to steal the show.

Through the crowd came Ellis and Raz.

"Oh my god, Vera, well done *you*." Izzie pinched my arm and I instinctively pinched her back. I looked over at Vera and was overcome with love. She was just so powerful, sitting atop a barstool in one of her cape dresses, her hair tied up with what looked like elephant tusks, undoubtedly fake and ethically sourced, her face shining with joy and pride as her lovers approached her. They each kissed her once on the cheek and she made space for them at the table.

"Does she have sex with both of them at once?" Izzie whispered in my ear.

Vera heard her and jutted her jaw out at Izzie. "The sexual dynamics of my relationships are private and not to be fetishized."

Izzie's mouth dropped open.

"But. Yes," Vera continued, pulling both Ellis and Raz into her, "we all have sex and it is very, very hot." Ellis threw his head back and laughed, while Raz's knives-for-cheeks flushed pink. They looked very pleased with themself.

"Where's Nieve?" Ellis asked Vera. Both Candace and I whipped our heads to look at her. Now Vera looked embarrassed.

"I'm sorry, who is where?" Candace interjected, leaning over the table to stare harder at Vera, who was looking down, uncharacteristically shy.

"Nieve? Vera's girlfriend?" Ellis said, looking confused. He was not catching on.

Raz poked Vera on the shoulder. "You haven't told them, V?"

"It's new!" Vera looked apologetic. "We started talking over spring break, after Wes's open mic. I wanted to tell y'all, but it didn't seem like great timing to talk about it! You both have had, um, some tough . . . experiences? As of late?"

"You can say it, V. Our love lives have been train wrecks."

"I mean . . ." Vera trailed off.

"Speak for yourself!" Candace interjected. "I am absolutely crushing it in the love department. I swiped right on multiple lesbians this week, and neither of them bragged about having mommy problems in their bio."

"Apparently I spoke too soon. I guess it's only me who has made horrible, terrible choices over the past few months. I truly cannot be trusted romantically," I said.

Everyone's faces went blank, and Vera coughed a little, her eyes glancing behind me.

*Fuck.*

"Wes is behind me, aren't they?" I whispered.

"Bingo." Candace nodded awkwardly.

I turned to see Wes standing near my barstool, still holding my drink.

"Dude! So good to see you out of class!" Candace to the rescue. "Come join, come join!" Candy beckoned for everyone at the table to scooch, and then Wes did a horrible thing. They slid into the group, right between Izzie and me. Before I had a chance to find out what they had heard, Izzie jumped in.

"You must be Wes. I've heard so much about you," Izzie purred.

I practically kicked her under the table.

"You must be—"

"Izzie. We grew up together."

"That's so cool." Wesley was being totally genuine. "So awesome that you came to visit for Sav's birthday." Izzie was going to eat this up.

"Wouldn't miss it for the world!" Izzie took a sip of her drink. "So what makes you think you deserve my Savvy girl?"

"Izzie."

"What?!" She looked up at me innocently. "I'm kidding, I'm kidding! I know you two are just friends, right?" She wiggled her eyebrows at the group.

"So, Izzie, what are your favorite things to do?" Wes seamlessly moved on.

*God, they were perfect.*

"Oh!" Izzie squealed and clapped her hands. "Great question. Well, I'm an art history major, so honestly I could live in a museum for the rest of my life and be happy."

If Wes was surprised, they didn't show it.

"If you had to pick one artist's work to look at for the rest of your life, whose would you choose?"

"Glory Roberts, hands down. She is completely underrepresented, and I've only gotten to see a few of her paintings in person, but my dream is to curate an actual show so other people can really appreciate her. Her paintings have, like, changed me as a person."

I was shocked. I knew Izzie loved art, always had, but I guess I never really asked her more about it. What it meant to her. I felt guilty thinking about the times I'd just assumed she liked the idea of being in the art world. Going to the parties, making the commissions. The status of it all. Here she was talking about an artist I'd never heard of.

"I got to see her show too. Did you go in Barcelona?" Reg and Lara were back from the bar.

"Oh my god, yes! I went last summer!" Izzie was delighted.

"Me too. I traveled after my study abroad and was *this* close to missing the exhibit." Reg measured with her fingers. "I'm so happy I didn't."

"Wow, honestly, none of my friends are ever interested in talking about obscure artists, or, like, any artists. This is amazing." Izzie turned to me. "Your friends are the best, Savvy."

She was right. I looked around the table and it dawned on me that I, Savannah Henry, had a real fucking *friend group*. Like, multiple people who were cool and kind and interesting and actually cared about real things. And me.

"I'm really lucky," I agreed.

"Anyway, Wesley, Savvy was just joking about her love life before. She's always had lots of luck with dating, I mean how could she not, have you seen her boobs?"

I rolled my eyes. A slight look of panic flew across Wesley's face.

"I have! I've seen them!" Candace cheered.

"My little hopeless romantic." Izzie grabbed my chin playfully. One of her nails was sharp against my skin.

"When we were little, I swear you never met anyone so boy crazy in your life. So, you're perfect for her!"

My stomach dropped.

No *no no no no no.*

"Sorry, what?" Wes was still smiling, but it was covering confusion in their eyes.

"Oh, you know what I mean! She's gay and everything but will always be boy crazy. So, you're perfect for her!"

"Ah, well, I'm not a boy."

"Well, obviously." Izzie laughed.

"Hey. Dude." Candace snapped in front of Izzie's face to get her attention. "You need to stop talking now."

Izzie cocked her head to the side, not getting it.

"What? I wasn't trying to be offensive—I was just saying that she's, sorry, *they're* perfect because—"

"Let's go, Izzie," I said quietly.

"What?"

"Now," I said louder, firmer. I grabbed her elbow and her purse and yanked her toward the door and back to my dorm.

•

I WAS QUIET the whole walk home, walking ahead of Izzie, her calling out behind me.

"Sav, I don't think anyone understood what I was saying—you know I'd never—"

"I don't want to talk about this here."

We were silent in the elevator. Once in my dorm room, I threw off my heels and reached for my makeup wipes, desperate to get the gunk off my face.

"Sav." Izzie sat on my bed, staring at me.

"What?"

"You know I'd never mean to say—"

"I don't know that, Izzie."

"I feel terrible! What I was trying to say was, like—"

"I really don't need to know, Iz. Okay? I'm exhausted. And I have to apologize to Wes now."

"I can apologize! Savvy, I know how much you like them—"

"No, you really don't." I turned to face her. "You don't know me like you think you do, Izzie. You don't know what kind of man or woman or human I need, what I like, what I think about love, or sex, or what I want. I am not the person I was in high school."

"Neither am I! I know that. That's not what I'm saying."

"Well, it is what you said. Even if you didn't mean it. Intent verses impact, you know? And honestly, you don't have the best track record with this shit."

Izzie sighed. "Not this whole thing again."

Anger seared through me.

"This whole thing?"

"Savannah, how many times can I apologize for that whole mess?"

"That whole mess?! You turned the whole school against me, Izzie! You fucking cyberbullied me and made that year a living hell. For something that you didn't even understand."

"I can't take back what I did, okay?! It was fucked up. So fucked up. And I'm sorry. I've told you over and over that I'm sorry about it. But I was angry at you. I told you not to and you did it anyway. You had sex with him, Savannah."

"No. He had sex with me."

Izzie looked down. I stood there, unmoving, and felt my teeth grit together.

"I get that, like, it wasn't something you necessarily wanted—"

"Listen to yourself. Listen to what you're saying to me." Thick tears started to drip down my cheeks.

"We were all so drunk, Sav. You were throwing up, we were all so—there was too much alcohol. It was just a really, really fucked up night."

"I know you don't want to hear it."

"NO. Stop." She put her hands up and squeezed her eyes shut. "I *can't* hear it. He's my brother. I don't want to hear it. He is my family." Her voice was breaking.

"So am I."

Izzie opened her eyes.

"Savvy, you know it's different. You don't have—I mean, you're an only child—it's just, like. He has to be my brother my whole life, you know?" Izzie was crying now. "And of course, I mean, you're my best friend. This is, I don't know, this whole thing is so fucked. I just want everything to be okay again. And if you call it that, it just can't be."

"It has been a very long time since things were okay."

"You were *fine*, for years. You saw him. We all hung out."

"I can't do this. I can't defend myself. This haunts me every waking day of my fucking life. Yes, I saw him. Yes, we hung out. It doesn't matter. It doesn't change anything. I can't unknow what I know now. I know what he did to me, and I will never, ever, have the privilege of forgetting it. He—"

"Please don't say it." She was begging me now.

I paused.

"I don't even have to."

I blinked the tears from my eyes, and I turned around and walked toward the door. Before I left, I could hear her whisper under her breath.

"I'm sorry."

It was far, far too late.

I walked out into the hallway and just stood there, frozen. I didn't know what to do, where to go.

"Savannah?" I heard a voice whisper.

I turned to see Candace and Vera standing there.

"Did you . . . ?"

Vera nodded. "Sav, we had no idea." She looked so sad.

My face crumpled, and I burst into tears. Candace ran toward me and threw her arms around me.

"It's not your fault. It's not your fault."

"Come on, let's go." Vera pressed her hand against my back and guided us toward the elevator.

# 33

"SAV, WHEN WAS the last time you and Izzie *felt* like you and Izzie?" Candace asked me gently. The three of us were crowded into Candace's bed, leaning against the wall. Vera had texted Izzie that I was staying in Candace's room, and to please give me some space.

The question hit me like a ton of bricks.

"I don't know."

"I know that you love her. Like, I get that. That this friendship is a deep part of you. But from everything you just told us, it sounds like you all have not been the same since you were basically kids."

I hugged my knees closer and rested my chin on my kneecaps. "Yeah. Not since before he, um. Yeah. You're right."

Vera put her hand on my shoulder. She spoke softly, "Sav, it's been a long time since you were sixteen."

I had never thought of it that way. I had tried so hard. I had wanted nothing more than for us to go back to what we were before. I had played the part so well too, and now it was just . . . exhausting.

"I'm so tired of pretending things are the same."

"Dude, I can't even imagine." Candace kneeled in front of me and lifted my chin.

"Being friends with you is the easiest thing in the world, Sav. And I hope it feels pretty easy with me too."

"It does."

"And you deserve that. This 'time heals all things' just doesn't work with every situation. You can still love someone and have to let them go. Not my quote, but, like, that shit is deep." Candace shrugged.

I laughed a little.

"I'm really fucking sorry about Nova. I lost myself for a while. And that's not an excuse for not telling you. I know I can't magically erase any of it."

"I overreacted." Candace shrugged.

"No, you didn't." I shook my head. "She hurt you, badly, and I shouldn't have gotten caught up with her again. I know it might take time to trust me again. And I know that all this"—I gestured to myself—"is a lot."

"It is, but I signed up for a lot when we became friends. I consent to a lot. I want a lot. Signed, sealed, delivered, I'm yours." Candace gave two thumbs-up.

"Me too. All of it, okay?" Vera reached for my hand.

I bit my lip to stop from crying more. "Okay."

Now that I knew I could tell them anything, the words kept pouring out.

"Sometimes I wonder if I'd even be here if it hadn't happened," I whispered. "It's why I started caring about other things. College. My future. It's like, it's like I don't know who I would be if it hadn't happened. Is that so fucked up? That I had to be raped to be awake? To care?"

Vera nodded. "I think trauma does that. Makes you grow up

really fast. Remember that girl I told you about, Raya? My best friend forever in high school?"

I nodded.

"I think we were toeing the line between friendship and love, and neither of us could say it. When she pushed me away, it was because she couldn't go there with me. And that really fucked me up, but it also was the impetus of me exploring my sexuality. Would I have figured that out without her? Probably. But it didn't happen that way. You would have gotten here eventually, Sav. I know you would have. And you deserved the chance to do it on your own terms."

Maybe Vera was right. But if she was, if I was always meant to be this person, I still didn't know if Izzie and I could have survived. Maybe it would have been something else. Maybe it would have been gentler. Maybe it would have been slower. But it would have happened. That kind of closeness isn't meant to last. We're told that that kind of closeness is a strong bond. But it isn't strong at all. It's so easy to break.

It wasn't that I didn't love Izzie anymore. That was the hard, confusing part of all this. Everything that had made her choose the life she was living now had cost her the ability to be the person I needed her to be. The person I needed her to be all those years ago.

Izzie was never going to cut her brother out of her life. And that was a fair choice. But it was the one that made it so that we could not be in each other's lives anymore. In Izzie's world, which had spun in an entirely different direction than mine, she was choosing her brother. And in mine, she was choosing my rapist.

My eyes filled with tears. I looked up at Candace.

"This fucking sucks," I whispered.

"I know, Sav. I know," Candace said, before wrapping me in another hug.

# 34

## Sixteen

THEY NEVER CAUGHT us. Not the first time we tried sneaking out, freshman year of high school, when we only had the guts to make it to Frankie Melger's garage, where we shared a single beer and ran home immediately after. Not when we were brave, the summer before sophomore year, taking the Metro-North all the way to Grand Central for a concert we didn't even get into because our fake IDs were so bad. And they didn't catch us any of the nights after that, after we got the good fakes, and when sneaking out became our well-oiled routine—thrilling but easy, the thing we did almost every weekend.

But this night, I did not meet you. I did not call a cab to take us to the train station. We did not board an eleven p.m. train to New York City, did not share a plastic water bottle filled halfway with warm vodka from your parents' liquor cabinet. We did not flirt with the boys our age whose parents had no reason to fear them leaving suburbia on a Saturday night. We did not meet up with some prep school kid who knew of a Columbia frat party her sister could get us into, or go to a bar that didn't card, or meet a skeezy bouncer who brought us into the clubs as long as we promised to stand by the table of old businessmen for most of the night. We did not finish the water bottle by the time we got to Grand Central, laughing uncontrollably as you tripped over the Jimmy Choos you stole from your mother. We did not race to the dance floor, grinding on each other the same way we did watching music videos in our pajamas. We didn't shove each other into a finance bro who was just cute enough for the story to be worth telling during free period on Monday. I didn't check my almost-dead phone at two a.m. and wrestle the tongue of the finance bro out of your mouth. We did not gallop, bare feet on dirty cement, toward Grand Central, praying we'd make the last train until morning. We did not collapse into our train seats, utterly relieved, with sweat streaking cheap mascara down our cheeks. We did not fall asleep on each other's shoulders. We did not hug each other as we got out of the cab at our spot between our houses.

I still slipped my nightgown over my clothes. I tiptoed down the creaky stairs. I wrestled out the window. I crawled down the driveway. I walked to our spot halfway between our houses. And when your brother pulled up, I got in his car. It was the fall of our junior year of high school. Thanksgiving break. It had been three months since the barbecue at your house when he raped me.

There were all kinds of love stories. That's what I told myself before I snuck out to meet him. People didn't always remember having sex. It could be a funny story, actually. And then we would get married, and you and I would be sisters. Real sisters. And you would forgive me, I knew, when you realized it was true love.

The sex was horrible. He took me to his friend's empty house and fucked me in a guest room with no heat on. And all I really remember is his vodka breath blowing hot on me, and the bed thudding underneath me, and the rawness of my vagina, and how

I couldn't even look him in the eyes. I never stopped shaking. Afterward, we had nothing to talk about. Except you.

"It'll be good for her to go to college. Get out of here," he said.

"Yeah, definitely."

"Guys here are really shitty to her. It sucks." He blew his nose into a dishrag. For the first time, I looked at him and felt nothing.

# 35

I TEXTED WES before I fell asleep.

> Last night went the opposite of how
> I wanted it to go. I'm so sorry.

I waited for a few minutes to see if those magical floating bubbles would appear, but they didn't. I knew I had fucked things up for good.

I woke up to Candace snoring. She had fallen asleep on the floor, Vera's spider blanket (with terrifyingly realistic spiders crawling all over it) pulled up to her neck and just her feet peeking out from underneath. I was in Candace's roommate's bed. She had stopped by late last night and found us all crying on the floor. She told me to take her bed, she was going to stay over at her boyfriend's anyway. Vera was already up, sitting cross-legged on Candace's bed scrolling through her phone. She must have felt me looking at her because she looked up. She waved.

"Happy birthday," she mouthed.

"Thank you," I mouthed back.

I dug out my phone from under the covers and tapped on the screen.

*Holy fuck.*

Wes had texted me back.

> I'll be outside your dorm at 10 :)

"Oh my god."

At the sound of my voice Candace shot up from the floor, attacking the blanket and then throwing it across the room.

"Fucking spiders! Spiders!"

Vera burst out laughing. "Candace, it's the blanket. They aren't real!"

Candace looked like she had been electrocuted.

"Jesus fucking Christ." She slunk back down to the floor and covered her face with her hands.

"I'm sorry for waking you up!"

"Any other day, I'd kill you. But it's your birthday, so I'm gonna kill you with loooooove." She leapt up onto the bed, squeezing me tightly.

"Candace, we have to celebrate Sav later. She has to go. Wes is waiting for her."

I looked up at Vera, confused. "How did you—?"

She crossed her arms.

"When are you both finally going to believe that I'm psychic?"

Candace got up and looked out the window.

"Dude, that's fucking freaky, they're literally outside."

"What time is it?!" I tapped my phone again: 9:58.

"Fuck! I have to go!"

"Go!" they both yelled at once.

I ran down the hall to the bathroom to inspect the damage from last night. I was wearing one of Candace's oversized tees and some boxers. Not great, but not terrible. Luckily, I had cried so hard that my makeup had washed off but not too hard that my face was puffy. I rubbed some moisturizer on my face.

I managed to brush my teeth in under fifteen seconds before catapulting myself down the hall and into the elevator. I took three deep breaths and quickly prayed to the gay gods before I hit the lobby.

*If birthday wishes are real, please let them still like me. Please let them somehow see past the misery that was Izzie last night and all associations they have of me with her and remember that I am a semi-decent person with a cute butt. Please, whomever I'm talking to, throw me a bone. A Wesley-shaped bone. I like them so fucking much.*

When I got out of the lobby, Wesley was waiting for me on the bench closest to my dorm. They wore a light green beanie and a striped shirt. I adjusted my top, sliding my boobs a little out to the side so my cleavage didn't fully terrify them.

They looked up just as I approached the bench. I was so relieved to see them smile.

"Hey, I hear it's your birthday?"

"Hey, I think you heard right."

From behind their back, Wes revealed a single cupcake. White frosting, chocolate cake. My favorite.

"How?"

"You have very attentive friends. Who text back quickly."

*Ah, Vera the psychic.*

I bit my lip, smiling.

"Thank you. You really didn't have to—" I reached for the cupcake, but they stopped me. They pulled a little pink candle and a lighter from their pocket.

"You have to make a birthday wish."

Tears attacked my eyes.

Wes's mouth dropped open.

"Oh god, sorry, Sav, is this too much? I thought—"

"It's amazing. I just. I'm sorry." I was spluttering.

"Can we sit?" I asked.

"Of course."

Before Wes's ass even landed on the bench, the word vomit came.

"I'm so sorry about last night."

"Hey, it happens."

"It shouldn't. And I can't believe I exposed you to a person who—"

"Sav, you couldn't have planned that."

"But I should have."

"If only life worked that way!" Wes was smiling again; little creases hugged the skin around their eyes. "Look, Sav—"

"I really like you," I blurted.

Wes's eyes doubled in size.

"And I should have said that the other day, when you said it to me."

They opened their mouth to speak, but I cut them off before they could.

"But I also like the way you see me. A lot. Like, the way you see me is how I want to, how I am, like, trying to see myself. But there's a lot you don't know about me. And last night, the things that happened and the things she said, I'm so fucking sorry, that was just. So bad. But. No, not but. AND. I grew up in a place where those things were okay to say. Where a lot of things are okay that shouldn't be. And I hate that, and I'm still from there. And I don't want you to ever have to be around people like that. But I still go back there, to that world. Even though I don't want it to be, it's still a part of me. And Izzie . . ." I trailed off. "She's a part of me too."

Wes was quiet for a second.

"Sav, did you know that I'm a transfer student?"

That caught me off guard.

"Um, no, I didn't."

"Yeah. I did a full year at a different school. In the South. And I was in a sorority."

That *really* caught me off guard.

"I'm sorry, what?!"

"Oh yeah. All of this?" They pointed to their face and body and made a wide circle with their finger. "Imagine in it in florals."

"No."

"Bold prints."

"*No.*"

"Glitter."

"Please. Stop."

Wes laughed.

"But, you, how?" I asked, bewildered.

They shrugged.

"I have three sisters. They did it, so I did it. I love them. I'm nothing like them. They thought I'd love it because they did."

"And did you?"

Wes laughed again.

"Uh, no, I would say it was hugely traumatizing and I'm almost positive it took years off my life."

"I'm so sorry."

"It's okay. It's why I came here. It's why I came out. But I still did that, Sav, and I've done a lot of other things in my life that feel weird and don't really mesh with who I am now. But they're still a part of me."

"Yeah."

We were quiet for a moment.

"Savannah?"

My whole body glitched when they said my full name.

"Yeah?"

"I don't see you a certain way. I just see you."

*FUCK.*

"And," they continued, "I really want to see more of you."

My eyebrows rose.

Their sweet expression quickly shifted to complete horror. "Wait. Not in like a creepy, I was trying to be, um, GOD, Wesley, when will you learn how to STOP?" They scolded themself and covered their face with their hands.

I laughed. I reached toward their palms and drew them away from their face. They peeked their eyes open.

"I'd really like to see more of you too," I said quietly.

Wes took a breath in. They looked relieved.

"That's. Awesome."

I was still holding their hands. We both looked down at our skin touching, and then back up at each other. They were looking at my mouth.

My phone rang.

*Fuuuuuuuuck me.*

Instinctively, I went to grab it, breaking our gaze and pulling my hand from theirs.

"I'm so sorry, Wes—" I scrambled to turn off the ringer. I glanced down at the screen.

It was Izzie.

"It's her, she's about to go, I have to, um—"

"No worries. At all. I'll see you in class?"

"Yes, definitely. I'll definitely be there."

*Class feels so far away.*

I started to speed walk toward the dorm lobby. I heard running behind me. I turned to see Wes sprinting and holding out the cupcake. I covered my mouth with my hand, trying not to laugh.

"You have to make a wish," they said, out of breath, shoving the candle into the center of the cupcake. They swiped at their lighter and held the flame to the wick. They looked up at me.

*GreenGreenGreenGreen.*

I leaned in and closed my eyes. Took a deep breath and blew. When I opened my eyes, Wes was staring at me.

"Happy birthday, Savannah Henry." They handed me the cupcake.

"Thank you."

When I turned back toward the lobby, I could see Izzie through the doors, wearing her massive bug-eye sunglasses she only used when she was hungover. I pushed the doors open.

"Hey," I said.

"Hey," she replied.

The adrenaline from seeing Wes had worn off instantaneously, and now I was in that special kind of stomach-clawing, vomit-inducing place that only morning-after conversations like this could elicit.

"Sav—"

"I think we should give this all some air."

"You do?" She sounded surprised.

Honestly, I'd surprised myself. But what was there to say in this situation? Was Izzie really going to tell me anything I hadn't heard before?

"Yeah. I don't really feel like I have the energy to talk this out right now."

"Okay, but when?" Izzie chewed on her bottom lip. She was picking at a hangnail.

"I don't know, Iz." I sighed. "Just not now."

"Are you still coming to the wedding?" The question came out in a yelp.

"Um, I. I think I need to—"

Izzie reached out and grabbed my hand.

"Savvy, I cannot get married without you. I can't do this alone." Izzie's cheeks were wet. "Please, please, don't make me do this alone." She was shaking.

"Oh, Izzie." Instinctively, I hugged her. Her body crumpled against mine.

She let out a small sob.

"I don't know what I'm doing, okay? I don't know why I'm getting married at twenty, I don't know why we're rushing this, his mom definitely doesn't like me, and I don't even know if he likes art."

"What?" I pulled her from my shoulder to look her in the eye. Her hair was matted against one cheek.

"Art," she croaked. "I realized last night, when Wes asked, I don't even know if Ben likes art."

"Everybody likes art, Izzie."

"You don't."

Honestly, she wasn't wrong.

"Well, you still love me, don't you?" I asked.

"But I'm not marrying you!"

"Right."

"Please come. Please. I know none of this has gone the way we said it would, the way we promised. But, Sav, the whole thing only counts if you're there."

Suddenly, we're nine again on the floor of her room.

I quickly wiped my eyes.

"Of course. Of course I'm coming." The words tasted bitter as I said them.

*Don't make promises you can't keep, Savannah.*

Izzie took a shaky breath and leaned her forehead against mine.

"I love you, Savvy."

"I love you, too." It was true.

I walked her outside and called an Uber. We sat on the sidewalk, our shoulders resting against each other, quiet.

As the car pulled up, I turned to her.

"He'll learn to love it."

"What?" she asked.

"Art. He'll learn to love art."

"How do you know?"

"Because he'll never be able to look at it again without thinking of you."

The driver opened the trunk, and I loaded Izzie's weekender bag inside. We hugged goodbye and her hair smelled like citrus.

·

BACK IN MY room, I got a DM from the Girlfriend. She had been heart-reacting to my Instagram stories for the past two weeks. I hadn't responded to any of them. The new message lit up my phone screen, taunting me.

> Saw you on Izzie's story!!! Happy
> birthday!! Looking forward to hanging
> at the wedding.

I stared at the message for a long time. I wanted to hate her for sending it, but to be honest, it made me feel good that she liked me. I had liked her too, that whole time at the bar, and as much as I didn't want to admit it, her pottery was cool. In an alternate reality, my rapist's girlfriend and I would be friends. We might even be more than friends.

My iPhone screen was dirty. Foggy. Greasy fingerprints all over it. I rubbed at it with my sleeve. By accident, I hit the keyboard with my wrist.

Bkjds

I had DMed her "Bkjds."
And she had seen it.
*Fuck*.

My bad, typo lol, hiii sorry

I started to hurriedly type an excuse for not responding. Something about being so bad at messaging back. But then I kept typing.

So this is really weird, and I've been debating telling you this, but the reason I left the shower early that day is because your boyfriend and I have a history. When I was 16, he raped me and he's never taken accountability for that, and Izzie doesn't acknowledge it, and so I can't really be around him. I think you're amazing, like so cool and I felt instantly connected to you, so this is probably so jarring to hear. I just thought you would want to know the whole story. I'm sorry, this is probably a lot. But it's why I haven't responded much. I haven't known what to do.

My finger hovered over the send button. I felt like I could throw up. What was I doing? What would this do? Tear apart this girl's life and bring me into it with her? I didn't want to be a part of her story, their story. She was happy. He seemed like a good boyfriend to her. In a twisted universe like this one, I guess you could be a good boyfriend and someone's rapist. Who knew?

I held my finger down over the delete key. I watched the message disappear.

> Thanks for the birthday wishes.
> Hope you're well! Xo

I tapped on her profile and then hit the unfollow button.

## 36

THERE WERE ONLY two more GSS classes left before the end of the semester. And today was presentation day. One by one, we got up to present our topics. Vera brought three cis men from her major and covered their naked bodies in red paint. She had asked Professor Tolino if she could collect various people's period blood as the paint, but apparently after an incident on campus two years ago, menstrual blood was no longer allowed to be used for creative purposes. Instead, Vera had spent the past two weeks mixing combinations of red and pink and brown paint together until she got the shade she wanted. Unfortunately, Candace and I had been the test subjects, which resulted in a very awkward encounter with my RA in the bathroom two nights ago. While she painted the three men, Vera broke down the definitions of consent as described by three different dictionaries. She then had each man read written accounts of how teenage and adult men had described consent on a Reddit forum. When they finished, she stopped painting.

"The blood on these men is the blood their parents drew when they taught them non-consent for the first time. When they were circumcised."

*Don'tlookdon'tlookdon'tlook.*

I looked.

Mercifully, Wes was next. They gave a presentation on gender euphoria, showing us a collection of interviews that they'd filmed asking folks all around campus what aspects of their gender made them feel euphoric. Many of the people in the interviews were trans, but a lot of them were also cis. It was incredible. I spent most of the time watching Wes watch the video, and I could see that it lit them up from the inside out. The last clip of the film was of Wes alone, talking to the camera.

"There's far too much focus on dysphoria, on the pain and trauma of the trans experience, and it's time to change that narrative. We should not have to prove that we are lacking joy in our gender to get the gender-affirming care that we need. We deserve care, period."

After the video ended, I started clapping, which was not a good idea because there was no precedent of clapping for the first presentation, but now I had to commit.

"Hell yeah, Wes!" Candace whooped, joining in with me. The rest of the class cheered for them, and a wave of relief passed through me. Before Wes sat down, I could see that the tip of their nose had turned pink.

Reg's project was, by far, my favorite. She brought in pillows and blankets, had us push back all the chairs and desks, and laid out the blankets. We were invited to gather on the floor. Wes sat down next to me, and when my knee briefly brushed against their leg the inside of my elbows got sweaty.

Reg passed around juice boxes and animal crackers, and then pulled out a book from her backpack. She looked at us mischievously and brought a finger to her lips, shushing us.

"Okay, class, it's story time."

My heart skipped a beat. This was the cutest thing.

She cleared her throat and opened the book, holding it up for us to see. She had written and illustrated a children's book about bodily autonomy. It was so beautiful and gentle and deeply necessary. As she read from the last page, my skin bloomed goose bumps.

Lara's presentation was on the desexualization of women in the United States as they age, and it was surprisingly captivating. She had compiled visuals, stories, folklore of women from all different areas of the world, to show cultural differences in honoring and revering older and elderly women—and compared this to how our culture discounts women over forty.

"I read a story about this woman"—Lara gestured to a photo of a person on the screen, a gray-haired woman with chin-length hair—"who described her forties to be the most sexually empowering time of her life, because it was the first time society finally left her alone." Lara shook her head and was quiet for a moment. "I get that. It's like this double-edged sword. You spent the first chunk of your life being told to savor your beauty and youth, but how can you savor it when it's the final fucking countdown?"

"I want to be like this woman," Lara said, turning to face the photo, her back to us. Her hair was up today, which was different, and she was wearing a black tank top. She had strong shoulders. I had never noticed that before.

"I don't want to wait till I'm forty to feel empowered."

Still facing away from us, Lara reached up and undid the scrunchie securing the bun on her head. Her hair tumbled down her back. When she turned around, she was crying a little.

"I know what I look like." Her voice was breaking. "I do. And I know I've spent too long using it as a mask, because everyone and their mother told me that I should. Because a *boy* told me I should. And I'm not saying this will remove my privilege or that it'll make me ugly, but I also know it will change things, for me. And I want that. I'm ready for that."

Candace kicked my foot under my desk. I shot her a look that said "Dude, I don't fucking know."

Lara parted her hair from the back and brought equal chunks in front of her shoulders. She reached into her bag and pulled out a pair of scissors. I gasped.

"Oh, FUCK yes," Candace screamed, shooting up from her seat and jumping on her chair. "You got this, Lara."

Before I knew it, I was standing too. Everyone was. Lara looked at me and we locked eyes.

"Fuck him," I mouthed.

"Fuck him," she repeated, as she cut through her perfect blond hair with the scissors. It fell to the ground and she stared at what was left in her hand in disbelief. No one moved. And then Lara burst out laughing. The rest of us erupted into cheers.

"CUT IT! CUT IT! CUT IT!" Reg started chanting, and we all joined in as Lara cut her hair above her shoulders. She was beaming the whole time. When she was done, we helped her sweep her hair into the trash. When we all finally sat back down, I looked over at her. Her hair looked rough, jagged and frayed at the ends and completely uneven. But she was glowing.

"Okay, my dears, we must continue." Professor Tolino gestured to me. Instantly, I started sweating. I took a deep breath and walked to the front of the room.

The night before, I had submitted a paper for my project. It wasn't cutting my hair off in front of the class, but it was what I was good at. Writing was what I was good at.

I stood in front of the class. "I did something very rebellious for this project and hoped to push some boundaries, so I wrote a paper."

I heard Wesley chuckle and I blushed.

"Don't worry, I'm not gonna read the whole thing. Just one part."

I looked down at the page and began.

"At the beginning of the semester we were asked to define justice." My voice was a little shaky. "I really didn't know how to answer that question. But now I do." I looked up at the rest of the class. "I don't believe in justice. At least not in the way that it exists now. Because I think justice centers the abuser." The room was quiet.

"Sometimes I feel like what we do in this classroom is bullshit. We've spent this entire semester sitting here talking about how rape kits need to be more accessible, how there shouldn't be a lull between accusation and trial, how jail time should be longer and the prison facility should be stricter, and in none of these conversations have we talked about what the survivor is doing while they wait for their abuser to be held accountable. The conversation so quickly jumps to justice, but there is a difference between justice and healing."

"Truth," Vera said, nodding at me. Everyone was looking intently at me. I felt something settle inside my belly.

I took a deep breath.

"It took me three years to understand that I was raped." My voice was firm. "And I think part of that was because it was easier to stuff it all down than think about what I was 'supposed' to do. Because what I was supposed to do sounded like hell. And for most survivors, it is hell. Fuck proof. Fuck trial. Fuck the police."

"Fuck 'em," Candace echoed.

"The system sucks. But there are ways to change that. With

free therapy. Safe places to heal. Community care." I felt tears prick my eyes and looked down. "That's what I needed." I took another deep breath and balled my hand into a fist. I swallowed and looked up again.

"That's what I deserved. That's what we all deserve."

I caught Professor Tolino's eye. She was smiling at me.

When I left class, Wesley was waiting for me by the door. Candace noticed first and dragged Vera away by the elbow. I looked at Wes nervously. They had both their hands looped in their backpack straps. We walked silently out to the quad.

"It's hot out," Wesley said.

"It is hot out," I repeated.

"Do you like lemonade?"

I gulped.

"I do, in fact, like lemonade."

"Sweet. Let's go." Wesley grabbed my hand, pulling me toward Owen's. Their palm was damp but not clammy, and there's a difference. I liked it. They squeezed my fingers.

Owen's was practically empty, it was a weird time of day, and I was nervous at the thought of not having to scream over other students pounding iced coffee and arguing over group projects. I hoped I could make my voice sound alluring and sexy, but my hands were still shaking, and I could feel my heart in my throat. Wesley gestured for me to sit, and I did, thudding down into the seat. I watched them order our drinks. When they came back, they wordlessly slid the sweating glass into my hands.

I realized, in that moment, how fucking thirsty I was. I lifted my glass and drained it within seconds. When I looked up from my drink. I was practically panting. I wiped the liquid from my chin.

"Thirsty?"

"Thirsty." We were both quiet for a moment.

"We don't have to talk about it or anything, but that was really amazing, Sav."

"Thank you," I said, glancing down.

"You're brave as hell."

I looked up at them and they had their chin resting on their fists, elbows up on the table. Their eyes were soft and full of admiration. I realized I hadn't ever seen their face this close. Those eyelashes. Those fucking eyelashes. I wondered if they ever wore mascara.

"I'm not polyamorous," I blurted. Wes's brow furrowed.

"Oh, okay," they said.

"I know you are," I went on, "but I'm not. And as much as I like you, I just am not evolved enough to have multiple partners and not, like, die of jealousy. And that makes this really suck and I'm probably going to regret it, but I just can't—"

"Whoa, Sav, I'm not polyamorous either."

I fell silent.

"What?"

"No, I'm, uh, kind of boring like that. One-and-done kind of human over here."

"Oh."

"Why did you think . . ." they trailed off.

"The person at the protest. With the pink bowl cut? I saw you together, and I also saw a photo of you two in your room, and I saw you holding hands after that party at Roula's? God, now I sound like a creepy stalker, but I'm not, I just—"

Wes was smiling.

"Oh, that's Gia. My best friend."

*Best friend.*

"Oh god," Wes continued, sounding slightly alarmed. "I can see why it could come off that way. We're not together. We've just been friends for ages. She's the one who encouraged me to transfer here."

"Oh."

"Yeah." Wes shrugged, sheepish.

"So you're single."

"Well, technically. But I, um, hope not to be for too much longer." They looked down shyly.

My heart was racing again, but in a good way. I felt like my whole body was swelling. Like I couldn't sit still for a second longer. I stood up from the table. Wesley stood up too. We looked at each other for a moment, and then I grabbed their hand. I pulled them toward the door and out onto the quad.

"Where is—" I started to ask.

"West Campus parking lot. Right there." They pointed to the lot, which was, magically, behind me.

We didn't talk in the car, and I didn't want to. The drive was quick.

Outside their apartment door we stopped. Wesley fumbled in their bag for their keys. It became clear that they couldn't find them fast enough, so they dumped the entire contents of their backpack on the sidewalk. I lunged first for the flash of silver and slammed the key into the lock. The door opened and I felt the cold from the AC unit in the window hit my skin. I yanked my hair down from its bun. Bits of hair stuck to my forehead.

"Is anyone, um?" I asked, gesturing vaguely. They shook their head.

We stared at each other, panting from sprinting up the stairs.

"Do you ever wear mascara?" I finally asked.

"On special occasions," they said, and pulled me in.

Everything was citrus all at once and we were, we were, we were finally kissing. I opened my mouth a little and they slipped their tongue inside. The best amount of tongue.

And then, in a horrible twist of fate, I leaned in harder as they pulled away to say something, and in an attempt at politeness and to acknowledge that I wasn't quite done, they leaned back in, and

too fast. So fast that their face collided with my nose and a ridiculous crunching sound escaped from my face.

"Oh no, oh my gosh, Sav, are you—?" they asked, frantic.

I tried to make my face look like I wasn't experiencing searing
pain.

"I'm fine!" I just wanted to go back to kissing.

"You're not."

"It's just, like, a tickle of pain."

"Your nose is bleeding, Sav."

My hand flew to my face. It was instantly wet.

"No, it isn't."

"I mean, sure, it might not be," they offered. "But some sort of
red liquid *is* seeping from your face."

"Oh my god." I felt more blood pooling into my palm.

"Does this happen a lot? Should I get you a tampon? Like they
do in the movies?"

"No, it doesn't, and yes, okay."

"Okay! I don't have one!" They were speaking very loudly.

"I don't either, I don't have my bag with me!"

"Oh no. Like, I, um. I don't get my period. Oh, this is a weird
way to tell you I'm on testosterone! Okay! The tampon search
commences."

I laughed and felt a gush of blood seep into my hand. I lifted
my face up to the ceiling.

"Please go."

"Going!"

Wes ran to the bathroom. I wiped my wrist against my upper
lip and my skin came away bloody. It wasn't polite blood either. It
was purple and brown goo, thick and gloppy. I doubled down and
added both hands to cup my nose.

"I GOT ONE!" they yelled, zooming back into the room. They
thrust a loose tampon into the air in victory.

"Yes! Wait, don't look at me!" I whirled around.

"Sav, I'm the only one with free hands. I think you might need some help."

Fuck, they were right.

I slowly turned around.

"I know you have to look, but, like, metaphorically, can you not look?"

"Absolutely. In a literary sense I am not looking."

"Okay."

"Okay. Now, I'm going to be honest, I haven't practiced my tampon-to-nostril aim in a while. But I'll do my best."

"I trust you. But now I'm not gonna look." I shut my eyes tight.

I felt them gently insert the tampon into my left nostril, twisting it a little until it was as far in as possible. After a moment or two, I heard them give a sigh of relief.

"It's in," they whispered.

"Thank god." I slowly moved my palms away from my face. "I never thought our first time would be like this."

I blinked open my eyes to see Wesley's mouth agape.

"Too much?"

"Not enough," they said, smirking.

I looked down at my hands, and then the floor, and then their hands.

"I have massacred your entire apartment."

"It's okay. I have towels. Cloth and paper. And Clorox wipes. And the best of all wipes: wet wipes," they said, proudly.

"Those really are the best."

Wesley reached into their kitchen cabinet and pulled out a Pyrex filled with an absurd number of wet wipes. They shrugged. "Jewish mother."

"Got it.

"Hey, Wes?"

"Yeah?"

"You have a shower, right?"

"Oh. Yes. I do have a shower."

"Can I?" I asked, trailing off.

After my shower, I successfully dislodged the tampon from my nose and resisted the urge to flush it. *You are not going to bleed on their floor and clog their toilet on the same day, Savannah.* I took inventory of my face in the mirror. A slight brownish color was forming just under my eyebrow, which meant that I'd have a nasty black eye later. My nose was swollen, and apparently there was only so much crusty blood you can excavate out of your nostril after mass trauma. Otherwise, I looked okay. My hair looked nice wet. Not quite a Kim K wet look, but definitely hot lifeguard at the pool. I wrapped myself in the light blue towel Wes had given me and then made my way to their room. I knocked lightly. I could hear Frank Ocean playing behind the door. I bit my lip to stop from smiling. Frank Ocean was, unquestionably, baby-making music. If Wes was playing Frank Ocean, then maybe my guest appearance on bootleg *Grey's Anatomy* hadn't totally disgusted them. Maybe they wanted to make a proverbial baby with me. Wes opened the door wide and almost pulled off pretending like they didn't think it was a big deal that I was wearing their towel.

"Hi," I said.

"Hi," they said back. "Come in."

Their room was the same as I remembered it from the open mic. Only this time they had invited me in. They closed the door gingerly behind me. They had placed an oversized T-shirt and a pair of boxers on their bed.

"This time I really won't look," they promised and closed their eyes.

I slipped on the clothes and walked over to where they were standing. And before I let myself think twice about it, I kissed them. Miraculously, it didn't hurt.

I tugged Wes toward their bed, and they fell back onto it, not so gracefully, and I climbed over their body and down onto their hips. They grabbed ahold of my waist, and I pressed my chest into them, snaking my hands up into their hair. Wes groaned a little, and my skin erupted in goose bumps. We weren't kissing politely anymore, pretty much just mauling each other's mouths the way you do when it isn't about being good at sex, it's about the sex itself. I felt Wes tentatively tug at the base of my shirt, and I hastily sat up and yanked it off, knowing full well that now they could see most of me. I slid off the boxer shorts. Their mouth went slack.

"You make me feel like a teenager again," they said, reaching up to touch me.

*You make me feel like the teenager I never got to be.*

They slid their hands from my chest to my stomach, staring at my body, and then moved down to my hips. All of a sudden, they stopped and looked at me.

"Is everything okay?" I asked, slightly terrified.

They moved their head from one side, then the other, scanning my lower body.

"Where's your tattoo?"

"What?" I said, entirely confused.

They scratched their head.

"Of the chair? Your grandmother?"

My hand flew to my mouth. I had completely forgotten. I burst out laughing.

"It's a long story," I said. "I promise I'll explain, but please don't stop."

They moved their palms to cup my chest, and I lowered myself to their mouth, breathing heavily. I moaned softly into them as they reached for my ass, and then swiftly flipped me over so that my head was resting on the pillow.

"Nice!" I said, apparently not in my own head but very much out loud.

"Honestly, I'm impressed with myself." Wes laughed before leaning back in to kiss me. I stuck my hands under their shirt, not trying to be sexy, not trying to be anything, just needing to touch them. I felt the fabric of their binder, fit tightly to their chest, and I stopped. They found my hands with theirs and gently slid them away from their skin. They pulled away for a moment.

"Should we go over house rules?"

"Oh! Yes. For sure," I said, a little embarrassed that I hadn't thought to ask what was and wasn't okay first. Wes rolled over and we both sat up.

"Great. Okay. So, uh, as you may have noticed, I wear a binder. Which I love! It makes me feel really good and masculine. I don't like to take it off when I'm having sex, and if I do, that's not a place I like to be touched."

"Got it. Makes sense."

"Okay, you go."

I go? Right. I have rules too.

"Um, I like to talk. Not like, dirty talk. Although I like that! But I mean, if we can keep a conversation going, it helps me stay present. Not get in my head."

"I love that. Totally, can do."

"And, um, sometimes stuff flashes in my head, and I can't really control that. And if it does, I think taking a break would be good. But it wouldn't be because of you. I would just need to take a break."

"That also makes sense. Breaks are good." Wes shot me some finger guns.

"Your turn."

"Right." They thought for a moment. "Oh, duh, okay. So with, uh, down-there stuff? I like the word 'crotch,' or 'groin,' but no specific genitalia talk, if that makes sense."

"I can do that."

"Any words you like? For your body?"

I paused. I hadn't really thought about what words I liked. I scanned through words I'd heard other people use to talk about my body in bed, or words from porn.

"I like 'pussy.' I don't like 'cunt.'"

"Perfect. 'Pussy' it is. Very into pussy. Yours, I mean, not, um. See, you know, talking is not an issue for me! Not talking is something I could work on."

"Don't," I said, pulling them into me. "I love it."

We kissed again, and for a long time. And even though we'd gone over house rules, neither of us seemed to be in a rush to do anything more than kiss. And that wasn't weird or unsexy. It was actually very sexy. And then, at some point, we stopped. We stopped, I think, because we could. Because we finally had time. I rested my head on their pillow and Wes pulled a throw blanket over us. I was overcome with exhaustion. I closed my eyes.

"Do you want to take a nap?"

"Is that okay?" I whispered.

"Anything's okay."

I was pulled into sleep. I woke up only once, when I felt their breath in my mouth, and blinked my eyes open to see their lips inches from mine. I breathed with them, matching the rise and fall of their chest. The lemonade scent was gone and what replaced it was unnamable. Essence of Wesley, I guess. A bodily thing, so human and delicious. It was the most intimate thing of all, to share breath like this. I dozed off again.

The next thing I heard was their voice in my ear.

"Sav. Sav?"

They were pushing the hair that had fallen across my face off my cheek. I opened my eyes and couldn't believe this wasn't a dream. They were staring at me, a lopsided smile on their face.

"Do you need me to go?" I whispered.

"No, that's the last thing I need."

They leaned in and kissed me. I felt hot, everywhere, and pushed off the blanket, my mouth still on theirs.

"I'm so hungry." They spoke into my mouth.

Um. That was unexpected, but still hot, I think.

"Me . . . too?" I narrowed my eyes.

"Thank god." Wesley sat up. "Do you like Chinese food?"

"Oh!" I burst out laughing.

Wesley looked at me confused. "Oh? Oh what?" They searched my face, and then it clicked. "Oh! Oh. Oh no. Oh as in *oh*? You thought I was, wow, no—"

"No! No! That was me. That was all me. I'm hungry! Food hungry!"

"I don't think it's possible to feel this embarrassed."

"You should try giving birth through your nose. Believe me, this is nothing."

Wes laughed. We were staring at each other again, sheepish and toothy.

"Okay, I think Golden Wok is still open," they said.

"What? Why wouldn't it be?"

"It's nine p.m., Sav."

"*It's what?!*" I lunged for my phone. "Oh my god, I'm so sorry," I yelped.

"Why are you sorry?"

"I fell asleep in your bed for five hours, Wesley."

"Why in the world would I complain about that, Savannah?"

"You probably had plans?"

"If the girl you can't stop thinking about ends up in your *bed*

with you on a Friday night, you cancel all of your plans immediately."

*Oh.*

"You really can't stop thinking about me?"

"Not since the second you confessed to me that your water
bottle was from Amazon. Now please come read this menu, because if I don't eat soon I *will* have to kick you out."

"Okay, okay!" I went over to their desk and they pushed their
computer screen toward me.

## 37

THE NEXT AFTERNOON, I called home.

"Mom?"

I could hear the dishwasher going in the background.

"Hi! Can you hear me? I'm on my cell. Call the landline?"

"I can hear you fine."

"Well, I can't hear you."

"Really?"

"Really."

"Then how did you hear me say 'really'?"

"You're going in and out, Savannah. I'm calling you back."

I sighed. How could I be annoyed before a conversation even started? I sat back on my bed, stuffing a pillow into my lap. The contact for my house phone lit up across my screen.

"Hi," I mumbled.

"Can you hear me?"

"Yes, I can hear you."

"Well, don't you want to know if I can hear you?"

I groaned.

"I'm just kidding. Hi. How are you, sweetie?"

I bit down on my lip. "Uh, so, remember how I came back to school early for spring break?"

"Yes?"

"It wasn't because I was stressed."

"I know that," she said.

"What?"

"I knew it was for some other reason."

"You sound smug."

"I'm not smug! You're so quick to tell me what I feel."

I didn't respond. I heard her sigh.

"Sav, what's going on? Did you want to tell me why you left early?"

"Well, why do you think I did?"

"You want me to guess?"

*Why are you doing this, Savannah?*

"Yes."

"Well, I guess I thought it had to do with Izzie. Maybe feeling jealous of all the attention?"

My jaw fell open.

"Are you kidding?"

"You asked me to guess! That is my guess! I don't understand why you won't just tell me."

"Why the fuck would I be jealous? You think I want to get married?"

"No, I don't think that." Her voice was quiet.

"Okay?"

"I think maybe you're jealous of Ben, for taking Izzie away from you. You've been close for so long."

"You're wrong. That's literally so far from why I left early."

"Okay, I'm wrong, then! I don't understand—"

"We're not close."

"Who? You and Izzie?"

"Yes. We're not close."

"All right. That's news to me."

"Do you have any idea why we might not be close?"

"Why are you interrogating me, Sav? You called me!"

"Just think, Mom."

"I'm not a mind reader, Savannah!"

"We weren't in love."

"Of course not, I know you and Izzie were always just friends."

"No, no, that's not what I—her brother and I. We weren't. In love."

The line went silent for a moment.

"Okay, you weren't in love."

"We weren't dating at all. We never did."

"So when you told me—"

"I was lying."

"All right."

"We had sex."

"I figured that much, yes."

"But it wasn't regular sex."

"What do you mean?"

"I, um, I didn't want to. Have it."

*Just say the fucking words.*

"Because you weren't dating?"

"No, because I. I um. I wasn't awake when it—"

"Oh god."

"I need you not to freak. As much as you want to. Please don't."

"Okay, I'll try."

"Um"—I took a deep breath—"yeah, he, um, he raped me, Mom. At a party at Izzie's."

"Why didn't you tell me?" She sounded like she was about to cry.

"Because I didn't think it counted. Because I was drunk."

"Was he drunk?"

"Um, yeah? Why does that matter?"

"It doesn't, I guess. I don't know. I'm sorry, this is—I thought you two were—that's why I tried not to press, I thought you loved him."

"I know."

"But I remember, I asked you, I know I asked you—"

*And what would you have done? Called the police?*

"I didn't know. It took me a while to get it. Get that I could call it that."

"I understand." Her voice was soft.

I didn't know what to say now.

"I'm so sorry, Savannah."

Tears clawed at my eyes.

"This wasn't your fault," she said.

*Waterworks.*

"Sometimes I think it was. I don't remember—" I said, trying to swallow my tears. "I don't remember what I said to him. I don't remember any of it, Mom."

"I should have known." Her voice small, like a child's.

Anger seared through me. She should have known. She should have seen how different I was after. How I hid myself.

"It's okay," I said.

"I guess I thought you were so upset over you and Izzie fighting—I didn't think . . ."

"Yeah."

"What can I do?" she asked.

The question made me pause.

"Nothing," I said quietly.

"Okay."

I wiped my face.

"So will you go?" she asked.

"I don't know."

"Whatever you decide, I love you."

# 38

A WEEK AFTER the school year ended, Candace, Vera, and I went to the city for the weekend. We left on Friday, took the subway to Brooklyn, and walked to a bar that Candace had been to last summer. It had the best queer night in New York, she said.

"You can tell that so many of these lesbians are mean as fuck and I'd let any one of them spit in my mouth."

"Oh my god, Candace." I gave her a look. She played innocent.

"You know I love a bossy femme. They are my downfall. Why do you think I'm in love with Vera?"

"Candace, what the fuck? I am not a femme." Vera pinched Candace's arm.

"Ow! See what I mean? Bossy as fuck."

"Come on, let's go to the bar out back." Vera marched in front of us, leading us through a sea of queer people. "I'm hungry. I think they have food here."

We made our way through the dim-lit room and out to the back. The bar was set up along a redbrick wall and had a huge neon light strung across in the shape of a cocktail glass.

*Holy shit.*

I had been here before. Last year, with Izzie, for New Year's. She had been invited by her Big, and we had just come from a pre-game at her friend's apartment in SoHo. I hadn't wanted to come to the bar, and I spent the night avoiding drunk frat bros wearing shorts even though it had hit the low thirties that week. I hated it. I sat at the bar the entire evening, staring at that neon sign.

But now the bar was totally transformed. There were no frat bros in sight. Instead, it was filled with, well, gay people. It was sort of like school, but everyone was obviously older, and no one was lugging a backpack around. It was a sea of mullets and under-cuts and nose piercings, overalls and leather jackets and danger-ously high Doc Martens, tall city femmes with slicked-back ponytails and red lips and tattoos winding down their arms, norm-core skaters with their boards propped up along the fence of the bar, smoking cigarettes and comparing bruises, a horde of cottage core lesbians playing Settlers of Catan, two drag queens posing in an open-air photo booth, a terrifying group of what could only be described as androgynous aliens in one corner, so beautiful and so intimidating I could barely take my eyes off them, and a very hot masc4masc couple furiously making out by the kitchen. I stood, stunned, unable to tear my eyes away from the scene in front of me. And as I kept watching, these groups started to move—one of the city femmes ran over to the cottage core Catan players, throwing their arms around them. The drag queens sidled over to the skaters and bummed some cigarettes; one androgynous alien leaned over the bar to kiss the cheek of the bartender, clearly a regular, and the two looked elated to be reunited.

And, of course, there were people who didn't really fit into any stereotype. They were just existing. Drinking or playing darts or nervously laughing on a first date. The sensation of it all was like a warm hum beneath my feet. I couldn't stop smiling.

"Sav, we have to pee, can you order for us?" Vera pointed inside, where the bathroom was. "I'll text you from the bathroom line."

I nodded and waved them away.

I stood at the back of the patio waiting for our food, a burger to share and two orders of fries. When it came out, the food was steaming hot, and I scooped a handful of ketchup packets onto the plate, balancing them on top of the tower of fries.

The bartender looked at the pile and laughed.

"Oh, they're not just for me. My friends—" I gestured behind me, turning to see if I could find them in the crowd. They were by the DJ now, the only ones on the makeshift dance floor, twirling each other round and round, laughing at each other's worst dance moves. I couldn't help but grin.

"They're for all of us," I said to the bartender.

They chuckled, amused by the antics.

"Hey"—they gestured to the fries—"even if they were all for you, that would be cool too."

"You're right," I agreed.

Before I could turn around to join Candace and Vera, they were both beside me. Candace's arm reached over my shoulder and grabbed a fistful of fries, cramming them in her mouth.

"Can you hold on for, like, one fucking second?" Vera asked, ripping a ketchup packet open with her teeth. She started squeezing it onto a clean corner of the plate.

"So glad you got more than one." She looked at me gratefully, as she tore into the next packet. "You can never have enough."

Candace stole another fry and then used it to lure us back toward the DJ. We all started dancing, me still carrying the plate, and Vera passing the burger among us. I couldn't stop laughing, hamburger bun hanging out of my mouth, watching the two of them dance with their fries waving in the air. In my pocket, my phone vibrated. I knew it was Wesley, and I felt my heart skip a beat. They were coming tomorrow, for the rest of the weekend, and we were going to the queer beach.

*How is this my life?*

Along the perimeter of the patio, people had started to watch the three of us. The group of androgynous aliens were making their way to the dance floor now, and behind them more and more people joined in. Vera was offering our fries to everyone.

A few states away, Izzie was probably dancing by now too. She wasn't at the Plaza, I knew, but for a moment I closed my eyes and imagined her there, just over the bridge, dancing in the same white dress we chose from a torn-up magazine. She was happy, truly happy, and I was happy for her. I believed she was happy for me too. Or that she would be one day. Because I think the promises that we made to each other were never really about weddings or forevers. They were about a commitment to each other. A commitment to each other's joy. I think we both believed that joy could not exist without us being together, but we're old enough now to know otherwise. We're old enough now to know that joy is not dependent on another person, no matter how much we want it to be.

"Sav?" Candace came up to me, cupping my face in their hands.

"Yeah?" I asked, doing the same with mine. We locked eyes.

"You good?" they asked. "You're just standing here with a goofy look on your face."

I laughed.

"I'm good. I'm really good." I was.

"Good."

Candace pulled me in to the center of the crowd, where Vera was, and suddenly we were lost in the sea of what finally, finally, felt like my life.

# Acknowledgments

I go wild for book acknowledgments. I always have. They make me weepy and hopeful, and vacuum-suck the New York City jadedness right out of my heart. I can't believe I get to write my own.

To Ayla Zuraw-Friedland, my firecracker of an agent, when you pick up the phone I breathe easy. You get this book in the way I needed someone to get this book. Your mind is sharp, your heart is sweet, and you are very weird and gay, which is all this writer could have hoped for. You are my North Star. To Hannah, who I asked for help—I am indebted to you. Thank you for taking a chance on me and helping this book land in Ayla's safe, bisexual hands.

To Frances Goldin Literary Agency, it is an electric feeling to be a part of an agency with tremendously important values.

Thank you to the steadfast and most supportive team at Dutton. John Parsley, for your guidance; lovely Lisset and your hasty responses to my panicked emails; to publicity pros Lauren Morrow and Amanda Walker; Isabel DaSilva and Stephanie Cooper, for your marketing magic; and LeeAnn Pemberton, for your production prowess.

To my editor, Pilar Garcia-Brown, for your fervent gentleness, your curiosity, your affirmation, and your inherent understanding of the heart of this book. You are a beacon of calm, and it is my great privilege to work with you. Thank you for the biggest yes of my life.

To my teachers: Nancela, my mentor, who taught me that writing is a holy practice; Lynn Steger-Strong, whose wisdom on writing has been my phone background for two years; A.E. Osworth, who reminded me I could not write this book without joy. Everyone at Catapult and the peers I've met along the way. Especially Katie, my plot wizard.

Huge thanks to the folks I interviewed about what real college is like (one day I'll write a book about acting school); Teresa Tran, for your generous and essential authenticity read; and to my killer copy editor, Eileen Chetti, who informed me I used the names Josh and Matt for multiple characters in this novel. You have humbled me greatly. I appreciate you and hope we never meet.

To Jody, thank you for being my witness. You once told me that therapy has chapters, and this novel is an ode to every page you helped me turn. I am indescribably grateful for your care.

I can't fathom that there was ever a moment, a singular speck of time, that Jake Murphy was not my best friend. Those first few weeks at college, us tucked into my twin bed, laughing till our ribs were sore—those nights altered the course of my life forever. You've made my book so much better. Not only because of your immensely thoughtful notes and insights, but because I wouldn't be able to write—really write—about friendship without knowing how profoundly yours has changed me. Thanks for telling me to quit being a party girl and own how smart I am. That was a good call.

To my Wes, who was once named Carter before you so sweetly asked if you might borrow the name, thank you for loving me in all my forms. Especially my bitchiest ones. You are a master class of patience, and your soft, steady love has carried me through this process. Thank you for staying up past your bedtime to brainstorm with me, making me crispy chicken, for holding me on the nights I ugly cried for fear this book would never go anywhere, and for reminding me that we are never beholden to the people we were yesterday. It is a forever humblebrag that I scored a hot therapist with perfect green eyes.

To my father—my brilliant, tender father—who taught me funny and instilled in me a fervor for language that has made me the writer I am today. You are the blueprint, Pops. I love you desperately.

To my mom, who believes in me so fiercely that I have never had a choice of whether to believe in myself. Thank you for reminding me when I was twenty and very sure that I wanted to be an actress and nothing else (queasy just thinking about that) that I've always been a writer. Sorry I was pissy about it—you were right. Most often, you are right. Remember the book we used to read together, *Guess How I Much I Love You?* I couldn't possibly stretch my arms out wider than they are right now. I love you in every lifetime.

To my grandmother, who would have said this book was absolutely divine. To my family, who love words.

Thank you to my exquisite, expansive, and bighearted queer chosen family and the few fantastic straight friends I have left. I am quite lucky to be able to say that if I listed you all, I'd far exceed the word count permitted here. You're all sexy and smart and I love you.

Thank you to my ride-or-die online readers, some of whom have been hanging with me since I wore my hair in a very deep side part and wrote love poems about boys. I owe you and the internet a whole lot. In so many ways, you got me here. Thank you for listening.

To femme friendship in all its captivating complexity. I have earned an infinite wisdom from the friendships that could not last.

To the bisexuals!!!

To survivors. May we continue to heal together.

Lastly and always, thank you to sixteen-year-old Haley. Everything I write is for you. <3

# About the Author

**Haley Jakobson** (she/her) is a bisexual author and playwright living in Brooklyn, New York. She often writes about girlhood, bisexuality, brains, and bodies. Her debut novel, *Old Enough*, was named a *New York Times* Editors' Choice and described by *Vogue* as being full of "winsome bisexual chaos." Haley is a gemini, eats a lot of bodega sandwiches, and is a killer follow on Instagram.

# Readers Guide

1. *Old Enough* explores many themes—queerness and identity, chosen family, friendship breakups, sexual assault and healing as a survivor, and girlhood. Which themes resonated the most deeply with you?

2. The novel switches from past to present throughout the book—the chapters set in the past are in second person. How did this tense shift affect your reading experience? Why do you think the author made the choice to reflect Sav's past in second person?

3. What was your impression of Izzie and Sav's friendship? Have you ever experienced any friendships that you outgrew? Did you understand Sav's choice to not attend the wedding?

4. In what ways does the author reinforce and challenge romance and coming-of-age tropes? If you were to write the story of your coming of age, what tropes would make sense for your story and which ones would not?

5. The phrase "old enough" appears several times throughout the book, and, of course, it serves as the book's title. In the context of this book, what does being "old enough" mean? In the context of your life, what does the phrase mean to you?

6. What roles do Candace and Vera play in Sav's journey through *Old Enough*? How are their friendships different from Sav's relationship with Izzie?

7. Discuss the theme of friendship breakups. Has a friendship breakup impacted your life? Did your perspective on having one "best friend forever" shift as you continued to read?

8. What do you think of Lara's evolution in *Old Enough*? How did her opinions over the course of the novel impact Savannah? How does Lara's personality and world view affect Savannah?

9. *Old Enough* investigates the way society addresses sexual assault post #MeToo and is a novel that centers on survivors, not their abusers. What was your experience reading a novel that explores themes of healing from sexual assault?

10. What does Wes represent to Sav? Why do you think she's instantly drawn to them? Ultimately, do you think they are a good match? Why or why not?

11. For most of the novel, Savannah resists sharing with her new queer friends what happened to her in high school and what she was like as a teenager. We watch her push away the integration of past and present until it overwhelms her. Why do you think this was so difficult for Sav? Did you relate to this struggle?

12. What was the reading experience like immersing yourself into Sav's big, bisexual world? What was the impact of reading a queer narrative that doesn't delve deeply into the process of coming out or the painful parts of queerness?